Jordan Harper was born and educated in Missouri. He currently lives in Los Angeles, where he works as a writer and producer for television. His debut novel, *A Lesson in Violence* (*She Rides Shotgun* in the US) won the Edgar Award for best first novel.

Also by Jordan Harper

A Lesson in Violence
Love and Other Wounds

JORDAN HARPER

THE LAST KING OF CALIFORNIA

SIMON & SCHUSTER

London · New York · Sydney · Toronto · New Delhi

First published in Great Britain by Simon & Schuster UK Ltd, 2022

Copyright © Jordan Harper, 2022

The right of Jordan Harper to be identified as author of this work has been asserted in accordance with the Copyright, Designs and Patents Act, 1988.

1 3 5 7 9 10 8 6 4 2

Simon & Schuster UK Ltd
1st Floor
222 Gray's Inn Road
London WC1X 8HB

Simon & Schuster Australia, Sydney
Simon & Schuster India, New Delhi

www.simonandschuster.co.uk
www.simonandschuster.com.au
www.simonandschuster.co.in

A CIP catalogue record for this book
is available from the British Library

Paperback ISBN: 978-1-4711-5901-5
eBook ISBN: 978-1-4711-5900-8

This book is a work of fiction.
Names, characters, places and incidents are either
a product of the author's imagination or are used fictitiously. Any resemblance
to actual people living or dead, events or locales is entirely coincidental.

Typeset in the UK by M Rules
Printed and bound in Great Britain by CPI Group (UK) Ltd, Croydon, CR0 4YY

In memory of Matthew and Mary Rogers

'He who is saved, is saved by fire.'

Origen of Alexandria

CHAPTER ZERO

See a scar of smoke across the belly of the sky.

Follow it down to the trailer burning on the desert floor. Smoke boils up black as the void, greasy with particulates, fluming from the vent Troy Gullet hacked in the fiberglass roof a few years back during a failed attempt at brewing crank. Moths of grey-orange ember float on heat currents. Sparks cough out with the smoke, come to earth, briefly jewel the scrub before dying out. It is the brief and shrinking time between California fire seasons, and nothing catches. Not now.

Hear no sound but the gobble of the fire. The cracking and snapping as its slow teeth chew.

The men watch leaning against the truck, close enough for the heat to water their eyes. They watch until Beast is sure the job is done.

Beast Daniels is newly unleashed on the world, so fresh from a ten-year bit in Calipatria that he still has gate money in his pocket. Everything about him is brutal and blunt – even his gut is a hard hillock tenting his T-shirt.

On his left bicep ride four blue thunderbolts. Each blue bolt marks a killing.

When he is sure the job is done he points to the rising smoke.

'As close to heaven as that fuck will ever get.'

The men laugh – at least they make a noise like laughter. Some of them, their eyes do something different and they're glad that Beast is watching the fire and not their faces. As they climb in the truck Beast rubs his arm where the fifth blue bolt will go, soon as he finds the time.

Later, when the firemen find Troy, his corpse still smokes like a blown-out candle. Much of him has burned away. What's left is still shaped like a man, face up on the floor of the trailer, legs curled into a crouch by the heat, arms still spread-eagled thanks to the twelve-penny nails driven through his palms into the melted linoleum beneath.

Later still in a cold and windowless room, a medical examiner will work open Troy's lipless mouth, careful so the brittle burnt jawbone doesn't crack off in her gloved hands. She will find his mouth full of ash. It is an important thing. Ash in the mouth means Troy was alive as the flames took him, that he died breathing fire.

A terrible death. As Beast Daniels built it to be.

Murder is a type of magic. It has powers so a single person killed with intention can haunt the world more than a million lives ended by car crashes or cancer. Beast Daniels knows this. It's why he and his men Christed Troy to that trailer floor and left him there to burn alive. So his ghost will infest the minds of every plugged-in peckerwood from here to Bakersfield. In Victorville, Pomona, Fontana, Devore, everywhere white trash outlaws huddle and do dirt, they'll talk about Troy Gullet and his terrible death.

They'll wonder what sin Troy committed against the Steel to earn this terrible death. But in truth Troy was no more guilty than the oxen burned for Odin back in Viking days. Troy's ghost was needed is all. The power of his fear and pain.

Aryan Steel used to hold every SoCal whiteboy in its hand. That was before the McClusky War and all the infighting, bushwhacking and splintering that followed. Beast Daniels has come to make that open hand a fist again. To do that he must be known. He must be feared. To begin his work he needs a herald to announce him. Someone to sing his song.

Now Troy will sing it with an ash-filled mouth.

PART ONE

DOOMER

CHAPTER ONE

If the world is flat like the Internet says, then this is the edge. The mountains on either side of the Cajon Pass are crumbled and cracked ruins slumping under a starless sky. It looks like where the earth runs out, the place before no place. Not that Luke really believes the earth is flat. But just now it seems like one of those online ideas – like the one about how the government and corporations are run by lizards only playing at being people – that's true enough to make a point.

Luke is nineteen, tall in a way nobody ever seems to notice, everything about him drawn thin like he's been stretched on a rack. His hair is getting long in a way that looks unplanned, odd bits sticking out all over. He's got the eyes of someone outnumbered, even when he is alone – maybe then most of all.

He's driven for sixteen hours now, that long slow fall from Colorado to California, stopping only to piss or buy food. He drives slumped forward so that he steers with his forearms resting on the wheel, so tired that ghost rabbits dance at the corners of his eyes. His stomach burns, his gut flora roiling in open rebellion. He figures they've earned the right. He's been firebombing them all day with energy drinks and bags of flamin' hot extruded whatever.

Or maybe it's something else that's riled them. Something that's been bubbling in him since he passed into California for the first time in twelve years. Something thick and black that tastes like root beer.

He is coming home.

His head snaps up, a trance breaking. How long had it been since he'd thought about the road? Weird how the body can drive without you, how there is a stranger in your brain that keeps you from drifting across the center line while you are somewhere else.

He cracks the window to let the cold air slap him awake. In his memories of this place – the ones he lets himself have – the Inland Empire is a place of unending heat. He forgot how cold the nights can be, how sometimes the desert holds no ghost of the heat that rules it during the day.

The music he's streaming feels wrong now. Skittering mumble rap he got into at school, echoing weirdness that sounded right in his cave of an apartment in Colorado Springs. Here on the edge of the world it sounds tinny and bad. He pokes at his phone to shut it off.

He drives in silence.

His teeth harvest the skin off his lips in thin strands.

His hands drum against the wheel.

He jabs the radio button. A blast of static. He jabs again, his radio scanning to find a station. A man bellows – *Low cost insurance even if you have a DUI* – an air-horn choir behind him. It is demonic as fuck. But better than the silence.

Luke's phone tells him the turn-off is coming. He checks behind him to switch lanes, catches a rear-view glimpse of the back seat crammed with everything he owns. His clothes piled in a hamper, his skateboard. The box with his single pot and his single pan, the plastic spoon and spatula. His box of books, his Algebra 101 textbook poking out of the top.

Looking at the math book fills him with hot shame. Maybe that's why he brought it, gave it this place of honor in the rear-view mirror. To remind him how he wound up here, the only place he has left to run to, the last place in the world he belongs.

The exit to Devore looms ahead.

The pulse in his neck thumps *turn-back turn-back turn-back*.

Turn back where? To his apartment in Colorado Springs that he fled owing two months' rent? To his mother's people who had passed him around like a serving dish from the time he was seven until exactly the day of his eighteenth birthday?

Again he has that feeling like he's standing with his toes poking over the edge of this flat earth. He thinks on something he read in a novel in Intro to World Lit, before he quit going to class altogether. About how when you peek over the side of a cliff and get that swooshing feeling in your belly, that it isn't a fear of falling. In fact, the book said, it is the opposite. Vertigo is the fight in your mind between the part that wants to save you and the part that wants to fall.

The exit lane slopes down from the highway. He takes it down into the dark.

His only memories of this place are a child's, so that it feels both familiar and strange at the same time. Like the rooms in a dream.

Luke's wheels spit gravel as he leaves the paved road and heads up into the hills. Rock walls dotted with greasewood and mummified monkeyflowers rise up on either side. He looks down at his phone. Here in the crevices there is no signal. Something inside tells him when to turn. He drives in submarine dark for three football fields before he sees the lights.

Home. At least it was once.

The sheet-metal gate that dead-ends the gravel road is pulled shut. Past the gate, up the hill, Luke can see the house with its broad front porch. He remembers a swinging loveseat. Now there's only a row of fold-out camping chairs, the kind that look woven out of seat belts. A couple of big trucks sit in the gravel in front of the house. Lights burn behind the curtains of the front windows. Behind the house the box canyon stretches, and in the half-moon light he can see shadows of junkers and brush piles, and something new, something like a second house against the far back wall of the canyon.

Luke knows there's no nerves in the meat of the brain, so this feeling of a thumb pressed deep into the center of his head is just bullshit. But he feels it anyway – the pressure that is almost always there, juicing his adrenal gland. You cannot smell adrenaline, but Luke's sure it smells like root beer.

Luke stops his car and climbs out to lift the hitch and open the gate. He's too tired to lift his feet clear. They shush through the gravel as he walks to the latch.

'Hey now,' a voice says in the dark.

Luke freezes, his hand inches from the latch. He has this feeling like being dunked in cold water.

This scuzzy kid comes out of the dark. The kid, old enough to drive but not much more, is a head-and-a-half shorter than Luke, but stocky. His dark hair hangs greasy down to his shoulders; he has a sad teenage mustache. He wears a heavy metal T-shirt under a jean jacket with the sleeves hacked off. He carries something long in his hands.

The pit bull that runs ahead of him is the color of a bad day. Her ears are combat-clipped into tiny triangles and her muzzle carries old scars, but when she pokes her head between the wide slats of the gate her tongue lolls out of a friendly idiot grin. The kid follows behind. When he steps into the slashes of headlight Luke sees the thing in his hands is a rifle.

'You're in the wrong place.'

No shit, Luke almost says.

'I'm Luke.' He tries to say it strong and clear, but it gets caught up in his throat and comes out a rasp.

'You're what now?' The kid is not pointing the rifle at Luke, but he holds it at the ready. Luke can't meet the kid's eyes so he studies his shirt, the words 'POWER

TRIP' written in electric letters, a skeleton king underneath the logo.

'I'm Luke,' he says again, better this time. 'They know I'm coming. Del's my uncle.'

The kid spits into the dark.

'You're Luke Crosswhite?'

Luke almost reaches for his wallet, like he's going to show this kid ID to prove it. He catches himself, thinks about how lame that would be. He nods instead and mumbles some sort of *yes*.

The kid works his jaw like he's thinking of spitting again but can't wrangle the sputum to pull it off.

'Kathy said you was en route. I thought it was like next week is all. You're a college kid, right?'

'I was.' He doesn't say, *Before I blew it all up*.

The kid scratches himself under the chin with the barrel of the rifle, as if thinking on casual suicide. He looks Luke over, like he's trying to make sense of how this skinny kid with scared eyes could be the seed of Big Bobby Crosswhite.

'You even know what goes on down here?' he asks.

'Yeah.'

The kid laughs like *the hell you do*.

'So you're coming to join the Combine then?' the kid asks, but Luke's pretty sure he's fucking with him, that even in the dark this kid must be able to see from the sweat on Luke's forehead and the pulse of his neck that Luke has no place in his family's business, no matter who his dad is.

'I just need a place to crash, get my head above water, you know?'

The kid blows across the rifle's muzzle, drawing out a low sad tone.

'Well, they got a place laid out for you. Hell, it's your dad's land anyway, right?'

Luke can almost see the thoughts splash across the kid's face next as he has them one by one: *But your dad's not here – ten years left on his sentence at least – oh shit oh shit—*

'Oh shit,' the kid says. 'You were there. At Arrowhead.'

Luke's face must do something. The kid whistles low like *goddamn.* Luke worries he's going to want to talk about it, maybe ask questions that Luke can't handle. But instead the kid moves forward and reaches for the gate latch.

'I'm Sam,' he says. The pit bull goes through the gap in the gate as soon as it's wide enough to fit her. She hits Luke with her body, that way dogs do like they love you so much they want to mix their atoms together with yours. Luke kneels down to take her hungry affection and give some back.

Sam comes through the gate behind her.

'That's Manson. She's a stone killer. Only thing is she doesn't know it.'

Luke rises, looks towards the light spilling from the house. In the windows, shapes from inside project against the closed curtains. Men standing close to the light so their shadows fill the windows, making them giants, the way they'd always seemed to Luke back when he had lived here and the house was often filled with the huge roaring men of the Devore Combine.

'Del and them's talking with this dude Pinkle from out in the desert,' Sam says, talking low, his eyes gleaming like he's sharing juicy gossip. 'Some shit went down out in Hangtree, I think. I think maybe somebody got got.'

A dark thrill runs through Luke at those words, and he thinks about asking more, to find out *what really goes on down here*. But a wave of panic washes through him at the thought, and he studies the gravel until the moment passes.

'It's black hearts only, so they got me on lookout.' Sam touches his shirt over his heart. 'I'm due mine soon, for real.'

Black hearts kick up memories of black-ink hearts tattooed over real ones, men laughing and lifting Luke into the air, the taste of ice and root beer.

Luke swallows the memories before they swallow him first.

He thinks, *Please don't let it happen here.*

'So, should I wait?' Luke asks. 'I've been driving since dawn, mountain time. I just want to crash.'

'Don't think you're meant to stay in the big house. Kathy fixed up the trailer out back for you.' Sam nods to the shape back against the canyon wall.

Luke wants to say *But my bedroom is there*, but he knows it would come out weird and childish. Something about this feels right anyway, that he wouldn't be let inside. He just nods again.

'I'll let them know what's up when the meeting's done,' Sam says. 'There's room to park right next to the trailer.'

'Thanks.'

The kid touches his shirt over his heart again. 'Blood is love.'

Somebody says *Hey Bobby what's up Bobby blood is love Bobby* in Luke's head. He's worried that if he stays out here much longer he's going to say something strange. So he mumbles some sort of *seeya* and climbs back into his car.

Luke drives up onto the property. As he passes he looks behind him to the back of the house, at the back right corner, the window of his childhood bedroom where he thought he'd be sleeping tonight. The window is dark. He drives through the skeletons of old cars, junk, shadowy and unidentifiable on either side of the gravel. He parks next to the trailer that is his home now. It is covered in brown siding, lifted off the ground with cinderblocks, spear grass growing tall around it.

He kills the engine. The dash lights glow for a while. Then they go out. He sits in the darkness and tries to make sense of his insides. Other folk seem to know right away what it is that they're feeling, have words for it and everything. Luke hardly ever knows how to name the things that swim so huge inside him. He doesn't know if he is smart or dumb, happy or sad. He doesn't know what he's doing or where he is going. All he knows for sure is that he does not belong here. That he is his father's child but not his son.

He watches in the rear-view as Sam pushes shut the gate. It's like he can hear it shut from here. But of course he can't.

He lets himself into the trailer, bringing in just his

backpack and a half-drunk bottle of water. He doesn't turn on the lights. In the dim he sees the hotplate kitchen, the bathroom with its toilet and shower in the same stall, before falling onto the bed. Sleep comes fast for once.

He wakes to the sound of meat and bone colliding.

CHAPTER TWO

Thud.

Thud.

Thud.

He rolls over on the thin mattress – he'd fallen asleep in the clothes he'd drove here in. He sits up, thick with dreams, lost in this strange new dark. He grasps for the near wall. The trailer is still unset in his mind.

His tongue lays heavy and too large in his mouth. He gropes for the plastic bottle on the floor by the bed, gulps stale water. Not even sure what it was that woke him. If it had come from the outside or from within.

Thud.

Thud.

Thud.

Overhead the stars are blotted and dull.

A single light burns from the window of his childhood bedroom. It seems too far away for the sounds to have come from there. But he knows how noise can be funny in a canyon.

Rocks bite the bottoms of his feet as he walks towards the house. From the house to the back of the canyon, an asteroid belt of junk, old cars, weeds and brush. Some cars have been there since his childhood. The old once-white Dodge. Luke, maybe only two, had once pried loose a wasp's nest that hung under the rear bumper. He remembers stings like a wave of fire all over him, his mom mumbling something like a scream, moving sloppy, moving slow. Although maybe that last part is made-up, a fake memory created after he learned the truth about his mom.

He passes the old shed, the red siding now faded to dullness by twelve summers. A duct-taped punching bag hangs from the metal T of a clothesline hitch just behind the house. Under it, a circle of dust made by scuffing feet.

Twelve years ago he'd sat here in the backseat of a strange car, not talking – he had barely talked for months after Arrowhead – just looking out, seeing Uncle Del and Kathy, the other men of the Combine, his play-cousin Callie looking back at him waving goodbye with these big sad eyes. His Uncle Ted, his mom's brother and a stranger to all of them, drove him away.

Thud.

Thud.

Thud.

The sounds bring him back to now. He walks softly to the house. He brings his face to the window of his childhood bedroom. He's awake but he thinks on sleep-walking, and on the stranger inside you who steers when you don't.

The man standing in Luke's old bedroom is shirtless. His back is to the window, muscled up, slick with sweat, his skin sheeted in ink. An eagle soars between his shoulder blades. A skull with vampire teeth on one shoulder. At the center of his back grins a devil's face made of flame, sinners spilling from his jaws. 'BLOOD IS LOVE' in gangster script across the small of his back.

Behind him, the same wood paneling, pinpricks all over where Luke had used thumbtacks to hang up pictures of Wolverine and the Diaz Brothers and anime spaceships.

The man's head tilts back. He raises his fist. He drives it down into his own stomach.

Thud.

The man puffs out loud air. Luke's stomach muscles spasm like he's the one taking the punch. Inside, the man's fist rises again.

Thud.

Luke moves closer to the window. His reflection rises up against his face. Luke looks through himself to the man living in his bedroom.

Thud.

Luke feels like he's peeking at another world, one without Arrowhead. A world where Luke didn't shatter and they hadn't sent him away, where he'd stayed and grown up solid and strong, a member of both his father's families. Like he's seeing the ghost of what should have been, a world where he is not cracked and weak. He watches until the man's hands fall to his sides and his fists unclench. Luke backs away from the window so that his reflection melts away into nothing, leaving only the man standing there. Like maybe Luke has it backwards. That man in the room is animal and alive. If anyone here is a ghost, it's Luke.

CHAPTER THREE

Convertibles are for a different California than this one. The California of white surf and wind off the ocean, rich folk eating funny little food arranged on plates just so. Not the sprawl of San Berdoo, this place of sun and scrub and dust. On the 5 with the top down the wind whips Callie's hair so it batters her face, so it flies wild in its roots, so later when she and Pretty Baby stop moving she'll feel each follicle in her head individually aching. But Pretty Baby loves having the top down and Callie loves Pretty Baby. Anyhow, this whipping feeling matches how she feels inside just now.

We could do it.

See her, twenty-two, these wild eyes that used to make the other girls' moms cluck their tongue like *that one's trouble*. She clacks her nails on the shotgun window. She takes three breaths, slow in, slow out. It helps to dull the skittering feeling all over her. She does the math in her head. If they did it, they'd clear six thousand dollars. Enough to achieve escape velocity.

We could do it.

She turns her face up to the sky, gun-metal grey from smog-trash in the air. The Inland Empire is always burning, even when it isn't. It's just it burns so slow most people don't know they're on fire. But Callie knows.

She turns to Pretty Baby, driving slouched, his left leg bent up so the foot is wedged up on the dash. Her hand steals over to him of its own accord, the way it always does when he's near. He's pale, bleach-blond hair with pink streaks and these heavy-lidded deep green eyes. Eyes that shine like the light goes out instead of comes in. He is scribbled all over with careless ink – to him his skin is so much notebook paper to be doodled on. Over his real heart sits a black ink one, the same tat as the one above her left boob. Only his is a little shinier on account of being newer.

'So what are we going to do?' she asks him.

Pretty Baby smiles that numbed-out way he has. Her hand climbs up him to touch the rose inked across his cheek. The one with *PRETTY BABY* written around it. It's no lie. He's prettier than she is. So goddamn pretty you can feel him pressing against your eyeballs when you look at him.

'There's nothing to do.' His voice is soft and Xannie-slow. He's higher than he'd admit to being. 'Bet Scubby was talking shit. You know, talking like he's big time. I mean look at this sad shit right here.'

He fishes in his pocket, pulls out the wad of bills Scubby has just paid them for a baggie of percs. The bills are wadded to dirty softness.

'Think he's got twenty thousand more of these laying around so he can buy a pound of crystal?'

He's right of course. Scubby has white-guy dreads and teeth like a mouth full of dog kibble. She knows he was probably lying when he said he had this big-time friend looking to buy serious weight. But it gave her this little dollop of hope and she doesn't want it to melt yet.

She turns, looks out the window. Next to them is a mini-van. The backseats are a riot of kids. One presses her nose against the glass of the window, streaking snot, licking the glass. The woman behind the wheel has the face of a person driving a hearse.

Not me, never me, she thinks.

Pretty Baby puts a hand on her leg to soothe her. She doesn't want to be soothed.

'What do you want to do?' he asks, turning it around on her the way she knew he would.

A tricked-out hatchback swerves past them. The guy driving wears a polo shirt with a corporate logo on it, on his way to work or getting off work. His cheeks puffed up, his neck tight, like he's holding his breath. She thinks on how all the people around them are running and they don't even know from what.

'I got this feeling, you know?' she says. 'Like the world is spinning faster and faster every day. Like it's getting closer to the sun and picking up speed. Like if things keep going the way they're going, pretty soon stuff's gonna start flying off into the void.'

'Truth.'

A bright red teardrop of a car roars past on the right. The man behind the wheel is squat, his face the color of ham. She thinks on how the ugliest men drive the prettiest cars.

'And it's like, when Scubby told us the deal, my first thought was, we could do it. We could get together some money and run. I don't want to grow old here. I don't even know if there's going to be an old to grow to, you know? Like is there even a future? Doesn't feel like it. I want to run with you, baby. Run while there's still places to run to.'

They sit in the roar of the air for a while. When Pretty Baby talks again it's so soft Callie has to lean an ear towards him to catch it.

'You want to run with me?'

'You know I do.'

He takes her hand and kisses her chewed-up fingers.

'If we went? Where would we go?'

She looks up at the Inland Empire's dull grey sky, the smog-dimmed mountains.

'Someplace the sky ain't dead.'

CHAPTER FOUR

Uncle Del drinks coffee like it is the cure. He sits in a big brown easy chair with the cupholder built in. It's not the same one that Luke's dad had, that one had been grey, but it serves the same purpose – Luke knows a throne when he sees one.

'So the prodigal son returns.'

Uncle Del in his memories: shaggy black hair and a tight goatee, arms ropey with muscle, eyes that stuck you like pushpins.

Uncle Del now: the hair and mustache thick with rags of grey. His arms are ropey, what little fat has started to cling to him all in a little pooch at his belt-line. Gray stubble on his cheeks, with the mustache big and droopy in a way that would be funny on the wrong face, the kind of face that would let you laugh at it. The eyes have some lines around them now, but they still stab at you. Luke was too young then to see the cleverness in Del's eyes. The searching.

'Thanks for giving me a place.'

'Couldn't leave you to the wolves, now, could I?'

When Luke lived here the walls had held mostly family photos, the kind of frames that can hold four or five snapshots apiece. There was usually some sort of electronics opened someplace, car stereos or speakers with wires like veins and all sorts of video game consoles – all of it stolen, Luke would realize much later as the truth of his family slowly dawned on him as a teenager.

Everything is different now, down to sofa and rugs. His aunt and uncle have a taste for paintings of wolves and moons and Indians on horseback, black velvet built into ornate wooden frames, antlers and shellacked fish and the like. There are bookshelves scattered around – the only books around before had been true crime paperbacks, the kind with black covers and lurid red titles. The one thing that sits unmoved is the old walnut gun cabinet in the corner, fuller now than in Luke's memories, every slot full of long guns.

'You like it up there in the mountains?' Aunt Kathy asks him. 'It's awful pretty, huh?'

Aunt Kathy then: blonde hair, usually with a stripe of brown at the roots, thin so her knuckles protruded from her hands like helmets and her fingers were always cold. A laugher, a teaser, quick to bribe a kid with candy and treats. Now she is blonde to the scalp and speckled by a life in the sun. She wears camo tights and a T-shirt three sizes too big so it hangs like a dress. Her voice is coarser now, living more in her throat. She'd woken Luke around eleven this morning, hugged him like a handshake and brought him down to the house for what he now sees is an audience with Uncle Del.

'Sometimes it was nice,' he says. 'Then sometimes it snowed all the way into May.'

'Gawd. That'd just about get me to take the toaster to the bathtub.' She puts one of those skinny menthols in her mouth and sparks a flame on a plastic lighter. The scrape of the flint raises chills in Luke. He stands far enough outside himself to know he is not okay. That doubled-up feeling Luke had the night before is back and stronger than before. That feeling of being in two places at once is growing stronger and stronger. All around him in the living room, with the kitchen in the far corner, everywhere memories are crowding in around Luke like zombies.

Please don't let it happen here.

'So didn't quite make valedictorian, huh?' Del asks.

'Something like that.'

'School's a scam, boy,' Del says. 'Only thing it really teaches you is how to live on their clock and do as you're told.'

'Now you tell me.'

After high school he moved to Colorado Springs, a few towns away from his mom's people who had fed him and clothed him and kept him from foster care but hadn't done more for him than that. He was thankful they'd done that much but didn't feel much else towards them either. His cousins went off to colleges all over the country. They took on six-figure debt like it wasn't even real. He took what money he'd saved working in a pizza place all through high school and moved to his first apartment, a basement deathtrap with thin carpet over concrete floors and a single window the size of a loaf of bread, but it was his. He took out some small loans and he started the fall semester at Colorado Springs Community College.

He'd met Julie the second week of classes. They'd fallen together so easy it almost fooled him into believing in fate. She was kind, the sort of kind that can drive a person crazy in these cruel days. She composted and reused plastic bags and didn't eat meat. She wrote postcards to politicians in faraway states about ocean levels and carbon footprints. She told him about how polar bears are falling through the rotted ice. How they are drowning. She told Luke that this time we are the comet crashing into the earth. And it hurt her so much to be part of that evil without even getting a say in the matter, it made Luke want to press himself into her as much as he could. And for some reason, she pressed right back. Sometimes he worried that to her he was another drowning polar bear, another thing to try to pull to safety from this melting world. But maybe that's what he was and maybe there are worse things than being saved.

The first semester he managed As and Bs, better than anyone thought he could manage. Him included. Julie told him how her plan was to transfer to Colorado University in Boulder in two years, that community college was just a stepping-stone, a way not to get completely crushed by student loans. She told him he could do it too. And maybe he even believed her. And those memories he had fought so hard against, memories of root beer in his mouth and blood on asphalt, they went away mostly.

And maybe there were still those nights when sleep wouldn't come, those nights he would stare at the computer screen with burning eyes, googling 'gangs of Inland Empire' and 'Devore combine' and reading weird little webpages, databases of gangs, old news articles with headlines like 'Guilty Plea in Bowling Alley Attack'. Or he'd dig up the Facebook pages and Instagrams of people who in another life he would be friends with, like the twins Trent and Tyson or his old play-cousin Callie. And maybe he'd never tell Julie or anyone about those nights, how they brought him right up to the edge of terror, but right up to the edge of something else too. That he was equally enthralled and repulsed by the people he had come from, this perfect orbit of push and pull. And as the semester went on those nights came less and less.

One night he had this dream, the best dream he has ever had:

He is in a green biplane, a little one only as long as he was tall, tractor green with yellow trim, and he flies in it nice and slow. And he doesn't feel the terror of being in the air – Luke has never been in an airplane – but instead it feels like swimming. He flies in long loops over the campus of his school. Below him the other students run out – there's Julie, there's Jess from his lit class, there's Woody, always shirtless with the frisbee, there's Joe and Rebecca and Jamila and Allen and Shelley. They all look up at him and wave. He waves back. And he's flying and he's floating and he's never going to fall.'

And then he woke up.

But the feeling stayed, at least a little of it.

Winter semester he signed up for Algebra 101, a math requirement he needed to transfer to CU. It crushed him.

He knew a couple of the other students got tutors but he didn't have the time and he didn't have the money. His brain whispered to him that anyway tutors were for people who just needed a little extra, and that he was dumb, that this was beyond him and always would be.

Julie fell in with a group of political kids, and more and more her conversations were about boys who'd read the same books she had and didn't have to work a double shift every Saturday, and he started to think the only reason she hadn't ended it with him yet was because she was sweet or because she was a coward and sometimes Luke wondered if there was a difference. And anyhow, he figured the time to save a polar bear is before the ice cracks under its feet, not when it's already in the water.

The first time he skipped class that semester, it was because of a head cold, but the day spent hiding in his cave watching old network sitcoms on endless repeat was like floating in one of those blackout-dark tanks of salt water just the temperature of your skin, floating in nothing, and Luke found the nothing suited him just fine. So he did it the next day too. He knew he was fucking up and he watched himself do it, like when you drop something and you have time to watch it tumble but no time to catch it.

He slept and slept but he never had any more airplane dreams. One day he rallied himself enough to go to campus, and he walked into algebra class just a little late. Everyone in class was writing in silence so Luke walked up to the teacher and said, 'Do I need something?'

'You mean the test?' the teacher asked. He kept his face calm as he said something like *Yeah I mean the test.*

Even as he took the test he knew it was over, that he was already heading towards a D at best and now it was an F for sure. The next week he gave up class altogether, and then work, not even calling in, just no-showing, ignoring the manager's angry texts. He missed rent and he hid as his landlord pounded on the door and yelled his eviction notice. It was only after it was too late to do anything about it that he realized he had to run, and that he only had one place to run to. He opened up a DM on Instagram to his aunt Kathy and sent her a message. Her message back was brief, so full of emojis it was hard to parse, but the message was clear: We'll find a place for you. It took him a night to pack what he could fit in his car and say goodbye to his couple of friends and Julie – there were tears, which was nice of her, but under them he could see the relief.

He left his basement apartment only half-cleaned with a note to the landlord saying *Sorry* on the floor, written on the back of a junk-mail envelope. Everything falls apart, Luke knows. Chaos and entropy pester everything to dust in the end. It's just somehow everything crumbles faster in Luke's hands.

CHAPTER FIVE

'You keep in touch with Amanda ever?' Del asks him.

'I got a card around Christmas from Clearwater. In Florida.'

His mom's writing on the back had been scrawled, childish – 'MISS YOU BABY DOLL MERRI CHRISTMAS'. The ink sat in deep grooves in the paper, like she'd pressed the pen down hard, like the effort ought to count for something.

She'd left California when Luke was young, so young that in his memories she was mostly shapes and smells, memories of warmth and being held. There'd been talk at the very beginning that as soon as she was able his mom would take him in, that his stop in Colorado was temporary while his mom got a nest ready to fit them both. Luke had believed it for the first few years. He waited for her and pretended not to hear the whispers from his aunts and uncles, how a long time ago she burned herself serving coffee at a chain diner, how she took the pain pills the doctor gave her until those ran out, then she took whatever she could get her hands on, until it unmoored her and Bobby kicked her out and from then on she floated through life facedown like a corpse. Luke had held out hope that she would beat it, that she would come to Colorado where it was so cold and wrap him up in her arms and take him away.

It took a lot of lies and disappointments, but after a while he'd learned how a dope habit hangs a mirror in front of a person's face, so no matter which way they look, even if they're looking straight at you, all they can see is themselves.

'Sometimes she calls,' Luke tells Del. 'I think she's . . . I think it's got her by the throat these days.'

'So she is not an option. You come to us as a last resort.'

'This is my family land, isn't it?'

It comes out wrong. When Del answers, there's anger in his voice.

'I've maintained what your daddy built all these years. Grown it, too. And taken care of him as well. Your daddy's books are full and the hacks are bribed to make sure his ride is turbulence free, and there's a spider out in Apple Valley sitting on a bank account filled to the brim so when he walks out that gate he'll be well ahead of the game.'

'I didn't mean anything,' Luke says, not understanding half of Del's words, feeling like it's already gone wrong.

'Anyhow, the two of you have been incommunicado for years,' Del says. 'So I'm not sure how much you can trade on him.'

'Your daddy talks about you,' Kathy says. 'Why don't you ever reach out to him no more?'

Because of this, he wants to tell them. Because of how just by being back here he can feel that other world bleeding into this one. Because the first time *it* happened had been after a phone call with his dad.

Please don't let it happen here.

'I guess what I'd want to know is,' Del says, 'what you're looking for? Are you just here for shelter? Or are you looking to join up?'

He touches his chest, over the black-ink heart Luke knows is there. And Luke wants to answer him *No*, tell him *I couldn't join even if I wanted to*, but he's scared to open his mouth because maybe if he does the night will pour out of him and fill up the house.

'You all right, honey?' Kathy asks him, and before he can answer Kathy looks past him and a voice calls out behind him.

'Goddamn, you must be Luke.'

Luke turns to see the man who he had seen last night – the one he thought must have been a ghost. But here in the room with him Luke's surer than ever that he himself is the ghost, he's the stranger visiting from the world of asphalt and sodium lights, that Arrowhead Lanes is his home and this is someone else's.

'Come here brother,' the man says. His face is anchored by a beaklike nose on a strong face, sharp blue eyes. He is wearing only tight boxer briefs. And the man walks straight to Luke, and Luke sees his black heart tattoo as he takes Luke in his arms so that Luke can smell the unbathed spice of him.

'I'm Curtis, brother. Blood is love.'

Voices in Luke's head like *Hey Bobby what's up Bobby blood is love Bobby.*

Luke wants to run. The one thing he has learned for sure is that there is no running from it. The thing he wants to run from is both inside him and it is everywhere outside him too.

It was a mistake to come back. This place is so close to the nexus to that other world, the one where time runs in tight loops, where it is always night and it is always hot and there is blood and bone on the asphalt.

'I been hearing about you for years,' the man says.

'Curtis here is family,' Del tells him. 'He was brought into the fold by your daddy on the inside.'

'Big Bobby saved my life in there, 'bout six different ways. Best man I ever knew.' Curtis slaps his black heart. 'I was lone wolfin' it before I got down with him – would have wound up stiff or running with the Hitler-huggers if he hadn't put me on the path.'

Curtis looks at Luke and it's like he's got X-ray eyes, it's like he sees everything. Like he can see that other world that's rising up in Luke.

Curtis walks to the kitchen area, opens drawers, yanks out a loaf of bread.

'You hungry, Luke? These two only eat coffee for breakfast.'

'I'm good,' Luke manages.

'You're a Crosswhite all right. No love for food. Not me, man. There's a hunger that if you feel it long enough and hard enough, it eats a hole in your stomach so you'll never be full again, not really. That's how I grew up. Out in Agua Dulce, you know, among the shitkickers? Never enough to eat, and not anyone who cared. My folks had a hunger all their own. Like your mom.'

Curtis pops slices of bread in the toaster. Luke tries to breath *in-out in-out*, like he's a person that is living in this world right here. But that other world is rising up.

'You coming aboard the Combine, right?' Curtis asks him.

'Don't push the boy,' Del says. Luke hears the warning in his voice.

'But we need you, brother. Things are shifting around. There's pebbles rolling down the mountain. Could be nothing. Could be an avalanche.'

What had Sam said last night?

Somebody got got in the desert.

Luke wants to know more.

Luke wants to run.

Curtis pulls the toast from the toaster. He ladles up the knife with margarine. His knife scrapes against the toast. Luke can feel the *scrape* of it in the roots of his teeth.

'Your dad pulled me up. Rescued me. I thought I was hot shit. He showed me, he showed me what real power was. He put this black heart on my chest himself. Del here bribed a CO to sneak some dead man's ink inside. So when I call you brother, believe it.'

All these words and phrases come at Luke too fast, this feeling of a half-remembered language – *the Combine* and *dead man's ink* and *blood is love*.

'I don't know . . .'

Sweat pops on Luke's forehead like a squeezed sponge. There is root beer sweetness at the back of his throat.

'There's plenty of work with the Combine,' Curtis says.

Luke can see the *shut-the-fuck-up* in his uncle's eyes.

He can see Del's already made up his mind about Luke and his place in this world – that he doesn't have one. Luke wants to say he agrees with his uncle. He doesn't say anything at all. Everything is too loud. The knife *SCRAPES* butter onto the next slice of toast.

'Your daddy loves you,' Curtis says. 'He's a good man, strong man. And he misses you. I think he's gonna be glad you're back here among your people.'

'He's got a place to stay,' Del says. 'But as for the rest of it . . .'

'Blood is love,' Curtis says, talking straight to Luke. His eyes are too alive, making Luke think of preachers and street freaks. 'Your daddy said it to me, on a real dark night inside, and it was rain in the desert, brother. "Blood is love", he told me. Love is the blood we share. Love makes us brothers and your blood is Bobby's blood so he loves you, and the blood we spill, we spill for love of our brothers. It's all right there in those three words. Your daddy's words. Blood is love, Luke. You feel me?'

Luke nods without thinking. He does. He feels something inside him, something small but vital. Like what a baby bird feels, maybe, that he has these wings for something. These fluttering things are there for a reason. And maybe he can be a part of it, become the person he was supposed to be, his father's son—

The thought is killed by this *scrraaaaaping* sound. Root beer sweetness at the back of his throat.

It's happening.

'Grab a seat,' Curtis says. 'You're looking a little green around the gills.'

Fingers of night poke through the noontime sun.

The taste of root beer blooms in his mouth.

'Come on sit down,' Kathy says.

Luke says something, a noise like *nu-uh.* He hears how high-pitched it is, like it's a little kid saying it. The world is dropping around him, making room for that forever night.

'Hey man we're all family here,' Curtis says, and he reaches out to Luke. But Luke's not in the kitchen anymore.

It's happening.

He runs without seeing, knocking open the front door with a flailing hand. Over the thuds of blood in his ears, the last thing he hears from the world of right now before he is swallowed up by the night in his head, is his uncle's final judgment:

'I told you he was soft.'

CHAPTER SIX

Luke is seven years old and he is drinking the last root beer he'll ever drink. The cup is white Styrofoam so he can leave half-moons in it with his fingernails. The ice is the good kind of ice, crushed so flecks fly up the straw and sting the back of his throat. The good kind of hurt.

Every chair Luke's dad sits in is a throne, even the plastic bench at Arrowhead Lanes. He is almost too big for Luke's little eyes to see all at once. Sun-bitten brown everywhere not covered by cut-off jeans. A black heart inked over his real one. He is king, not of the whole world but of their world. Luke knows if his dad is a king then he is a prince, and that is a good thing to be.

Dad drains the last of the beer from his plastic cup. He has drunk three pitchers worth, one for each of the three frames they have bowled. He palms Luke's kiddie ball with hands that can tear an apple in half. He walks Luke to the line, shows him how to move his arm like a pendulum. Luke lets go too late and the ball arcs up and then slams down loud, but it stays true all the way down the lane and it kisses a pin and sets off enough chaos to knock down a couple others. Dad's laugh cracks the room in two. He lifts Luke high like a trophy. Luke laughs giddy-scared, his heart so big with love and fear. He is young and there is nothing between him and the world yet. The scorekeeper screens shine so blue, his nose full of smoke and spilled beer and popcorn, all set to the calamity of pins crashing and crashing, everything alive alive alive.

Men from other lanes come and pay their homage. Men with ragged beards and shaved heads, white skin and brown skin scribbled with tattoos – some have a black-ink heart over their real one, just like Dad does. The men have hard eyes and yellow teeth. These men are with them almost always. They come to the compound, sit on the porch drinking and talking with Dad and Uncle Del. Here at the bowling alley Luke's dad stays seated and the men come to him, shake his hand and say *Hey Bobby what's up Bobby blood is love Bobby.* They clap Luke's back hard enough to hurt. Luke knows better than to let the pain show.

'You're gonna be big as your old man someday, ain't that right?' Teller with his billy-goat beard asks Luke.

'Goddamn right,' Dad says.

'Goddamn right,' Luke says. The men roar. The men lift their beers so foam slops the air. Luke sees the family one lane over look at the men and then look away fast. Luke can see the fear in them, and part of him is with them, scared by all these big barking men; but the other part of Luke loves it because he is with these men and someday he'll be big like them, and if Luke is a prince then someday he'll be king. And that means never being scared. Luke laughs not because it is funny but because of how good the night is.

This is what it is to be a prince, and Luke has never known another way.

On the way back to swap shoes, Dad leaves him with a quarter at the Ms Pac-Man machine and heads towards the bathroom with Teller and his billy-goat beard. Luke rests his root beer – his last-ever root beer – above the Player One button and slips his quarter in. The ghosts eat him fast; he hasn't learned the tricks of how to run from them yet. Luke's dad comes out of the bathroom snorting like a stallion, the rims of his nostrils red.

When they give their borrowed shoes to the man behind the counter, the man will not look Dad in the eyes. While they wait for their own shoes, Dad drums his fingers on the counter, faster than the music playing overhead. He wears a smile that could be a snarl.

It is the thick of summer and coming out from the air-conditioned bowling alley into the parking lot is like stepping onto Mars. Music spills from a half-dozen cars. People lean against them, older boys and girls laughing. A couple of teenagers walk past with their hands in each other's back pockets. The outside of the building is bright red, framed by bearded palm trees.

The men standing around the pickup next to his dad's Mustang laugh too loud, a mean laugh. The sound of it makes Luke take his dad's rough hand. Dad shakes it away. The men pass a bottle of brown liquor. A man in a yellow tank-top leans against Dad's Mustang. Dad walks straight to him. Dad puts his finger against the man's chest.

'The fuck you think you're doing?'

The man's speech is slurred so that Luke can't understand it, doesn't know what he says, will never know even though this moment will live in him forever. Whatever the man says makes Dad squeeze Luke's shoulder so fast and hard Luke wants to say *ow*. But he knows better than to ever say that. He swallows root beer instead.

'Back the fuck up,' Dad says. A vein pulses up on the side of his head.

The man answers in drunk babble.

'I ain't messing around,' Dad says, and the man talks back even louder, smears of words. The cigarette drops from Dad's hand as it clenches to a fist. Time is funny now for Luke, slow, and he watches the cherry twirl tracers against the night as the cigarette slow-dives to the pavement.

'All right then,' his dad says. He puts his hands on the man. Brings the man's face down into his knee. The man pops back up, drooling red. Dad hits him dead center of the stain. The man goes backwards. His head *thocks* against the concrete. His eyes go cue-ball white. Luke burps up sick-sweet root beer, swallows it back down his burning throat. He will never taste it again. He will never stop tasting it.

A woman screams, something between terror and joy. Somebody says *Hey Bobby no Bobby he's had enough Bobby*. Luke's dad pulls the man to the curb of the parking lot. Oh how the man's teeth *scrape scrape scraaaape* against the concrete. Luke feels a cold hand on his neck, like one of Ms Pac-Man's ghosts has caught up with him.

Hey Bobby no Bobby come on Bobby somebody says. Nobody moves. Nobody but Dad. His foot rises over the man's head. Time's still funny and he moves so slow. Luke has time to memorize every inch of his father's face. There is something so scared in his eyes. But there's something else behind the fear, something hungry and free. Like his father is a man riding a tiger, but also, he's the tiger too.

Dad's foot comes down.

CHAPTER SEVEN

He is on the asphalt in front of Arrowhead Lanes.

He is on the gravel in front of his childhood home.

It is night.

It is the middle of the day.

He is seven.

He is nineteen.

People are screaming.

There's no one here.

He is scared.

He is so fucking scared.

He remembers how to breathe. He rolls over onto his ass. The world fixes itself back into the now. The gravel under him. The slickness of tear-snot down his throat. His hands in front of his face.

All the moments of a life come and go, all of them but that night at Arrowhead Lanes. That night is always there. It hangs in Luke's life like the sun, something so big and burning he can't look at it, but it lights everything around him.

*

Halloween of his junior year of high school in Fort Collins, Luke and his friend Matt went out pumpkin stealing, going house to house, running softly to porches and front stoops, snatching pumpkins and running back while choking on the laughter they couldn't let out. They'd loaded them in the back of Matt's old Jeep. Near midnight they found a real prizewinner from in front of a craft store: a pumpkin big as a beer cooler, so big they struggled to lift it high enough to get it in the car, laughing at the mayhem, laughing so hard their eyes lost focus from tears. It had been too big to fit into the back seat so they just wedged it in like a beauty queen in a parade. They got down to Mountain Avenue where they could get up some speed. Luke leaned back from the shotgun seat and pushed the giant pumpkin up and out of the back seat. He watched as gravity took over. The pumpkin rolled down the back of the Jeep. It exploded as it hit the street. Luke vomited down the front of his hoodie, a sudden squall followed by sobbing tears.

Luke made excuses to Matt, something about drive-through burritos and rotgut wine and carsickness. How could Luke tell him that the sound of that giant pumpkin exploding at forty miles an hour was the exact same sound from that bowling alley parking lot a decade before, the sound of the man's head coming apart under his dad's boot. How when the pumpkin smashed, it made Luke a little boy again, made him watch a man die again and again.

Sometimes on late nights with his laptop he has gone searching for answers, found pages with words like 'flashback' and 'disassociation' and 'post-traumatic stress', those hard cold words that can't hold what it is like to live with the night inside you. Sometimes he thinks he was the one who died that night, that he was the one with his skull smashed on the pavement and everything since then has been the long last dream of a fading brain. But other times he sees it another way. There's two Lukes – the one who was a prince who laughed and ran and knew he would be king, and that is who died. And the Luke who lived absorbed him like a twin in the womb, and maybe there's a tooth or piece of flesh of that kid still in his brain but mostly they're dead and gone for good.

Luke sits in the gravel and looks up at the house, thinking maybe someone will come out and talk to him, to see if he's okay. He doesn't want them to, he can't take them seeing him as he really is, but there's still an empty feeling inside him when it doesn't happen. After a while he picks himself up off the gravel and walks back to the double-wide. It is a place to stay for a little while, and now Luke knows for sure that's all it will ever be.

CHAPTER EIGHT

Callie does inventory on the dinner table. She lays out the baggies, one by one. She counts Percocets, she counts benzos. She scrunches her toes in the crunchy carpet, the dull oatmeal color of the carpet in every apartment she's ever lived in. She jots numbers on the back of a receipt, just like Mr Martinez taught her in junior year accounting class. Inlays and outlays. Profit margins. Reserves. She waitresses at a bar called the Creepy Crawl – sometimes Pretty Baby barbacks. Hustling for the Combine keeps their noses above water, lets them sock a little cash away.

Pretty Baby slouches on the couch. His eyes are Xannie-glazed. He's playing his cowboy game, riding a horse through electric mountains. It's raining in the game – sometimes she thinks he plays it just to have weather in his life. He was born in Ohio and didn't move here until his parents split up while he was in high school, so he'd grown up with things like storms and snow and thunder. He's never fully got used to a place where rain is nothing but a memory nine months of the year.

I wanna steal a car for you.

That had been his pick-up line. And it was just a line, he told her later, just something he thought sounded cool and sexy and rebellious enough for this girl with long brown hair and wildcat eyes. For all his tattoos and illicit chemicals, *outlaw* was just a word to him.

She was different. She had been raised in the Devore Combine, her uncle a founding member and her mother a hanger-on who clung to the makeshift family after Callie's father split or evaporated or flew off into space – Callie was never quite sure which. She'd spent her childhood playing in the jungle of rusted junkers and speargrass with Luke Crosswhite while the grown-ups did dirt inside.

Callie's uncle had died when she was eight, found dead in his own pickup truck, a bullet through his temple, probably the result of a bad deal with some biker, although no one had ever been sure enough to pursue blood vengeance. Bobby had taken his ashes and mixed it with tattoo ink – the dead man's ink they used for their black heart tattoos.

Callie's mom had stopped coming around, but the older women had taken Callie under their wing, Kathy and Judy Del Sol, who now is doing six years in Chowchilla for receiving stolen property. They'd taught her as much as school had. When Callie was fifteen her mother had taken up with the manager of the restaurant where she worked, a divorced man who never wanted kids. Her mom made her choice and so had Callie. She moved out, couch-surfed with high-school girlfriends, then later, when hustling for the Combine started paying enough, on her own. She and her mom texted some and saw each other on holidays, but when they talk now Callie imagines she can see clouds of frost coming out of her mom's mouth.

About two years ago this pretty boy with his impossible green eyes had said *I wanna steal a car for you*. She'd called his bluff. She'd said *Okay*. How surprised he'd been a few hours later when it had been her hand that held the brick and cracked the driver's side window, her hand on the screwdriver, popping the ignition cap just like Apes had taught her. She'd looked over and seen his face in that moment, and that's when she knew. He'd looked at her with the brick in her hand and broken glass at her feet and she'd seen his face change – that this wasn't a one-nighter anymore for him.

They'd driven the stolen car into the Wash where the scrub would hide them and fucked in the backseat. After, glued together by drying sweat, she savored how their smells mingled together in her nose. Even in the cramped back seat she fit right into him. And the sex was good good good, but even better was a few weeks into it, when she'd drank too much on a night out with her girlfriends and then puked in the hallway of his apartment. She'd taken a sit-down shower burning with embarrassment and come out to find he'd cleaned it up and never ever made a big deal about it. Maybe it was a small thing but no other boy she'd ever been with would even think about doing it.

And maybe, she had thought, *maybe this time it won't be a lie*.

And so far it hasn't been.

She weighs out shake-and-bake crank for the bargain fiends. She weighs out glass-shard crystal for connoisseurs.

She bags it into grams, teenies, a couple of eight-balls. Small-timer units.

Small-timer profits.

She thinks about Scubby with his whiteboy dreads and hippie smell. He's got a two-tooth gap in his smile – he says he caught a major ass-whipping from the head of a nitrous crew out in the desert. Pretty Baby is right – Scubby likes to talk. Scubby says he's been greenlit by Sun Valley skinheads. Scubby says he knew Nate McClusky and his crazy-ass daughter, who took on Aryan Steel all by themselves and won. Scubby says he was in the Chinatown shoot-out.

Scubby says all sorts of crazy shit.

And now he says he's got a friend who wants a pound of glass.

Pretty Baby's right. Total bullshit.

She does the math again anyway. Del Crosswhite could get a pound from the La Eme pipeline for maybe ten grand. He'd sell it to them for thirteen, and they could pocket seven grand just by driving it over to Scubby's place and doing the deal. Add that seven to the three she's already stashed for them, it's almost enough to start over.

Almost enough to risk a bullshit deal.

But not quite.

She makes twenty-bundle baggies of molly. The pills are home-tabbed, rough around the edges, dyed all these funhouse colors that always make her think of kiddie vitamins. She pre-bags party packs, molly and crystal for the uphill climb bundled with benzos for the downhill slide.

She breaks up grams of weed and wax. She pops a

ten-milligram gummy. She thinks of Erik Montrose over in Redlands. Erik Montrose who moves weight for the Nazi Dope Boys.

Erik could get them a pound of crank easy-peasy. Erik who isn't tied to the Combine, isn't any sort of family. Erik with his white-power bullshit and yellow teeth. Erik with his eyes that move over her like cold hands every time they're in the same room. Erik who she could fuck over and feel nothing.

She does new calculations. She does the math for a deal done wrong. Pretty easy math. Twenty thousand dollars minus zero equals twenty thousand dollars. Enough to go anywhere. Enough to do anything.

Big-time profit.

Big-time risks.

She bags everything up. She puts the stash in the hole Pretty Baby sawed into the drywall behind her shoe rack in the closet. She hides their savings in the pocket of Pretty Baby's funeral suit. She pockets her take and the Combine's take. She drops fifty bucks on the couch in front of Pretty Baby, his share of petty cash, and plops down next to him.

He drops the controller and starts rubbing her shoulders.

'Thanks, baby,' she says. 'We got to get going soon, it's our turn to get the chicken. Oh, that feels good. Can you feel that knot there?'

'Yeah. You worried about something?'

'Still thinking about Scubby.'

His hands slip from her shoulders, wrap her up from

behind. She feels him bury his nose in her hair, breathes deep. It blooms gooseflesh all over her, how he still drinks her in.

'We can talk to Del about it tonight,' he says. 'See what he thinks.'

'Maybe.' She's not ready to tell him her new idea, the dangerous one.

His hand slips under her shirt.

'We're gonna be late,' she says, but she's smiling and falling into him.

Together they make it all go away for a while.

CHAPTER NINE

Some folk have their families handed to them ready-made. Some have to put one together from a kit. And like anything you make yourself, sometimes those families that you cobble together mean more.

The Combine family meals start with food, always. Somebody brings gas-station fried chicken – a San Berdoo specialty. The chicken is spicy, heat-lamp dry in a way that makes it better, dense and crunchy. On the side, baked beans from a can that Kathy adulterates with crispy bacon and onions and barbecue sauce. Hot potato chips, nacho cheese chips, pretzels. Party mix, the rye crisps always fished out early by Ricky and the Chuck Brothers, leaving Kathy at the end of the night with a bowl of pretzels sticks, peanuts and Rice Chex.

Curtis and Teller drink beer with tequila backs. Pretty Baby just drinks soda. He'll take any drug made by God or man except booze. All Callie knows is his dad drank bad enough for it to leave a mark somewhere inside him.

The rest mix drinks in giveaway cups, white plastic with the insides stained red from Kathy's fruit punch.

Callie has learned to watch Sam, the kid, who has to go home to his mom and if not watched will drink himself into slop.

Everybody takes their usual seats, never talked about but ingrained in order – Del in his chair, the big brown one, and everyone else finding their places on couches or drawn-in chairs from the table or stools from the kitchen island. To his right, Teller, a Combine OG. To his left, Curtis sits splayed-legged on the couch, taking up two seats – one for him and one for his balls, Pretty Baby always says. Curtis had joined with them a few years back, a stranger with the same black heart as theirs, done with the same dead man's ink, inducted into the family by Big Bobby inside Folsom. They were all unsure of Curtis at first, Del most of all she thinks, but it soon became clear Curtis was a force of nature, someone to sit close to the throne. When his probation was over, both with the state and the Combine, he'd moved into the back bedroom of the big house, and taken the seat next to Del.

After Curtis comes the Chuck Brothers – Trent and Tyson Charles – in lawn chairs dragged in from the porch. They sit next to each other for maximum effect. They trade rabbit punches and head smacks. She's known them for years, knows in a glance that Tyson is the one on the right. Next, sharing the loveseat, Ricky with his thick eyebrows and hair thinning already at twenty-eight, the quietest, the workhorse. Apes with her blonde buzzcut and boy clothes, her heart-throb smile and never-ending string of girlfriends. She is the best car thief among them.

Callie and Pretty Baby sit on the floor so Pretty Baby can lean against the arm of the loveseat, and Callie can lean against him, sitting between his legs with his arms draped over her shoulders.

Sometimes there are others, who have to figure out where to squeeze in among the regulars. There's about twenty black-heart members of the Combine on the outside, although many – like Maddox, who runs the garage for Del and is about eighty-twenty a legit mechanic – rarely appear at family dinner.

The air is hazy with cigarettes and weed smoke and vape. Music, corny old rock and roll, Del's music. She's grown to love it because it is for these family nights, grown to love Def Leppard and .38 Special and Scorpions and all their yearning and big-haired bravado.

They eat. They talk shit. Trent and Tyson tell some story about drunkenness, in that overlapping style they have – they don't share a brain, but there are so many echoes between them, so much shared time and experience that their thoughts often overlap and so do their voices. They laugh. They all laugh. She never laughs so hard as when they're all together like this.

Manson, Sam's pittie, stares at everyone's fried chicken, watches the trip from plate to mouth, tensed up waiting to snuff the floor, vacuuming up whatever falls down. When that's done, Manson finds a spot where she can see them all, the pack all together, which is her pleasure. Callie knows how she feels. This is the part that will hurt if they leave. The part of their life they'll have to tear off like a bandage that has grown to the skin.

Apes and Sam talk something, probably horror movies, their shared passion. But Sam says something that makes Apes look to Del.

'Bobby's kid is here?' she asks. The murmur of the room goes quiet.

'Luke's back?' Callie asks again. He had been her play-cousin and a prince, this loud kid who ran for the hellfire joy of it. And then it all shattered. She only saw him once in the days after Arrowhead. He had been sitting in the back seat of a car belonging to some family member from his mom's side of the family. His eyes had looked overstuffed with something, like a garbage bag you walk fast with, worried it will split and spill before you get it to the curb.

'He has made his triumphant return all right,' Del says. A mean laugh hidden in his voice.

'Well, where is he?'

'He's staying out in the trailer.'

'He's not gonna come say hi?'

'Not sure his constitution could handle it,' Del says. Kathy pig-snorts, covers her mouth.

Curtis says something about *the weak sperm*.

'Don't blame Bobby,' Kathy says. 'It's the mom. She's weak, always was. It was the weakness that drew Bobby to her. That was his downfall right there. Something sad in her always, made Bobby want to keep her safe from the world. See how that turned out.'

'He seemed okay to me,' Sam says. Nobody pays him mind.

'What's he like now?' Callie asks Del.

'Skinny and spastic. Couldn't hardly talk without stuttering. Then Curtis came out to meet the kid, and Luke went and had himself a fit.'

'He tore ass out of here,' Curtis says. 'Laid down on the drive and had himself a big ol' cry.'

'What a little bitch,' Tyson says.

'He's got a place to stay,' Del says. 'But he's not one of us.'

Callie looks to the back wall, in the direction of the trailer where Luke must be right now, but of course it's just a wall and she can't see anything. She remembers that little boy running free. That little boy in a backseat, eyes overflowing.

Somehow Pretty Baby knows to squeeze her just when she needs it.

Del fidgets with his phone and cuts the music short. He says, 'Enough on the wayward son. There's family business to discuss.'

Everybody puts their food down. Sam looks unsure – he doesn't have his black heart yet and sometimes Del tells him to leave. But sometimes Del lets him stay, and sometimes he forgets that he's there altogether. Seems like this is one of those times.

'Dave Pinkle came up from Hangtree last night with some news. Last week a fellow named Troy Gullet got killed out in the desert.'

'I know Troy,' Ricky says. 'Real peckerwood trash. Burned my ass on a deal one time.'

'Well, then maybe karma is real, because burned is exactly what Troy is,' Del says. He spreads his arms like a man crucified. 'They nailed him to the floor of his trailer, left him there to burn alive.'

Somebody makes a sound like *goddamn*. Callie leans back into Pretty Baby. She feels horror like scratching hands inside her. To die trapped, to see it coming and not be able to stop it. A death worse than any she'd ever thought of. How fast or slow had the flames come? Struggling against the nails, wanting to run, but stuck fast. To die drinking fire. Burning up and knowing it.

'Pinkle know the whys of it?' Ricky asks.

'It was Aryan Steel. On the say so of their new street general. Beast Daniels, they call him. Just walked out of Calipatria, ten years down on ag-assault.'

'I remember that,' Teller says. 'He blinded some son of a bitch down in Del Rosa, gouged his eyes out with his thumb.'

He flicks his own thumb in a scooping motion, pops his tongue. Somebody whistles low. Manson misses the *holy shit* vibe. She puts her head between her legs to loudly lick her twat. Callie tamps down a crazy laugh. Sam nudges the dog to get her to quit.

'Pinkle says Aryan Steel is resurrecting,' Del says. 'The Nazi Dope Boys, the High Desert Blood Skins. Beast is unifying the dirty whiteboy tribes that all scattered after the McClusky War.'

'The what war?' Pretty Baby asks.

'McClusky War,' Teller says. 'Crazy Craig Holllington, President of Aryan Steel put the greenlight on this dude Nate McClusky and his daughter. Dude turned it into some guerrilla war, wound up with the Mexican Mafia taking McClusky's side and offing Hollington for him. He and his daughter took off for parts unknown. This was like five years back?'

Curtis nodded. 'Something like that. I was inside when it went off. Everybody thought a bloodbath was coming. The Mexican Mafia versus Aryan Steel. But turns out La Eme didn't care, they just stood back and let the Steel turn on itself.'

'From what Bobby tells me,' Del says, 'all the infighting is done. There's a council now instead of a president. And Beast Daniels is their avatar on the outside.'

'So what's it got to do with us?' Tyson asks.

'Pinkle, he came by the house last night, talked with me and Curtis and Teller. Says that Beast wants to parley. That he's taking sit-downs with all the peckerwood operators. Not just the big gangs. Even little fish like us. Most likely they'll want us to pay the dime.'

'What's the dime?' Callie asks, not because she doesn't know, but because she knows Sam doesn't and won't ask.

'Ten per cent of every dollar we make kicked up to them.'

'Fuck all that,' the Chuck Brothers say together.

'Hold up,' Ricky says. 'I don't much dig paying, but also maybe I don't feel like getting burned alive by Nazi shitkickers. Let's talk it through. What's the dime buy us?'

'Protection,' Del says.

'From who?' Ricky asks.

'From them.'

Apes snorts like *bullshit*.

'We've gotten by for a long time,' Del says, 'on being

small-time enough and prickly enough that it don't make sense to fuck with us. We try and make it so the juice isn't worth the squeeze. Could be we're about to be tested. Or we flop over on our belly and let the man feast.'

'That doesn't suit me,' Curtis says. 'Not a bit.'

'Fuck Nazis,' Apes says. 'Fuck 'em all the way.'

'Could mean blood,' Del says. 'Some of you are young. You haven't been through the fire before.'

'You talk to Bobby?' Teller asks Del.

'He's aware. And it doesn't sit well with him either. I just wanted to let you know, keep an eye out. Beast may try to make a point before the sit-down.'

'I don't do this shit so I can kick up to Aryan Steel,' Apes says. She cracks her knuckles. 'They're just cops who didn't make the varsity team is all. Fuck 'em.'

'Blood is love,' Curtis says, hand over his heart. And they all say it, their little ritual, and Callie used to think it was dumb but she's old enough now to see the point, that maybe it's empty but it holds them together.

After the talk the feast resumes. Folk drink harder than normal. Callie catches herself gulping her drink, trying to put out this burning inside her.

She steps out onto the porch to escape the thick air inside.

Callie has come here since she was a baby, this place that is not her home but is. She walks down into the gravel, among their cars and around the side so she can look up the hill. She sees the trailer in back, dark but for some flickering grey light from one window, like maybe Luke's watching something on a laptop.

The door to the house opens – she knows it is Pretty Baby without looking. He stands next to her, looks up the hill.

'You want to go say hi?' he asks.

'Yeah, but not now. It's late and I'm freaked. We used to play together, like all the time. My uncle would bring me by, or my aunt after . . .'

Uncle John slumped up against the driver side door of his truck, a bullet in his brainpan.

'We'd play hide and seek in the junkers,' she went on, pushing the thought away. 'He was there when Bobby did what he did. Like standing right there when Bobby caved that man's head in. Guess it fucked him up.'

'It'd fuck me up too, for real. I thought Curtis and them were pretty cold about it.'

'They're scared of weakness. They're men.'

'And what's that make me again?' He makes a show of being wounded to hide how wounded he really is.

'You know what I mean, baby.'

She looks at the window of the trailer, thinks about the poor broken boy in the back of an outsider's car and wonders why he'd ever come back here.

'You want to talk to Del about doing that deal with Scubby, we better do it now,' Pretty Baby says. 'His drinks are getting paler, you know?'

He mimes a heavy pour of vodka.

'I don't know. It's probably like you said,' she says, keeping her eyes on Luke's trailer. 'Scubby's probably full of shit.'

He probably is, she figures. But that's not the reason she doesn't want to tell Del about it. She's still thinking of that other way of doing the deal, of getting a pound from someone outside the family and not paying them. So they'd have enough money to run far away. But now's not the time to talk about it. Not yet.

'Let's go home, baby. Let's talk about the deal later. Okay?'

He nods *okay* and takes her hand. She looks at him, tries to see him for real. They've been together over two years now, and she's past that first wild lie of fresh love. She can see him clear now. She knows there's a splinter stuck in him somewhere deep down, and that he takes too much stuff too often because of it, and she knows better than to think if she could see the splinter and get her hands on it and yank it free that he'd ever be whole and healed. Even at twenty-two she's past thinking anyone ever gets healed all the way. She only hopes he can be strong enough that she can lean on him sometimes. She's strong, but no one's so strong that they don't need to lean sometimes.

PART TWO

RISING UP AND RISING DOWN

CHAPTER TEN

Luke lights a smoke with dead man's hands. He closed tonight at the Hong Kong Inn, loading the last of the plates and the glasses into plastic trays, spraying them with a hot water hose, sliding the trays into the mouth of the industrial washer, yanking them back out, unloading them while they still steamed. It leaves his hands water-logged so the skin puckers and tears easy, like a corpse plucked from water.

He takes Rialto to the 215, heads north. Thrash metal napalm-burns from the speakers. Since he's been here, the music he'd listened to and loved in Colorado hasn't seemed right, like something he should have left behind with all his winter clothes. This pounding music, fast and loud and angry, this feels right. He'd started with Power Trip, the band that had been on Sam's shirt that first night. Something in it worked, fit this place better than his old music. He dug into it online, found other bands, names like Jesus Piece and Left Behind and Year of the Knife.

Luke takes the turn onto the gravel road fast so that the car skids a little. He steers into the skid. He grips the wheel tight, sharp little pain in the webbing between index finger and thumb, where the wet flesh always tears first.

His jeans are stiff with the dirty mist that hangs in the kitchen. During a twelve-hour shift time passes in smears. Rushes during lunch and dinner, waves of dishes, eating the discount meal after the lunch rush, not even free unless he steals it. A carry-out container of orange peel chicken and crab rangoon sits next to him, made in the slow hours between dinner rush and closing, when the manager had stepped outside. On days he works Luke eats buffet leavings twice a day. Between that and the trailer coming rent-free he is managing to save a little. He figures in three months he'll have enough to go someplace else, someplace no one knows him where he can start again.

The days are long, never-ending boredom broken up by stepping out into the night for cigarettes, the smoke like gasps of air to a drowning man. The hours go slow but the days go fast. He has been back only a few weeks but already the Luke of Colorado feels distant and blurry, like a movie he maybe watched one time.

It is almost midnight when Luke reaches the compound. He hopes that's late enough that Del and Kathy won't be on the porch, maybe with someone from the Combine, watching him with blank expressions and mean smiles behind their eyes. Ever since that first morning they've spoken nothing but pleasantries, mostly just nods, like neighbors whose names you've forgotten. He cannot look at them without thinking about how he'd run, how the part of him he didn't want anyone to see was the first thing they'd seen. A few times there've been gatherings, loud music and muddled voices, and he's watched from his window, feeling like a sniper. Once he saw a girl who he thought maybe was Callie Gifford standing in the gravel looking up towards his trailer with a boy with pink hair, and he thought for a second that she would come up and say hello. Maybe he'd even wanted her to. But she hadn't.

He rolls down the gravel road fast now. He's learned its quirks, just where to gas it to skid just right into the dogleg so his stomach drops and the tires spit rocks into the night. His foot is already on the brake to stop and open the gate when he sees how it hangs half-open already. A pickup truck is parked haphazard in front of the house.

A man sits half-in the cab of the truck, the door open and his feet dangling into the gravel. The way he sits cupping his face in his hands, not even looking up as Luke's headlights paint him, tells Luke something is wrong. Then Luke sees the blood.

Luke kills his lights. The man doesn't move. Luke kills the motor. He gets out of the car. He slams the door shut. The man doesn't move. The front of his shirt is a bib of blood. Luke can see now at the center of the stain is a rip in the shirt, and inside that there is a rip in the man. A wound like a little red mouth drooling blood. Luke's within touching distance before he can see that the man is breathing.

'Hey.' Luke whispers it, so he can barely hear himself over the sudden roar in his head.

The man looks up at Luke, his eyes flat underneath bushy eyebrows. The reek of booze on his breath.

'At first it didn't hurt,' the man says. 'Then it hurt like hell. Now it doesn't hurt again. Starting to think I'm fucked.'

His voice is dull in a way Luke finds more alarming than the panic he expected. The man spits pink.

'Someone inside know you're out here?' Luke can feel the blackness rise up inside him. Panic like flecks of ice at the back of his throat. He tries to keep himself focused on the man's need, not the blood. He barely keeps it all inside.

'Felt like a punch,' the man says. 'Felt the wet before I felt the pain. Ain't that a bitch?'

When he talks Luke can see blood on his teeth.

Luke blinks and the light changes. Like the moon is a sodium lamp in a bowling alley parking lot.

'Let me help,' Luke says through a mouth full of root beer.

'Get away from him.'

Curtis comes down the steps from the house. He's got blood on the front of his jeans.

The air is sharp at the back of Luke's throat. He bites the inside of his mouth. The pain keeps him on just this side of his two worlds.

'Get up, Ricky. Kathy's got a bed made up for you.'

Curtis turns his eyes on Luke. Luke can't hold the gaze. He looks down. The blood blackens the gravel below the man named Ricky. Fat red drops on his dirty white sneakers. Shadows flutter, make Luke look up to the porch. Del stands in the doorway, looking down at them. His face tells Luke he can see how the panic has Luke in his grip. How pathetic he must look to them.

'You don't carry nothing by yourself,' Curtis tells Ricky. 'I got you, brother.'

Luke stands frozen in the gravel, afraid that if he moves, he'll run.

'This got nothing to do with you,' Curtis says to him, not looking back. 'You made your choice. Now get up to your fucking hidey-hole and forget you ever saw this.'

Luke stands in silence as Curtis gets Ricky up the steps. Del pulls him onto the porch, and the three walk in together. They don't look back. Luke stands there between two different nights, blood on the ground everywhere he looks.

Later, in the trailer, Luke strips down in the dark. He doesn't want to see himself, not a reflection or even shadow. He scrubs the crust off his face. He leaves the food uneaten on the counter. He lays down in the bed, naked against the chill, just to feel something. The cold keeps him anchored to this world.

Lights poke through the trailer window as more cars come up the gravel road. He listens to the sounds of car doors slamming. Folk talking muffled in the night. A few angry shouts. He listens, tries to decipher what's going on. But it all gets crowded out by Curtis in his head, telling him *You got nothing to do with this*, barely even seeing Luke, like maybe he wasn't even really there.

CHAPTER ELEVEN

Marshall Boulevard is a shitty skateboard surface, too pebbly, so that the vibrations thrum through the soles of Luke's feet. He finds the rumble soothing. Above him the sunset is orange blazed with pink. The shadow that skates in front of him is stretched skinnier by the setting sun.

In the morning there had been no evidence of the stabbing. Ricky's truck was gone, and the patch of bloody gravel was now clean. As he drove past the side of the house Luke could see the garden hose, which the night before had been stored in a neat coil on its hook now sitting in a tangled pile against the side of the house.

He didn't know who had stabbed the man, or if he'd lived or died. As he'd worked the lunch shift he'd become aware of a swelling sensation inside him, the same kind he'd felt in those last days of college, before he'd quit going altogether, and he knows that if he doesn't do something, he'll pop again and everything will spill out and wash away whatever vestiges of a life he's been able to build.

He'd seen the skateboard in his back seat – there'd been no reason to move it into the trailer – and as he stood in the restaurant parking lot the prospect of heading back to the compound filled him with dread so he'd driven a few blocks from work, parked in a strip mall and taken the board out. And he'd known right away from how the rumble of the wheels moved through his feet and up into his bones that this was what he needed.

He carves back and forth down an empty thoroughfare as the last of the sunset falls away into night. Outside a shuttered poke place an old guy sells al pastor, a hunk of meat on a vertical spit, slicing off chunks. A family is gathered round, taking tacos on white paper plates, leaning up against the dead building, laughing, talking in Spanish so Luke can only catch the feelings of what they're saying.

He has not skated in months, and at first, he falls too often to get into the flow of it. The tendons of his right foot, his pushing foot, ache almost instantly. He tries to ollie from street to sidewalk but comes in too low and the wheels catch on the lip of the curb, leaving him to breakfall on the sidewalk. But somehow the falling is good, the sting on his hands taking him away, getting him closer to that place he's trying to get to.

Luke loops, shifting his weight to cut long diagonals down the street. He ollies the curb. This time he lands it. The way the *grrrr* of the wheels goes quiet as they leave the earth with a slap. The rhythm of it:

Grrrrrr
slap
silence
slap
grrrrrrr

He was twelve when he'd gotten his first board. The way you had to practice a trick a hundred times – back foot shove down, front foot comes up, and the board pops up – suited him. He liked the way it locked his brain in, owned it so completely. He had neglected the board in Colorado Springs, his days taken up with books and work and Julie. It's why he's out of practice.

He kicks the ground, builds up speed. The wind finds every gap in his clothes, drinking sweat from his belly and the crack of his ass. He ollies again. It's like flying until gravity catches you. The night drinks his sweat. He picks up speed. Here, one bad bump from death, he is safe.

He follows gravity, picks up more speed, rolls onto a residential street. Plunging past quiet houses lit only by porch lights and television grey-light through blinds. He looks down at the pavement, thinks about how dying here skull-cracked on the road seems more real and possible and maybe even better than a life stretching out another sixty years. The thrumming at the center of him stops, or maybe it just matches the thrumming of the wheels on the road; they cancel each other out and there's quiet. Luke finds himself lighter, floating like a moon-man on a spacewalk.

A car backs out of a driveway to his right, not looking, pulling quick into the street right in front of him.

Do it.

Instead he shifts his weight to slide the board sideways, skidding to a stop. The guy behind the wheel hits the brakes too late to make a difference, gives Luke the *I'm the asshole* wave and drives away.

Luke crashes back into himself. He catches his breath and feels himself come back to the world around him and it's like putting wet clothes back on, heavy and damp and even colder than when you took them off.

CHAPTER TWELVE

He rolls downhill on E Street, slow now. He moves into a strip mall parking lot, a wide expanse of smooth asphalt where maybe he can work on getting his heelflip back in shape. Nothing here looks new. The cars, the sign for P&J's Liquors, the men hanging outside the liquor store door – everything looks like it's been baking in the sun for years.

He sees a beat-down pickup truck – not the one from last night, but still it seems familiar. He sees the pit bull in the truck bed, her paws hanging over the side, a rope tied around her collar, and recognizes her. He stomps the backlip of the board so the top jumps into his hand. He walks over to Manson. She rushes to meet him, as far as the rope will allow.

'Hey girl.' His voice is froggy – he realizes he's barely spoken all day. On his days off sometimes he doesn't talk at all. He gets close so she can kiss him, and he finds that spot between her ears so she gapes in pleasure. He talks doggie: *Hey girl, good girl, are we best friends, yes we are*. Her tail wags with love. He thinks on how good it would be to have a dog. Luke thinks for one crazy second about untying the rope and dognapping her.

‘Some fucking watchdog.’ Sam walks up from the direction of the liquor store, a soda and a bag of chips in hand.

‘Hey,’ Luke says.

‘Hey man.’ Sam nods at the board. ‘Nice.’

‘You skate?’

‘Used to.’

‘Me too. Thought I’d get back into it.’

Luke rubs the velvet of Manson’s little clipped ears. He realizes he is starving for talk, and to learn the story of the stabbed man. He’s trying to figure out a thing to say, a way to prolong the night. They stand there in awkward silence. He thinks on how Sam’s eyes gleamed when he told him somebody got got.

‘You hear what went down last night?’ he asks.

‘Maybe.’

‘I saw it.’

‘Horseshit.’ But Luke can see cracks in the wall – Sam knows he shouldn’t talk but he wants to. Luke realizes this kid must be the low man of the Combine. The only person he can hold any rank over is Luke himself. He needs Luke to talk to just as much as Luke needs him.

‘I was getting off work, he was in his truck out in front of the house. Blood and everything.’

‘Oh I thought you were *there* there. When they got him.’

‘Just the aftermath. Do you know what happened?’

Sam waits a beat. Luke figures it’s just for show, a way of saying *I shouldn’t be telling you this*.

‘Ricky was up at the Creepy Crawl, right up off the exit

there? There's some waitress up there he's trying to bang. A couple of these NDB guys from Fontucky—'

'NDB?'

'Nazi Dope Boys. Yeah, I know. Anyhow, these two guys come in, and I don't know if they were sent or got lucky or what, but they jumped Ricky right there in the bar. One guy held him, and the other one, *ga-goosh*, he fucking stabbed him, and then they split.'

'Is Ricky going to be okay?'

'Del says yeah. Said Ricky'll be fine as long as there's no infection.'

'He didn't go to a doctor?'

'Man, Ricky does all right but he don't have sixty-dollar-aspirin money. Anyhow they probably would call the cops, guy with a stab wound comes in.'

'There was a lot of blood. It looked bad.'

'Did you spazz out?' Sam asks him, and then gets this look on his face like he shouldn't have said it. 'Del and Curtis, they said you have like fits.'

Luke's not sure how to answer that, but something in his face must answer it for him, because Sam raises his hands and says, 'Sorry, whatever man, I get it.'

They stand there in the parking lot for a long beat. Luke scrambles for something more to say. The idea of going back to his trailer for another long mute night destroys him.

'I got Xbox and my mom works third shift,' Sam says, 'Wanna get a pizza and play *Call Of Duty*?'

They sit on shag carpet and get pepperoni grease on the controllers. They get their asses kicked by kids too young to know how to swear right, little jerks who call them *butt-asses* and *fartfuckers* and then no-scope headshot them. They get their asses kicked and laugh.

They pass a joint back and forth – Luke only takes a real hit the first time, knowing how weed moves from relaxing to terrifying so easily. After that he just lets the smoke sit in his mouth a second before puffing it out in a weak cloud that wouldn't fool anyone who was paying attention.

They talk about music. Luke pretends like he knows more than he does. He name-drops Power Trip – Sam doesn't remember he'd been wearing the shirt the first night they met. He buys Luke's line. Luke feels like a creep for manipulating Sam. He just needs this human moment so bad.

Sam buys it. Invites him to a concert in Pomona. Ricky was supposed to go with him, but he was laid flat by pain pills and general bitch-made weakness. Luke says *hell yes*.

They sit on shag carpet and Sam talks. Sam fills him in on the Combine. He lays out the whole criminal enterprise. Luke keeps his eyes on the game, nodding, filing all of it away. He tries to pretend he doesn't want to know everything about this life, this life he is sure he is living in other timelines.

Sam takes all the whispers and rumors Luke collected about his family and gives them a shape and heft. He talks about the Combine – how Del runs it on the outside, but everyone knows Big Bobby still calls the shots. He tells him Big Bobby's got occasional access to a cell phone. He breaks down the org chart – Big Bobby to Del, with

Teller and Curtis under them. On the side there's this guy Maddox who manages the garage – they funnel stolen cars, chop them up. Apes – don't ever call her April – is a car thief beyond compare. She likes to hot-wire old Hondas, big-time resale value. The Chuck Brothers like B&E, electronics. They're not above the occasional gas station stick-up – they also work laying rebar with a foundation crew. Callie and Pretty Baby are a couple, they move party drugs mostly, small-timer shit.

They all kick into a kitty, they all get paid out. It's all based on pirate contracts, shit Big Bobby and Teller and Del and some other guy who died came up with back when they were a bunch of teenage skate punks tired of getting their asses kicked by the white power gangs and Mexi gangs and black gangs. He names the OGs – Big Bobby, Del, Teller, and John Meadows, first of the fallen.

'John,' Luke says. 'Callie Gifford's uncle. I remember when he died.'

'He got shot or something.'

'I don't remember how he died. I was a kid.'

Sam explains how Del moves weight, meth mostly – he moves it out of state, working with bikers, him and Teller. It's not major – none of it's major. They stay small on purpose. They stay in that middle area, above the street people who get scooped up by local cops, but below the vision of the Feds.

They drink vodka with grape soda and Sam talks about Beast Daniels and Aryan Steel. He talks about how they want the Combine to pay the dime. He talks about a fight coming. Sometimes he talks to Luke like Luke is a part of all of it, and then he remembers that Luke is an outsider and stops talking for a while.

Manson snoozes between them. She has doggie dreams, ghost-running, half swallowed barks. Luke wonders if dogs understand dreaming, or if they just take turns living in two worlds, each one as real to them as the other. He gives her a little shake to break her from the dream.

'Whoever had her first, I think maybe they fought her when she was young,' Sam says. 'I got her from that shelter, the one in Agua Dulce. I don't know what they made her do before she was rescued but she came out the other side sweet as anything. But bitch fights in her dreams.'

They play the game in silence for a while. Luke can feel some question building in Sam, can see it coming in these sidelong glances. He's about to ask Sam *what?* when Sam breaks the silence himself.

'You really not going to join the crew?'

Luke shakes his head like *naw.* This feeling when he breathes like his lungs are full of fiber.

'It's your family,' Sam says. 'Your dad built it.'

Luke studies the screen. He is under fire. He dies. He drops the controller. He looks at Sam.

'Like you said. I have fits.'

'You got this family out there waiting on you man. You got a dad—'

'In Folsom—'

'Still a dad.' Sam looks at Luke, like he's not sure if he should keep going. 'My dad died. He was a fireman. Like he got sick in this way that only firemen get, all those years of breathing burning shit. Meso-something. His piss was brown when he died. His throat was swole up like a howler monkey's, swole up so he couldn't even breathe. And it was like the smoke, all of it for years, it was still in him even though he didn't know and it ended up choking him in the end.'

He looks at Luke like a challenge, like he dares him to make fun of him for his pain.

'That's fucked up,' Luke says. Sam nods like *yeah*. His shoulders drop from his ears, something released by Luke accepting it.

'I just don't get how you could still have your dad be here and not talk to him.'

Luke doesn't know how to say it – how to explain he's not his father's son, just the ghost of him.

'The Combine is a family,' Sam says. 'Sort of the best one a lot of us got. And it's yours, your dad started it. I don't get how you don't want to be a part of it.'

Luke studies his hands, the way they look like a corpse's hands. He chooses his words carefully, afraid of how much could pour out of him if he opens his mouth all the way.

'I'm trying real fucking hard not to want things I can't have.'

He knows if he says anything more, words like *ghost* and *forever night* will start to come out of his mouth like root beer foaming over the top of a glass. He stops talking and the two of them sit in a silence as heavy as Luke has ever known.

Luke drives home with his hands at ten and two. Not too fast and not too slow. He closes one eye to kill the blur of drunkenness. He sees ghost cops in his rear-view. He feels his heart in his throat. He thinks about the way Sam had talked to him. Like he could join the Combine. Like he wasn't a ghost, a mostly dead boy who just happened to float into Sam's view.

He trudges inside the trailer, looks around at his stuff scattered around. How it barely looks lived in. He tells himself that he is just here in SoCal because he has to be. Because he doesn't have anywhere else to go. Because he had flunked out of school and wrecked his life besides. Because he fucked it all up. He thinks maybe he should leave, right now, not even wait for sobriety.

He shoves things into the boxes he hadn't even bothered to throw away, like he's always known this day was coming. He thinks about Phoenix, maybe, or Flagstaff, someplace a tank of gas or two away where he can start anew with the little money he's managed to save. He wasn't ever supposed to come here, it was just he'd fucked up his life too much to go anywhere else—

He comes out of a trance, his head snapping up. He thinks again of the stranger that drives when you don't. It leads him to something new, something huge.

What if it hadn't been a fuck-up?

What if all his skipping class and ditching work and blowing his life in Colorado hadn't been mistakes? He thinks about the way it had felt sometimes, watching himself burn down his chances, watching himself blow up his life, as if he didn't have any choice in the matter.

Well, what if he hadn't had a choice? What if it had been the stranger inside him, steering him here? What if his fuck-ups were some sort of hidden plan?

He pops a full body sweat. He feels a thumb at the center of his skull. He knows now that it's true. That the stranger had been driving the whole time. Driving him back home, back to his family.

And all at once Luke knows why. Because the stranger knows him better than he knows himself. It knows that Luke wants to be here. He wants to be a part of this world, to try to become the person he was supposed to be. If Luke goes to Flagstaff or anywhere else he'll always be this floating thing that never even leaves a footprint on the world. Someone with feet in two worlds, that's what a ghost is, right? If Luke wants a chance of being more than a reflection in glass, he has to stay here and try and join his family. Because if you are going to resurrect somebody you have to go back to where they died.

He dumps out the boxes. He puts the things away. He is terrified, but it's a new kind of terror. This terror of hope. Maybe it will heal the crack in him. Maybe it will shatter him down to dust. But one way or another it will be decided here.

CHAPTER THIRTEEN

Pomona has time-warp vibes – small town Americana like you see in the movies. The crowds of metal fans come off like barbarian invaders. Shaggy metal heads, brown and white, with long hair and denim vests, patches sewn all over – 'Electric Wizard', 'Sleep', 'Bongzilla', 'Windhand'. Pentagrams, anarchy symbols, Baphomet with a scepter. Luke steals glances at a group of Latina goth girls with pewter jewelry and black lipstick and kohl-drawn eyes. Mixed in are college kids from one of the schools in Pomona, lumberjack beards on soft jaws, tight T-shirts – they make him think of the guys who hung around Julie, like that Adam kid she was probably dating now.

Death Valley winds blow in from the east, sweeping the sky so the stars shine through.

They trudge through the ticket line. Sam pulls a weed cookie from his pocket, breaks it in half, eats half in one bite, offers the other half to Luke.

'Homemade from Apes. She don't fuck around.'

Luke waves it away. He knows how badly edibles can go. Already there's a tightness in his chest. He has not told Sam that he plans to join the family. He doesn't know where to start, how to get a handhold in this world. But even having the goal has lightened him somewhat, helped pass the time washing dishes, waiting for this night.

Inside the club, the air is thick with vape smoke and body heat, everyone pressed together. The ripe smell of unwashed bodies and weed smoke.

The two of them press in close to the front of the stage. The back of the stage is a long semicircle of Marshall stacks. Two guitars on stands on either side.

'Where's the drums?' Sam says. The guy to his right laughs at him. Sam shoots a stink-eye.

'First time?' the guy asks. 'Y'all will want these.'

He reaches out to them. Four little squishy orange earplugs in his cupped palm.

Sam shakes his head *no thanks*.

'Trust me,' the man says. Luke reaches across, takes them.

'Thanks.'

Luke squishes the plugs into shape and jams them in his ears. Instead of getting quieter, it feels like the rush and roar of his blood gets louder.

Again that tightness in his chest. If the other world falls on him here he doesn't know what he will do. He is trapped by the mass of bodies around them. He thinks he should say something to Sam, some kind of warning, but of course he can't do that, he can't bear to look weaker than he already does.

Smoke machines hiss and hiss. The room grows thick with sweet vanilla. The house lights dim. The buzz of the crowd goes quiet. The fog is total. Luke shoots a look to Sam: even though they stand shoulder to shoulder, Sam fades away in the smoke until Luke is all alone.

The smoke machine hiss goes quiet. The lights go completely out. For a terrific moment there is total silence, total darkness. Luke floats in the void.

Nothing.

Nothing.

Nothing.

The *ROAR* of the guitar is distorted and deep and louder than anything. Red light blazes through the smoke, turning the whole world fiery red.

Luke is front row at the Big Bang.

He breathes in like surfacing from a lake after a deep dive. The sustaining chord of the guitar is so loud he feels it in the roots of his teeth, feels his uvula buzzing at the back of his throat. So loud it presses on his breastplate, his bones like tuning forks buried in his flesh. He can feel his individual cells rubbing together. It should be too much. But it isn't.

It's just enough.

He looks to his right. Through the glow of red smoke he can just make out Sam's head, his fingers jammed in his ears, animal fear on his face. Luke hands him the other set of earplugs. Sam jams them in. Luke turns away, wanting to forget Sam, wanting to let the music vibrate in each individual cell of him.

The guitars rise and fall in glacial chords. Luke lifts his shoe off the floor. His sock buzzes against the bottom of his foot. It makes him think of the rumble of skateboarding, how in those moments he feels whole and alive.

The light shifts from red to deep blue. The smoke clears a little. Luke can see two men in robes on the stage, guitars in hand, their faces hidden by hoods.

The press of the crowd is a comfort now. Like he's one cell in a big organism.

The man to Luke's left, his eyes closed, bliss on his face. Luke reaches up to his own face, feels the smile there.

The sound washes him down to the meat, each hair on his head shaking in its root. Luke fishes an earplug from one ear, just to test it – the sound pours in sudden and sharp like an icepick, and he plugs it fast again. He feels a shove to his right. Sam pushes his way out of the crowd, his eyes wild with the Fear. Luke lets him go. He stays where he is. He lets himself come to pieces. It feels right and good.

That other world, the world of night and blood, presses against him, but this time it does not swallow him. The vibrations keep him safe. The flashes of the bowling alley are blurred like old videos, weirdly beautiful.

Red-black blood on the asphalt.

White shards of shattered tooth bright against it.

The crowd screaming as his dad stood there in the muck.

The images come and go as if they're just memories. Which, Luke suddenly realizes, is all they ever are. The massive sound of the music grounds him in his body. He closes his eyes – the lids buzz against his eyeballs – his sweat joins him to the world, his body giving water to the wind. His shirt buzzing against his skin. The sound fills him, connects him to everything and everyone, all these vibrating particles. And even though it is loud, it is quiet too – a sound so complete it serves as silence. This is what the end of the universe will sound like, the last long vibration, the white-noise heat death of everything. It hushed the thing in Luke's head that hummed in him always. If the world is vibrating to pieces, somehow that fills him with calm, because that is the frequency Luke vibrates at all the time. The chords go on and on, buffeting him and abrading him. And it's like he himself is the thing to be scrubbed away, pieces of him sloughing off. He feels himself rising up off the ground, but when he looks down his feet are on the floor. He thinks maybe he is laughing but it is too loud to be sure.

He feels washed in the blood of something pure.

And then it ends. The house lights go up. It's like something breaks, and the world comes back to Luke, or him to it. The robed men hold up their guitars in benediction. The crowd cheers – a feeble sound compared to what had come before it. The organism falls apart. It's just a crowd again, pressing against him. Luke isn't a cell of some great beast. He's just Luke. But some feeling of it remains. The feeling that parts of him he thought were solid are in fact nothing but dust. Only the flesh is real.

The crowd trudges out slowly. Luke moves with them. He sneaks glimpses of faces, looking for someone else with some new secret fire in their eyes. Mostly they look exhausted by what they have been through. He finds Sam in front of the venue. Sam blows a vape cloud. He smiles to try and hide his dope-fear. Luke acts like he doesn't see it. He slips his hoodie back on and thinks of the robed men. He tries to think about how to talk about what they'd just taken part in.

Before he can figure it out, Sam says, 'That was lame as hell. Thought they were gonna be a thrash band or something. Not like the longest fart I ever heard.'

Luke just nods. He knows now he can't talk to Sam about it. Sam would just laugh at him if he tried to explain this swirl of thought inside him. If he tried to explain to Sam that the show had been a ritual. He's never been in a ritual before, not a real one. He doesn't count the dry motions he'd gone through with his aunts and uncles when they'd dragged him to church. This had been more like something done by firelight in ancient times. A rite of life and death. A way to control the mysteries of the world by acting them out in miniature.

If he says it to Sam in whatever mangled way it would come out of his mouth, he knows Sam will laugh at him. And this feeling in him, this weird bloody elation, is too fragile to survive the laughter of a friend.

He doesn't say shit. He just sits in the shotgun seat looking out the window at billboards and factories. He knows now that what he fears is not the world, not his family, but only and ever himself. That there is something struggling inside him, tearing him apart. But maybe it is struggling to be born.

Maybe he should help it come out into the world.

CHAPTER FOURTEEN

The mirror in the trailer bathroom is plastic with a thin reflective glaze that is peeling off, so when he looks in it his reflection is in shreds. He takes off his clothes. He thinks about that first night here: the thuds, hearing Curtis, seeing him through his own reflection. How he felt like a ghost, with his soul still living in that bowling alley parking lot.

He'd always thought that the night at Arrowhead had taken something from him. But maybe that wasn't it at all. Maybe instead it put something into him, like folks who get shot then carry a bullet with them the rest of their lives.

He looks at the shards of himself in the mirror. His skin unblemished. His scars are invisible.

He thinks again on how maybe his fuck-ups hadn't been fuck-ups. Maybe fuck-ups are just your brain's way of getting you someplace you don't want to admit you want to be?

There's this thing inside him, this part of the base of his brain, and it screams and it tears at him. He wants to talk to it, to reason with it, but how can he reason with this part of him that was shaped before language and will never learn how to speak in words?

And he thinks on the fear he feels in these moments, and that maybe he's misunderstood it. Maybe he's not afraid of other people, of the world. Maybe he's afraid of himself, and what he would be capable of if he let this thing inside him out into the world. And that maybe that's what the stranger wants him to do.

An idea bubbles up from someplace deep inside him. He thinks on how there are deeper rituals, rituals of the body. Rites of flesh, sun dances and human sacrifices.

He remembers the concert, and before that, on his skateboard. Those little tastes of danger, those private rituals where he can make the world vibrate at his frequency, where he can face the violence inside himself safely.

Let the pressure out.

He makes a fist.

He raises it above his head.

He tastes root beer and ice.

He brings it down.

Thud.

There's pain. But there's something else too. A warmth. It spreads from the ache. His stomach muscles spasm. That other night inside him fades a little. He lifts his fist again. This time he tightens his stomach, giving his fist something to collide with.

Thud.

In his head he sees a bird slicing through the air, afloat on its hollow bones.

He lifts his fist again.

Thud.

CHAPTER FIFTEEN

The vibe is *DEFCON Beast*.

The Chuck Brothers man the gate. Trent holds a shotgun with a drum under the barrel. Tyson holds a machete he found with the gardening tools up against the house, swinging it back and forth in front of him like he's chopping down ghosts. This goofy smile on his face under these scary eyes.

Apes sits on the front steps, a battered old .22 rifle across her lap.

Manson sniffs in the dirt in front of the house, scraping after something gone to ground. Pretty Baby sits with his hands in his lap. Callie knows it shames him to not be muscle in times like these. There's no way for her to tell him it's why she loves him, no way for him to believe it.

Curtis paces, veins popping, his shirt tight against angry muscles. In his head the war has already started. *That makes him dangerous*, Callie thinks.

Del stands on the porch, his long hair slicked back, shaved clean except for his mustache, almost regal in his

Pendleton plaid. Teller stands next to him, hair slicked back as well, a semi-auto long gun in his hands, radiating OG. It makes her proud of them. It scares her bad.

Ricky looks gaunt, his eyes glazed by pain-pills. His shirt puffs out from the gauze on his chest. So far the knife-wound is healing. So far no corruption has spread. He drinks pale vodka-cranberries. They don't sit well with the antibiotics they got from a bent doc in Victorville. He drinks them anyway. Callie pats his hand – he jumps a little, then smiles shamefaced. Eyes that say *don't laugh at me*. She gives him a wink like *never*.

'Can't believe this all started 'cause of me. Was just trying to get a little pussy,' he says. 'Didn't plan on getting stuck and starting goddamn World War Whiteboy.'

'Could have been any of us. You were just the first one to come within reach of them is all.'

He nods like he doesn't really believe her. She thinks on how everyone is the star of their own movie, for good or ill. All of them feeling like they brought themselves here, that they are carrying the load on their own.

A sharp whistle from Tyson tells them someone's coming. Gooseflesh pops on her arms out of nowhere. Pretty Baby's hand finds the small of her back. She gives him a grateful squeeze.

An SUV rolls up the gravel road. The sound of screaming black metal bleeds from inside it.

Tyson swings open the gate. The SUV rolls up to the space they left open in front of the house. Tyson comes in behind them and swings the gate shut. He makes a show of locking it, just how Del told him to. Trent with the shotgun and Teller with the semi-auto take position in front of the SUV.

Callie tastes a new thickness in the air, like the SUV brought its own atmosphere with it. Like hot winds from the desert, the kind that bring on fire season.

This is real in a way she wasn't ready for.

The guy behind the wheel is nineteen, shaved to the skull. His scalp is shaved, paler than his face. His knuckles too tight on the steering wheel, the sweat on his brow, a mean mug that doesn't quite fit his face. Everything about him screams *new fish*.

The man sitting shotgun screams something very different. Tatted everywhere, his body fully filigreed with prison ink, from his shaved scalp to the tips of his fingers. The man's eyes are flat – not dead. More like a reptile's. His T-shirt pops shocking white against the vandalism of his skin. He pays no attention to the long guns in front of him as he climbs from the car. A pistol pokes from his waistband. She thinks for a moment this must be Beast, until the man opens the back door and another man climbs out and she knows at once, *this* is Beast Daniels.

Beast is a head and a half taller than the other man, fingers thick as candy bars, mid-forties she guesses, thick with both muscle and fat. A face of hard angles, craggy flesh. He rolls his neck, shakes his limbs, like the SUV was too cramped for him.

He looks straight past the mass of the Combine, up to Del. He spreads his arms wide, palms out like *I come in peace*, a friendly smile on his face. But it makes Callie think of the man in the desert crucified in a burning trailer. It takes her another moment to realize that was Beast's intention.

'Del Crosswhite.' She'd figured on his voice being rough, gravelly. But it's musical, higher pitched than his bulk suggests. 'It's good to meet you.'

'Likewise,' Del says. 'Come on in. Your man can come too. But not the gun.'

Beast nods to the other man. The man pulls out the pistol – this knife-edge moment as he brings it up – and tosses it onto the shotgun seat.

Callie lets out a breath she didn't know she was holding.

'One of your associates used a knife on one of ours. Unprovoked.' Del speaks from his easy chair. Beast sits across from him in a kitchen chair dragged over for the occasion.

'Unprovoked? You sure about that?'

'I didn't do shit,' Ricky says. He's aiming for hard, misses badly. Del shoots him a look like *shut up*.

Beast laughs. Sitting in a roomful of enemies, unafraid. He nods to the ink-stained man sitting next to him. The man – Beast introduces him as Stainless – produces a rolled up sandwich bag, heavy with off-white powder.

'This is our offering,' Beast says. 'To make peace. One ounce. That ain't no Mexi shit snuck over the border in some beaner's asshole. We've got the Steel's labs up and running again. That there is American-made and duty free. Once it's gone we'll sell you as much as you need.'

'We're not looking for product,' Del tells him.

'We're offering more than just product. I come ordained

from the Council itself. I've been given this area as my own. You all is natural born white men.' He looks at Apes. 'Or close enough, anyhow. So it's time you joined up. Come under the protection of Aryan Steel.'

'And pay you the dime,' Del says.

'Well worth it. Nobody lives truly free. La Eme, Black Rag Mafia – you gotta pay somebody.'

'We've managed our own affairs up 'til now,' Del says. 'That's our preference.'

Beast smiles, friendly but he lets them see the falseness of it at the edges. He turns to display his left arm, rolling up the sleeve, the row of blue thunderbolts tattooed there. Callie's heard about how Aryan Steel marks its kills – each blue thunderbolt a murder.

When he talks it feels practiced, like this is a speech he's given before:

'This top bolt here, my first. You know Magoo up in Vacaville? He inked my first blue bolt, a homemade rig with a beard-trimmer motor. It was an order from Despot himself, a righteous kill. This chomo priest somehow landed in gen pop – usually they put them in PC. Maybe it was a fuck-up, or maybe some CO wanted the kiddie-raper to get iced. Either way I was happy to do it, a righteous piece of work. I got to hand out a little justice and secure my place in the Steel. Bolts two and three, those I got on the outside, in a for-real parlor. That's why they look so clean. Those were two fellows, they were Aryan Steel brothers who were double dealing, not paying their share up the ladder. Now understand, in the Steel you do not kill a brother. You correct him. I corrected those two with a three-pound hammer. That's the job got me the name Beast. Bolt number four, that one was a fellow up in Calipatria during my last bit who was dry-snitching to the Correctional Officers. Me and two brothers tossed him off the top tier. Fellow died a modern art masterpiece on the cellblock floor. And this last one –' he pats the bottom blue thunderbolt '– this one you've probably heard tell of.'

She sees Troy Gullet nailed down, breathing smoke, breathing fire. She makes up her mind about something.

'Hey, Stainless, what you packing?' Beast asks. 'Two bolts?'

Stainless pushes up his sleeve.

'For now.'

Beast scans the room.

'Now I've heard plenty about Big Bobby Crosswhite. His name carries heavy weight. But he's on the inside, isn't he? And you can be big and you can be bad, but on the inside he is touchable. Believe me on that. As for what you've got here? See now, Del, I look around at your crew and I don't see shooters.'

Curtis snorts like *fuck you*. Beast looks him over. Curtis gives him this look, this shift in the eyes. She reads it plain. She'd heard whispers about what he'd done inside. Now in his eyes she can see it is true. Beast must see it too.

'Come see me if you ever want to make a mark in this world,' says Beast. 'You could be a proper white man some day.'

Curtis slaps his chest over his dead man's ink. That's his answer. Beast turns to Apes.

'What about you? You a girl or a boy or one of them new models they talk about?'

Curtis stands. Apes is the one who stops him.

'Fuck it,' she says. She swallows something big and painful.

Callie also stands – it's not fair that Apes should have to hold someone else back. Callie puts her hand on Curtis – his arm vibrates under her touch.

'I'm a woman,' she says to Beast. It comes out strong and clear but Callie can still hear the rage Apes is holding down.

Beast laughs.

He's getting the best of us, Callie thinks.

'There's a hierarchy in this world, plain as there's days and there's nights,' Beast says. 'You'll pay the dime or you'll be buried, and whichever peckerwoods scavenge your corpse and take over your businesses, they'll pay the dime in your place. This is the way of things. You all have done well, and you think you can't afford to kick up, but I'm telling you that you can't afford to not pay. There's no shame in it, don't think that. Only two things change. Anything you sell, you buy from who we tell you to buy from. Any profit you make you kick up the dime. Anything you do otherwise, your cars and hot parts and whatever, you kick up the dime on that too.'

'And if we refuse?' Del asks.

'We can't have it. If you don't pay, then somebody down in Berdoo, or over in Apple Valley, or some such, somebody's gonna ask why if you don't pay then they do. So listen. If you choose not to pay the dime, you'll pay in other ways. Uglier ways.'

'I already conferred with Big Bobby,' Del says, and now it's his turn to deliver a planned speech. 'We anticipated what you'd say here. So I already have your answer for you. Our business is ours. You provide no services to us. We don't live like we do so we can pay taxes to you all. It's been a while since we've bled for what's ours, but we haven't forgotten the way of it. This thing Bobby and me built, it's family, and we'll stand together or we'll fall together.'

'All right then,' Beast says, rising slow. 'Fair enough. Next round of negotiations won't be done with words.'

'It won't be easy,' Del says. 'That much is plain.'

Beast is twenty minutes gone, but some part of him hangs in the air, fouling it so everyone talks with wrinkled noses and sneers. The way he bragged about his kills echoes in Callie's mind, showing her a future that might be:

The Chuck brothers shotgunned, their parts all mixed up on the ground.

Apes savaged with bottles and bricks.

Curtis, his throat slit, a lap full of blood.

Del stabbed and slashed, his tongue cut out.

Teller face down on the ground, a lake of blood spreading under him.

Pretty Baby with a bullet in his head.

'Way I see it,' Teller says, 'we can't win a straight-ahead war against them. They got numbers and they got pull. But what we can do is hold out, stay strong. Show the world you don't have to bend to these fucks. Beast showed us his ass, only he don't know it. It's just like he said. If we don't pay, it makes him look weak.'

'That's how we do it,' Curtis says. 'That's how we win.'

Ricky, reading Callie's mind: 'There's like twenty of us, and the Steel's got folk everywhere.'

'It's like when those Odin's Bastards tried to muscle us way back in the day,' Teller says. Callie sits up – rumor had it the bikers had been the ones who killed her uncle John.

'Bobby chain-whipped one of them, down to the bone. And that was enough for them. They walked away – they didn't want word getting out how weak he'd made them look.' Teller drums his hands on the table. 'We hold out, we make them look weak. It'll make others wonder what they're paying for. It'll make them want to rise up too. There's more of us at the bottom then there are of them at the top. Always are.'

'You mean everybody who doesn't want to wear the brand,' Del says. 'You're saying you want to unify the tribes outside the Steel.'

'I don't want to unify shit,' Teller says. 'I'm just saying, the weaker the Steel looks, the weaker they are. And folk will rise up, and they'll have a dozen fights on their hands.'

'It'll be ugly,' Del says. 'And part of that ugliness will come from us. Y'all ready for that?'

Callie isn't. But she knows the way this will go, she sees it on everyone's faces, and she knows better than to take a worthless stand.

'Blood is love,' Trent says.

And everybody says it, even Callie, even while the movie plays in her head, all of them dying and dying so bad.

Her feet dangle off the porch. Inside the family is loud, building up energy, coalescing into a war party. Outside the air is sharp, scraping the smoke and the ruminants of Beast Daniels off of her.

The sound of them gets louder as someone opens the door, and it hushes again as it shuts. Pretty Baby sits down next to her. He takes her hand, kisses her fingertips.

'I guess we're in a war,' he says. 'I guess this is how it feels.'

He's not a soldier. She doesn't care about that. But she thinks he can be strong in other ways. And she needs him to be. She made up her mind in there. It's time to show him everything. It's time to find out if the two of them are make or break.

'I want to try the deal with Scubby.'

'Okay,' he says after a second. He thinks she's changing the subject. 'We can check with him tomorrow, see if his buddy still has a need. And you want to talk to Del about getting a brick?'

'I don't want to tell the Combine at all,' she says. 'I have an idea. A way we could make way more than just six thousand. We don't buy the pound from Del. We buy it from that asshole Erik Montrose. Only we don't buy it from him. We get him to front us, and then we get out of town. We sell it for twenty thousand, and we keep all of it. Twenty thousand dollars. Enough to go anywhere at all.'

'You want to rip off Erik?'

'I don't want to be nailed down and burned alive. And goddamn if that's not how it is if we stay. Nailed to a place that's on fire. Fighting to protect . . . well, what? The Combine? Pretty Baby, I can't. I love them in there, but I don't want to fight for this place. Anyway what good am I in a fight? Or you?' She sees that last part bruise him and she's sorry but now's the time for bruising truth. She keeps going.

'And it's not about the Combine anyway. It's about this place. This dead-sky place. I'm going to leave. I want you to come with me more than anything. But I'm going to leave. I love the Combine and I love you most of all but I can't be nailed to the floor while everything burns around us. Combine's my family. But you, you're something different. You're a part of me, you mean as much as my own arm, and would be just as hard to lose. I love you all the way down. But I don't want to stay here. I can't.'

She pauses – she feels so naked now, in front of this boy who has seen her naked from every angle but this one. And if he laughs right now it will be ruined forever. If he shuts down, runs away from the moment, it will be ruined forever.

She can feel her tongue in her mouth, too big to fit inside her teeth.

He looks at her with those eyes, those eyes, those eyes – even in the dark they gleam. And those eyes tell her the answer, floods her with beautiful calm before he says a word.

'I love you too,' he tells her. 'All the way down. Let's do it.'

She holds him there in the night and he holds her too.

She'd never thought she'd ever have anything so right. She always thought she was too jagged to find anything that would fit her flush.

CHAPTER SIXTEEN

Callie takes shallow breaths to deal with the smell. Erik's place doesn't smell like death. Death doesn't smell like anything. It's the hungry slime of life that stinks. Erik keeps it cave-dark. Only the slashes of light at the edges of the blackout curtains hint at how Riverside bakes outside. He's like something from a cave himself, a lump of a man the color of fishbelly, his purple mohawk limp, the hollows of his eyes darkened by puffs of blood under the skin. He is sweaty and bug eyed. His sweat smells metallic from meth toxins. He is spun as all fuck.

She never gets used to it, the smells, the dark, or his crawling eyes. She tries hard not let herself be alone with him.

She is alone with him now.

Pretty Baby sits in the car outside. Close enough to keep Erik in check, but out of sight, so Erik won't get frustrated and angry, the way guys like him do sometimes when Pretty Baby is in the room.

Erik had been watching a movie when she showed up. It's one of those horror movies that is four-fifths about a woman getting sliced up and raped and then one fifth about the woman's revenge to make it seem like *that's* what the movie's about. He hasn't paused it. Every so often Erik's eyes drift over to the screen to check the action when the woman screams good and loud. Callie thinks about the things she's heard about him. That he was busted a few years ago for grave robbing, like somebody from a shitty Frankenstein movie, just so he could scavenge the corpses for buried jewelry and gold teeth. How he did three months for it and hit the streets afterwards as big and white and gross as ever.

Erik looks her up and down like he can see right through her clothes.

'Wanna get fucked up?' he asks. 'I got some K, straight from a vet tech, total purity.'

'Pretty Baby's in the car.' She hides her horror, the thought of being in a K hole with no one but Erik around. 'We got a thing.'

His face sours at the mention of Pretty Baby.

'What then?' His spun nerves turn to anger.

The most dangerous things in the world are a wounded animal and a rejected man.

'I'm looking to make a buy,' she says.

'Figure you didn't pop by to say hello.'

'I want a pound of ice.'

'A whole pound?'

She nods like *that's right*.

'You think you're big-time?'

'I met a guy in need.'

'What's he going to pay for it?'

'What you're going to charge me,' she says. 'Plus a little more.'

A woman on the TV screams. Erik grins. She's not one hundred percent sure that he's a human being.

'Del Crosswhite can handle a pound,' he says. 'Why you going outside the Combine?'

'My reasons are my reasons.' Let him think she's looking to cheat the Combine out of their taste.

'I'm getting my package from Beast Daniels now,' he says. 'Heard there's been beef. I don't need to get mixed up in nothing.'

'This has got nothing to do with that. Let's keep this between us. I'm just doing this once.'

'Maybe you ought to just tell me who you're selling to. Let me handle it. You don't want to punch above your weight class. Figure that's how you get knocked the fuck out. You let me make the sale, I'll throw you a finder's fee. Keep your pretty little nose clean.'

She shakes her head.

'He only trusts me.'

'Hey, this is America,' he says. 'You got a right to make a profit. I can get you a pound for fifteen.'

'Thirteen.' She barters because she knows he'll get hinky if she doesn't. It doesn't matter what he wants to charge her. She's never going to pay him anyway.

'All right, Big Time. You bring me thirteen and we'll get it set up. Gonna take a few days.'

This is the moment. She thinks about Pretty Baby. She thinks about getting the hell out of the Inland Empire.

She puts down the three grand.

'This is all we've got.'

'You want me to front you the rest, huh? Gonna need a down payment.'

'That's what the three grand is for.'

'Gonna need more than that.'

'I don't have more.'

'Hey, you help me out and I'll help you out.'

'I'm not gonna fuck you, Erik.' She somehow says it without screaming.

His lips curl up. Callie guesses you could call it a smile if you were feeling generous. Cavewoman warnings howl from the base of her brain. She holds steady. She looks for weapons with the sides of her eyes. Traffic noise breaks the moment. He picks up the cash she laid down.

'Come by on Tuesday,' he says. 'And when the deal is done, come bring me my money. Don't make me come looking for you. Figure you won't like it.' He grabs his crotch. 'Or maybe you will.'

She does her screaming on the inside.

The dirty air outside is the best thing she's ever tasted.

'All good?' Pretty Baby asks.

'Yeah.' Her voice sounds just right. 'We're all good.'

Anybody who thinks love means not having secrets doesn't know shit about love.

CHAPTER SEVENTEEN

Luke straps his skateboard to the back of his backpack. A camo off-roading dust mask pokes from his back pocket.

He skates around the block, carving slow, looking without looking. He passes the Hong Kong Inn, the lot crowded, someone else manning the wash station tonight. He passes the auto lot that's catty-corner to the restaurant.

Seven days since the concert. Seven nights of punching himself, feeling stronger, learning to take the punch, take the pain. Seven nights of learning to live with his memories, to break them off into chunks with a fist in his stomach. Seven nights for him to think on what he really wants.

The idea of what to do came to him fully formed four nights ago.

On his smoke breaks the last three nights he's marked the cameras at the auto lot, marked the security guard service's spot check times. Three nights of not knowing if he was serious at all.

He skates around to the side of the auto lot. He stomps the board into his hand, hangs it by its axel from his backpack. He scans the street. This 'No Credit No Problem' banner hides him from the street. He slips on the mask. He takes out the bolt cutters.

He feels his cells rubbing together inside him. Making fire, making heat.

He tries to get the cutter's jaws around a link of chain. He misses – his hands are shaking bad. He jabs the cutter again, misses again.

Cells rubbing together. Making friction, burning fuel. He moves his arms around in circles to burn some of it off. He's learning how to let things out of him before they burn him down.

He moves his hands up the cutter right up to the jaws. He moves the jaws around the link. He presses down until the jaws just bite into the metal.

This is the moment.

He can turn around. He can wash dishes and lay rebar and haul drywall until his knees go. He can forget about this place and his dad and whatever it is he thinks he can get here. He can go and live some hollow shell of what a life is supposed to be. He can find a series of jobs and a series of girls and marry one of them and have kids who he'll love and hate about fifty-fifty. And maybe the world will burn up first, or he will.

He makes his choice.

He snaps through the link. The fence rattles with released energy.

Walking in the lot, his footsteps so loud. A long string of plastic flags flap in the breeze overhead. He walks between cars, heads towards the back row up against the dealership. The mask kills his peripheral vision. He swivels his head to check. The street is dead.

He drops the skateboard. It rattles on the pavement. He curses himself for an amateur.

He kneels down and rolls his back onto the board. Friction tape scratches. He pulls his backpack onto his belly. His feet take little baby steps to roll him under the truck. He fishes out his phone, turns on the light. He traces the exhaust system from the back of the truck to the catalytic converter.

Luke had been seventeen years old, late for school, his wet hair freezing up in the Colorado cold. He climbed into his ancient Honda. He turned the key and the car *screamed* at him. It took a while to figure out – someone had stolen his catalytic converter. They're full of rare metals. Platinum, palladium, rhodium, mined in Africa by people living lives Luke couldn't even imagine.

His cousin Shane, laughing to his face: *They're big on the black market. Ask your family; they'd know all about it, I bet.*

The little shit had been right. The Combine knows all about hot parts. Sam has told Luke how the Combine moves them through the garage.

Luke fishes out the hacksaw. He saws fast. The saw kicks up bad dust – black snow falls on Luke. He's thankful for the mask. His shoulder burns from sawing at a weird angle.

He figures it's better to be loud and fast than quiet and slow. He saws through the pipe, then scootches the skateboard down a few inches so he can cut the pipe on the other side of the catalytic converter. After a minute it's free and he wrests it loose. He puts it in his backpack.

The next four go much faster.

He goes through the slit in the fence. He pulls loose the dust mask. The night is cold against his sweaty face as he skates back to the hatchback.

It's over. He's already thinking about doing it again.

He drives to the garage so very slow. His hands shaking now in a way they didn't before the job.

What if they laugh?

What if they close the door to him?

What if he can't keep the forever night from swallowing him up again?

The garage looks pretty much as he remembers it – an ersatz Woody Woodpecker above the bay doors, splintered wood painted brown with red trim. A new Smog Check sign where the old one hung.

Lights glow through the contact paper taped to the garage bay windows.

He sees Del's truck, plus a few other vehicles he's seen parked in front of the house.

He parks on the street. He gets the bag of catalytic converters out of the shotgun seat. He walks to the garage's office door – childhood memories springing up around him. He had been here many times with his dad, his dad and Del shooting shit with the mechanics while Luke would steal sugar cubes from the box beside the coffee machine, strawberry sodas from a cooler. He remembers a centerfold taped to the bay wall, his first naked woman – medical-textbook explicit.

He hears voices inside the garage – angry but hushed. A loud laugh he recognizes.

He stands in front of the door like someone with their toes poking off the edge of the world. This is where he jumps. The crime was nothing compared to this. He tenses his stomach muscles. They ache – the good kind of ache. It tells him that he is ready.

He knocks on the splintery wooden door.

The voices go quiet. They talk in urgent whispers.

The backpack in his hand, banging against his thigh as his leg bounces.

The door opens a crack. He sees a slice of Curtis's face.

'The fuck you doing here?'

It's not too late to run.

And then it is. Curtis opens the door. There's a flat black pistol in his hand.

'Answer me. Don't fucking tell me you drove out here just to have a conniption fit. Don't fucking tell me that.'

Luke holds out the bag. He fights the urge to look away. He blinks once hard, like a punch. He holds Curtis's eyes. He hands him the bag. Curtis looks inside.

'C-catalytic converters.'

'I know what they are.'

'I took them to sell. For the Combine. A hundred a piece, right?'

Curtis studies the converters, studies him.

Luke says, 'I want in.'

'That's what's up?'

'Yeah.'

Curtis thinks it over. Smiles.

'Fuck it.' Curtis holds open the door. 'Welcome to the party.'

Luke crosses the threshold. The air reeks with smoke and motor oil, rich mineral smells and smoke. The air is electric with something. Fluorescents make the world feel like a cheap movie. The first thing he sees is a man tied to a chair in the paint bay. The blood that flows from his broken face looks black in the weird light. His shirt is smeared with motor oil and dirt and blood. His hands are bound with electrical cords. His eyes are wide and white in his dirty face.

It's like Luke's insides have already poured out into the world. He stares at the blood and the dirt. And again it's like the world and him are vibrating at the same frequency. Where there should be fear in Luke there is something harder.

Del turns. He sees Luke standing there. He drops the hammer in his hand.

'Get the kid out of here.'

Behind Del stand the twins and Ricky. The twins pogo, *fuck yeahs* all over their faces. One has a helmet in his hands. The other one, a fungo bat.

Ricky's hands are empty. They hang loose at his sides. He looks seasick.

Curtis holds out the converters.

'Kid wants in. Brought us a gift and everything.'

'He's not one of us.'

Del eyes Luke. Luke holds the look. He thinks he does okay.

'I want to stay,' Luke says.

'He's already here,' Curtis says. 'Damage is done.'

'Not all of it,' Del says. 'There's still some damage left to do.'

The man in the paint bay moans. Nonsense words burble out on a wave of bloody spit.

'Shut the fuck up,' the twin with the helmet says. 'Just sit there and bleed.'

Luke can smell the guy from here. It's not just BO – the guy's body is sending out some kind of signal, some pheromone SOS. His breath is hitched and ragged.

'He's the one who stuck Ricky,' the other twin says to Luke.

'So we're turning him into a postcard,' Curtis says. He looks to Del. 'Can they get back to it?'

Something unsaid passes between the two men.

'Proceed,' Del says.

The twins put the motorcycle helmet on the man's head. The one with the fungo bat takes a few air swings, getting the feel for it. He gets into a batting stance. He swings the bat into the man's head. He swings home-run hard. The *thunk* is dull. So are the groans that come out from under the helmet. The twin tosses the bat to his brother. They take turns on the man's head. The helmet holds. The only sounds are the thud of the bat and the twins' giggles.

Luke stands in the back with Curtis and Del. The man under the helmet is awake; Luke can tell by the way his body doesn't slump all the way over. But he guesses the man is very far away. Luke himself isn't far away for once. Luke is right here.

After a while the twins drop the bat, out of breath.

'My hands are buzzing like a vibrator,' one says. 'I'm ever in a crash, that's the helmet I want. Jesus Christ. Want a swing, Ricky?'

Ricky shakes his head *nu-uh*.

'Maybe we ought to take it off,' the other one says. 'See what the bat can do without it.'

'Leave it on,' Del says. He's got a long gun in his hands. 'Let's do us an experiment.'

'Del,' Curtis says. Luke can hear the worry in Curtis's voice – he didn't know this was coming. Del waves him away. He steps into the paint bay. He bends over, leaning on the rifle like a walking stick. He lifts the chin of the helmet to look into the eyes inside.

'You're not the first fellow ever been in this paint bay. Not the twelfth, either.'

He points the rifle at the man's face. The man bucks to life, revitalized by the death so close to him. He tries to twist away from the gun.

'Turns out it catches blood just as well as paint. I reckon if there's brains, those we'll have to clean up by hand.'

Luke watches, planted where he stands. Something warm in his hands and feet. Cells rubbing together. Making heat, burning fuel.

'Del, come on,' Ricky says weakly. 'I didn't ask for this.'

The twins watch on in stunned surprise, smiles on their faces, like this is all a movie.

Del turns to the back of the room, looks to Curtis. Del turns back to the paint bay. He puts the rifle high on the helmet's temple.

GUNSHOT.

The helmet spits chunks. The echoes bounce cacophonous. Luke doesn't let himself grab his ears. There's no silence when the echoes fade – just a shrieking whine. The man in the chair slumps dead. He spasms back to life. He finds breath to scream.

'Holy shit,' the twins say as one.

Del drops the rifle. He takes the helmet off the man. The man blinks in the light. He looks like he's still doing the math on if he's alive or not. Del holds up the helmet to the light. It looks like the bullet missed skull by about a quarter-inch. He tosses it. He takes the man's smeared face in his hands again.

'Listen. All we want is to be left alone. The Combine is not worth how much it will cost you to take it. We won't come for you, but if you come for us, we'll turn the Inland Empire into a butcher shop. You tell Beast Daniels we're even. You tell him to leave us be.'

The twins drunk-walk the man out into the night – Del says to dump him outside the bar they found him at. Ricky hoses down the paint bay. Del and Curtis talk low in the corner, shooting Luke glances.

No one says *leave*. No one says *stay*.

He finds a new cooler where the old one was. He fishes out a strawberry soda. He sits on the floor. He can't tell if he's tired or not. Waves wash over him. He can't tell if they're hot or cold. But he knows this – he does not feel like a ghost. He doesn't know if he's ever felt this alive. He takes a drink of the soda, fizzy-sweet against his tongue. He takes another drink.

Alive alive alive.

Del comes over. He hunkers down – his knees *pop pop pop* – so he's eye level with Luke.

'This is what it is,' Del says. 'This is what it means to run with the Combine.'

His eyes probe.

Hold the look, hold the look, hold the look.

'You said you want in. That still the case?'

Luke thinks it over. What it would mean to stay. And what it would mean to leave.

'Yeah. I still want in.'

Del reaches in his pocket, pulls out a fat fold of cash. He deals out a stack of twenties.

'For the converters,' he says. 'That's a lucrative avenue to explore. Just don't get greedy like that. Hitting a dealership is too high-risk. Don't be crazy just to make a point. Don't be that much your daddy's son.'

Del had never before hinted he could be.

'I hear you.'

Del leans in close, talks quiet.

'You remember now – there's the Combine and then there's family. You and me are both. We're bound together twice, you and me.'

Luke nods like *okay*. He knows Del's buttering him up – and that means he's worth something.

'Figure the Combine's got a new prospect,' Del says to

Curtis. Curtis slaps Luke hard on the back. Luke knows better than to show that it hurts.

'Hell yeah we do,' Curtis says. 'Timing's great. We got family dinner tomorrow night.'

'I got a shift at the restaurant tomorrow night.'

'No,' Del says. 'You don't.'

INTERLUDE

A TREATISE ON FREE WILL

SCUBBY

Life grabs you in its jaws like a bear and all the flailing around and the screaming you do while it eats you, that's what we call free will. Like the bear's not there, like all this wailing and fury and fucking up everything is just what we choose to do.

Then maybe once or twice in a life you see someone slip loose from the bear's mouth altogether and walk free through the world, and it scares the hell out of you. Like Polly McClusky with her cherry-soda hair and Kurt Cobain eyes. I saw her walking like Athena with a teddy bear through a Nazi Dope Boys stash house. Her and her dad took on Aryan Steel and they won. Along the way they saved my life – I saw the shovel that was meant to dig my grave and the bag of lime that was meant to eat my flesh, that's how close I got to the big delete. But those two saved my skinny ass. They took on the world and they won. They walked free and clear.

I tried to walk free and clear too. I figured I owed it to the gods, you feel me? Like maybe they'd saved me for something. I kicked crank – a month spent like a corpse that can feel itself rotting. But I made it through. I caught work of a sort, riding along with a nitrous crew, following jam bands and dance festivals, hawking balloons of nitrous out the back of the van. Only it turned out bad – Viking funerals in the desert bad. And one night me and this other kid ran for it, escaped to Barstow, where crank is easier to find than fresh vegetables. I thought about what to do with myself for about two minutes. Then I broke my clean streak with two fat lines.

Barb-wire heaven.

Look, opiates grab headlines for killing white folk named Trevor and Becky, you feel me? Opiates and benzos and all that shit is self-administered hospice care for folks who don't even realize they're dying. But even in its death throes America is still in its shitkicker heart a Crank Nation. This grimy white powder that turns your blood neon and fills your soul with *yes* – it's as American as Big Macs and funding third-world coups.

And so I did my patriotic duty and lived that dirty life and took the pain of being chewed. I met this dude named Michael, his face acne-scarred in a way that made me think of dead planets, which of course had been a sign but I was too gakked and dumb to see it. I agreed to score him an eight-ball and to tell it true I knew I was busted before the other cops kicked in the door, I knew it from the shark-smile on Michael's acne-scarred face, his greedy happy eyes at having another life to ruin.

It ought to be illegal to be a cop.

'Don't take me in,' I said. 'I can help you out. I'm small time.'

Flipping before the cuffs were even on. Screaming before the bear even bit down. But it let me live, and it kept me out of lock-up. I fed Michael busts, I hated myself, I would get good and ripped, wash, rinse, repeat.

I am a three-day stranger from sleep when Callie calls me.

'Hey Scubby. How you living?'

'Like a bullet from a gun.' My laugh is too high, too skittery – she knows right away how spun I am.

'Bang bang. Hey listen, you remember that thing you was talking about? Your friend who was looking?'

Shit.

I like Callie and Pretty Baby. Even as I pitched them the deal last month I'd hoped they'd stay away. I owed Michael a solid bust, and Callie was plugged into the Devore Combine, a whole new web of folk for Michael to go after. But I hoped they'd say no. They'd always been cool to me. So I think, I'll steer her away from it. I'll tell her Michael isn't shopping for weight anymore. I'll tell her to forget it. Their lives will go on, and so will mine, and maybe we'll become better friends and I'll get cleaned up and cut my dreads and get a real job and she'll introduce me to one of her friends who is as hot as she is and exactly who am I bullshitting here, you or me? None of that happens. I don't warn her away. I say, 'Michael's always buying. I'll set it up. Call me when you're ready to deliver.'

When the call is done, I go looking in all my stashes for something from the downer side of the spectrum. Anything at all. Best I can do is a warm beer. I'd taken it out around 4 a.m. last night with intentions of drinking. I crack it now. I chug it staring at my phone. I know I've got to call Michael, let him know what's coming. But I can't stop thinking about that girl with the cherry hair. That girl didn't just escape the bear. She became it. And seeing her had made me understand everything in a way I didn't want to. I know the human brain wasn't built to handle enlightenment – even if you find those final truths, the ones that really matter, they're too big for the sloppy wrinkled meat of our brains to handle and it all just leaks out between the folds. That's why those eternal mushroom truths fade as you come down. But the truth of the girl won't leave me.

I can't forget how I've seen someone walk free. Seeing that makes you see the bear that's eating you, and it's terrible because I know I won't break free. The bear just chews and chews and I all but say *thanks*. And maybe if I never saw that little girl, how she walked free, maybe I wouldn't hate myself so much for how weak I am. Even though I know the world is chewing me hard I just can't help but hate myself for screaming.

PART THREE

BLOOD IS LOVE

CHAPTER EIGHTEEN

Luke spends the day antsy, waiting for night to come. He counts and recounts the cash Del gave him. He plays flashbacks of last night. The auto lot. The bloody man. The rifle. The way Del talked to him, like he was someone who mattered, someone with weight and heft.

Around noon he calls in to the restaurant to quit. The manager throws a shit fit to no avail. Listening to this pisspot dictator sputter impotent bullshit at him fills Luke's heart with helium. He rides the giddy joy into the afternoon.

His nerves return as the sun lowers. He's meeting the Combine. He's thrilled and terrified about half and half. He needs a time killer. He watches Internet porn. He jerks off medicinally. The subsequent chill-out buys him an hour.

Outside the sky is grey. The light from his window is soft and desaturated. He knows that California skies lie to you. Smog and cloud cover promise rain far more often than they deliver. So when the thuds start on his rooftop he is surprised.

He steps out onto the staircase.

Raindrops fall slow and fat. They slap the dry earth. They run fingers down the dust caked on everything. He lets the rain patter him. The cold little shocks of the raindrops goose him. He's lived here only a few months and already rain is precious to him.

He looks to the big house. Dinner's not for a half hour. He can't take waiting anymore. He walks around to the main house. He remembers walking this same path his first night here – seeing Curtis, feeling like a ghost.

Now his heart beats hard in his chest, full to bursting with blood.

He opens the door, sees Curtis in the kitchen.

'Hey brother,' Curtis says like Luke's done this a thousand times. 'Good to see you.'

He's boiling a pot of water. He's got a bag of nacho chips, some beef sticks, dry bricks of ramen noodles. He's squirting barbecue sauce into a gallon ziplock bag.

'What're you making?'

'Chichi. It's prison chow. The food inside is so bad you got to do what you can to get some flavor in your life. You get whatever you can from the commissary or the black market and you mix it together. That's chichi.'

'But you're not inside,' Luke says. The thought of all this junk mixed together curdles his guts. 'You don't have to eat like that anymore.'

'I know, it looks like a head-on collision, right? I just get to missing it some nights. Anything that was a comfort to you once tends to stay that way. Good or bad.'

'I get it.'

'Want to give me a hand? There's a million ways to make it, but I like the way your daddy taught me best.'

Curtis has this way of casually saying things that shatter Luke.

'What do you need me to do?'

'Break up those ramen noodles. Just enough to make them manageable.'

They get to work. Luke breaks up the dry noodles. Curtis adds them to the bag, pours some boiling water on top. They crush nacho chips, add them to the mix, then chop up the beef sticks, a little barbecue sauce and then a plop more of boiling water.

'Now we wait,' Curtis says, turning the burner off. 'Using the stove here is a bit of a cheat to be honest.'

'How?'

'Inside you don't have a stove, so no way to boil water. You got to make a stinger – you strip an extension cord and stick the wires in the water to make it boil.'

'That's crazy.'

'Desperate times, brother. Dropping a live wire into water was hardly the craziest thing your daddy ever got me to do inside.'

'What was?'

Luke sees Curtis's face change – he knows he has pushed too far. He sees the answer in Curtis's eyes.

'Your daddy brought me in from the cold,' Curtis tells him. 'And he gave me a family. And there's nothing I won't do for the Combine.'

They stand there a long moment in front of the plastic bag of cooking glop.

'Should be done now,' Curtis says. He opens the bag – this waft of salty steam hits Luke's face. Curtis gets out two forks. He hands one to Luke. He spears a mouthful. He tries it. He hisses air into his mouth to cool it down. He chews. He smiles.

'That's the stuff.' He nods to Luke like *now you*.

Luke eats a forkful. Salt-sugar-umami bombs explode in his mouth. It's disgusting. It's delicious.

'Nasty,' Luke says, 'in the best possible way.'

'We live in a trash world. That's how your daddy put it. He said, "You gotta take the trash of this world and make something beautiful with it."' His voice goes harsh and booming – he's doing Big Bobby Crosswhite. Luke shatters inside again. Curtis sees something on Luke's face. He slaps him on the arm like *atta boy*.

'Now that you're back, you gonna reach out to him, right? I know he's waiting.'

'I will.' He doesn't say, *When I'm worthy*. He knows Curtis hears it anyway.

The door opens – Kathy walks in with plastic bags – red cups, vodka, two-liters of soda, bags of chips, wax-paper boxes stained with grease, leaking a delicious spicy stink. Kathy smiles at Luke, wrinkles her nose like *who farted?*

'Gawd, Curtis, enough with the convict casserole,' she says. 'We got real food.'

'She means gas station fried chicken,' Curtis tells Luke. 'Swear to god, this family runs on gas station fried chicken.'

'Shut your piehole. The chicken is good.'

'I allow that it is,' Curtis says. 'But you still bought it

from under a heat lamp next to the boner pill display at a gas station, so I'm not sure that's a high horse you're sitting on.'

This guy walks in with Del. Luke recognizes him right away, even minus his billy-goat beard.

I will not let it happen here, he tells himself. He tightens his stomach muscles like a blow is coming. It breaks off the thoughts even as they rise.

'Hey Teller,' Curtis says, 'This here is Luke. Big Bobby's son, though maybe it took him a little while to remember it. He's blood.'

'We go all the way back,' Teller says. 'You remember me? From when you were a kid?'

The images come—

A quarter on the Player One button.

Ghosts chasing Luke.

A billy-goat beard, the smell of cologne.

Snorting like a stallion in a bowling alley lobby.

But they stay in Luke's head. They don't crowd their way into the world.

I will not let it happen here. This time the words have force.

'You used to have—' Luke strokes his chin.

'You got it. My old lady made me cut the soup-saver a long ways back. Good to see you again, little homie. Blood is love.' Teller takes Luke into a bear hug.

'Blood is love,' Luke says back like he's always been here, like he's always belonged.

More folk file in. Some of them he knows – Ricky, his thinness moving towards gaunt, a look now in his eyes that Luke recognizes from his mirror. The twins, introduced as the Chuck Brothers. They throw him a wink and make jokes about helmets – he tries to remember which one is Trent and which one is Tyson. Sam comes in with Manson walking slow behind him – he greets Luke with a pounding on the back and an *I fucking knew it*.

He meets Apes – this twentysomething girl with a buzzcut and a daredevil grin.

'Heard about your raid,' she says. 'Took a lot of scalps down at Frank's Auto Lot. Balls out.'

'Thanks.'

'Primo,' Luke hears behind him, turns to see Callie Gifford – a foot taller, but her eyes are still wild.

'Prima,' he says back, hugging her, smelling her wild rose scent, his brain crowding with images of hide-and-seek and skinned knees. 'It's so good to see you.'

She hugs him back and leans back to see his face and grins and all at once he knows if he had never left he would have loved her, that in some other world he does, maybe from afar and maybe up close, but either way it's another thing stolen from him.

'You're tall as hell, what the fuck? Anyway this is Pretty Baby.'

Luke has to admit the name fits. Pretty Baby is a beautiful space alien of a man, inked all over, a shock of pink and blond hair. His eyes are drug-frosted, but his smile is warm.

'Welcome home,' he tells Luke. They clasp hands.

'Welcome home,' echoes Curtis. Folk raise their red plastic cups. Folk cheer.

Luke smiles. Love hits him like a wave. It feels as good as Luke always guessed it would.

The family eats.

The gas station chicken *is* good. Luke eats it with a side of chichi. He drinks beers. He paces himself carefully – he already feels drunk.

The family laughs. They've got inside jokes – Callie explains them to Luke in asides. The two of them talk old times – they steer around the bad parts. He tells her a little about his old life, and about Julie, and she listens and nods her head and says *that bitch sounds crazy* in all the right places.

The family talks. They split off – little pockets form and reform. The Chuck Brothers and Ricky talk Lakers – they try to rope Luke in. He nods along, faking it. Curtis and Del and Teller talk in a tight circle, low voices – Callie calls it the big-boy circle. Apes and Sam talk horror movies. Pretty Baby and the Chuck Brothers talk video games. Sam and Pretty Baby talk pot. Ricky and Apes talk conspiracy theories. Everybody laughs. Luke laughs with them – he's getting used to the sound.

Luke offers Manson some chicken. She turns her nose up at it.

'She's feeling punk,' Sam says. 'Caught her eating dry bougainvillea leaves earlier – she does that when her stomach hurts.'

'Poor girl,' Callie says.

Luke retracts the chicken, scratches Manson between her ears.

Del leans forward. Everybody quiets down like it's a sign. Everybody shifts towards Del.

'There's family business to discuss. The fellow who stuck Ricky, we found him.'

'What condition did you leave him in?' Apes asks.

'He's still walking around,' Curtis says. 'But he's not having fun doing it.'

One of the Chuck Brothers – Tyson, he thinks – mimes a rifle shot. He throws a wink at Luke. Sam sees it. His eyes ask: *You were there?* Luke stonefaces – let him wonder. Luke knows it will drive Sam crazy – he's low man again.

'Could be they get the message,' Del says. 'Could be that's the end of it.'

'But chances are they'll hit back,' Apes says.

'That's the smart money.' Del pulls the lever on the side of his chair, the foot rest dropping, the back swinging up. Turning it back into a throne. 'How they hit back, that'll tell us everything. But we have to watch out for each other. And watch out for ourselves.'

'Hell,' Curtis says, 'we do this right, we could open up the Combine, franchise it, replace the Steel altogether. Bring a new way to the dirty whiteboys of the world.'

'Why we got to get bigger?' Ricky asks. 'Why do we got to be anything more than we are?'

'We could run SoCal,' Curtis says. 'I'm talking about freedom.'

'No you're not,' Callie says. 'You're talking about power.'

'Same thing.'

'The hell it is,' she says. 'Freedom's something you can have by yourself. Power needs somebody to piss on.'

Del steeples his hands in front of his face. Curtis and Callie stop talking. Luke sees how good he is at controlling the room with little gestures.

'We see what they do next. Beast has a lot of folk to fit under that big-ass thumb of his. Could be he forgets us. But that's not likely. We hold tight, we watch each other's backs. If you're ready, I'm ready.'

Luke looks around. He'd thought they'd all look tough, fearless. They look scared as hell. Scared as hell but they sit there anyway. Luke sees how unreal his life has been until now, how little the decisions he made up until now mattered. He sees now how life for most people is spent bundled up in bubble-wrap, and even the bad things that happen to them are decided in some faraway room and there's nothing to be done about it. Now he is in this room that is hot from all the bodies in it, all this shared air and shared food. When they talk about love, they mean it. And when they talk about killing, they mean that too.

CHAPTER NINETEEN

Curtis comes looking for him at dusk the next night. He has a sawed-off shotgun in one hand, a box of shells in the other. He says, 'School's in session.'

They walk up among the junkers. Luke throws a loose punch into the heavy bag. The clothes line creaks as the bag swings back – a little. Curtis laughs.

'That's not gonna do. Guess we got to teach you to throw hands too. Next time. Now I want to get you shooting.'

Curtis hands him the shotgun. The barrel and the stock are both sawed away, shitty work, the stock jagged, the barrel splintered and knurled.

'Regular shotgun, you got the perfect spread at twenty yards. You twenty yards from someone, the fuck are you shooting at them for? You only ever shoot at someone to kill them. So get fucking close. Ten feet away, this thing'll make 'em look like a wolf took a chunk out of them. The coroner'll be digging wadding out of the wound, you know? That's what you want. Fuck twenty yards. Anything more than twenty feet, get closer or get down.

Gunfights are for movies. Someone's shooting back at you, you fucked up.'

There's some echo of the Luke from Colorado in his head, yelling: *Three months ago you were me. Three months ago, you were in Intro to World Lit. Three months ago you had a girlfriend who wanted to be a veterinarian.*

'You think there's going to be shooting?' Luke asks.

'That's what we got to see,' Curtis says. 'Del's idea is, we come on like a porcupine. Show them we're more trouble than we're worth. They're fighting for a little bit more power. We're fighting for our lives. That evens the odds some.'

'And what if they come back at us?'

'No "if",' he says. 'Then we'll go big. Word is, Beast has set up a cook shop. A big one, like the one used to operate out of Hangtree. Enough to get all the dirty whiteboys off the Mexican Mafia tit. If we take it out, it queers Beast's whole deal. We make them look weak, we got a chance.

'Now, pick a car. That is, pick a victim.'

Luke scans the lot. He sees the once-white Dodge where the wasps had once lived.

'The old Dodge.'

Curtis hands him the gun. It's heavier than he'd thought.

'Don't we need earplugs?'

'Naw, that's the point. Got to get you used to the sound. You can't have a fit the first time you shoot a gun.'

In the grey sky above, hawks circle. Waiting to see if Curtis and him will stop moving so they can feed.

'I'm done having fits,' he says. His finger curls around

the trigger. The metal is cold, slick in his hands in some way he can taste, the cool oiliness in his hands somehow spreading in his mouth. He hikes the shotgun up to his shoulder.

Luke squints down the barrel like he's seen in the movies.

'Don't think on it. Shotguns aren't for thinking. That's their beauty.'

He pulls the trigger. The *BLAST* is like taking the world in his hands and ripping it in half. The buckshot chomps a jagged hole in the Dodge's bumper. It coughs up chunks of fiberglass. It coughs up little-kid memories—

a grey nest

wasps swarming

a wave of pain

Holes in the side of the car, little furrows.

holes in a wasp nest

He kneels down, runs his fingers across the holes. Nothing comes out of them. No wasps bloom.

'You shut your eyes,' Curtis says. Luke had forgot he was here. 'You shut your eyes just before you pulled. That won't do. Quit admiring the work and do it again.'

Luke rises up. The shotgun lighter now. He's learned the balance of it. He walks ten paces like in the old west. He turns.

Shotguns aren't for thinking.

He pulls the trigger. *BANG*. The car's corpse spits up chunks. Safety glass spumes. Paint flakes. The trunk springs open like a mouth.

He remembers Mom with her cigarette in her hand. The

slowness of her running. The wasps like a gust of flame all over him.

Luke fires again, blasting a hole through the trunk lid. It flaps up and down, a gibbering mouth.

The barrel smokes. The loudness is pain now, actual pain in the deeps of his ears.

Curtis smiles. He says something – Luke hears nothing but white noise.

The next shell, Luke thinks about that kid from three months ago. The kid on the gravel with tears on his face. He points the shotgun. He pulls the trigger. Buckshot rips that ghost in half.

CHAPTER TWENTY

It's dark when they're done. Luke feels that emptied out feeling – the rare gift of silence in his skull. Curtis says, *Burritos*. Luke says, *Let's do it*. They drive down into San Bernardino. Curtis drives fast, lots of lane changes, lots of curses. He keeps the seat belt buckled behind him so the car doesn't scold him. He likes drill music, deep bass and barked lyrics. They drive though Rosa Maria's. They order heavy – pork burritos with red chile, chips, salsa, a couple of quesadillas.

'Got to thicken you up,' Curtis says.

The smell, rich and spicy, maddening. Luke eats a chip to fend off the hunger.

'We taking it back to the compound?'

'Naw, let's give Del and Kathy a little peace. Let's hit the garage, maybe Maddox will be there; you must have known him when you was little.'

They take Sierra Way south. Luke reaches forward, turns down the music. Curtis shoots him a look like *my ride, my sounds*.

'Why'd you let me in the door the other night?' Luke asks before Curtis can turn it back up.

'Cause I wanted to see what you'd do. I wanted to see if maybe you had a little of your daddy in you. And turns out you do. How much is an open question, but he's in there.'

Curtis reaches out to turn the music back up. This time he stops himself.

'But to be real, I wanted to see what Del would do too. I wanted to yank on the bull's balls and see if he hopped. And brother did he ever.'

Luke flashes back: the rifle, the cracked helmet.

'It was crazy,' Luke says.

'Yeah. But you know why he did it, right? He was saying "I don't just run things because I'm Big Bobby's brother." He was saying "I'm still the craziest motherfucker in the room."'

'What do you mean?'

'If there's one thing you need to know about your uncle, it's he never does nothing without a reason. Like I know myself, I do things and if you ask me why, maybe I know and maybe I don't. Or sometimes I figure it out a week later. Like, until you asked just now, I didn't know I was being devious letting you in the garage.'

'I'm more like you.'

'No shit, my man.' Curtis laughs. 'But your uncle, he's that other type. Everything means something. Even when he's acting crazy, he ain't.'

'He could have killed that guy.'

'Hell yeah he could have. And then we'd be in the shit for sure. But you know why he risked it? Cause of you.

Don't get it twisted, your uncle loves you, but he's scared of you too.'

'Scared of *me*?'

''Cause you are who you are. The fucking heir apparent. That has power, you know it does. Del runs things outside and he does fine, but everybody knows Big Bobby is the king. Del's human – he's got used to sitting on that throne. Hardest thing in the world is to step down a notch. It makes him nervous of me sometimes. And it makes him nervous of you.'

Before Luke can answer, a siren rips through the night. Luke sits up straight.

'That's not a cop siren,' Curtis says. 'Unclench.'

Red lights flash up the street. Fire trucks everywhere.

'What the hell?' Curtis's voice is low and dangerous.

They can see it from a block away.

The orange glow of the garage on fire.

'Oh no, fuck no.'

Curtis floors it – invisible hands push Luke back in his seat. Curtis parks in between fire trucks. He's out the door before Luke can get his seatbelt off. A fireman puts a hand up like *stop right there*.

'Sir, you can't—'

'Was there anyone in there?'

'Sir—'

'Is there somebody inside, goddamn it?'

Flames lick up from under the lip of the roof. Flames lick up from the corners of the garage doors. Someplace inside glass shatters.

'We've got to save them,' Curtis says. His eyes so wide.

Luke gets it now. He knows what Curtis is thinking.

Somebody got nailed to the garage floor.

Somebody got burned alive.

'Let's go in,' Curtis says.

'We can't—'

Curtis kicks in the door.

Fire bursts out. Curtis plops on his ass. A fireman pulls him back. Curtis shrugs him off.

Kicking the door open feeds the flames. The garage goes faster now.

Fat orange tentacles reach up towards the sky.

'Somebody might be in there,' Luke tells one of them.

'If there is, it's too late for them now,' the fireman says. A stupid thing to say. Curtis turns to the man. Luke recognizes the look in his eyes. He remembers it from Arrowhead. A man riding a tiger, but he's the tiger, too.

Luke puts a hand on Curtis. Curtis turns. He is savage. Luke keeps his hand there.

'You can't go in there,' Luke tells him.

'I'll kill them all,' Curtis says. 'I'll fucking walk the road of death.'

And it ought to be funny, this line like something from a samurai movie – *the road of death?* – but he sees Curtis's face and knows better than to laugh right now.

And maybe there is someone in there.

Maybe somebody got got.

Firemen turn on the hose. They aim at the open door. The mouth of flame turns black. The mouth hisses, pukes smoke. Burned bits and ash flake off the garage and fall.

The fireman gets on his knees to control the hose.

Curtis paces, waves his arms, like he's trying to conduct the sky and bring down a rainstorm. Nothing comes. The hoses do their work. The fire dies a slow death. Luke takes out his phone, crosses the street, stands in front of the Mexican bakery.

'What?' Del answers, his voice thick with sleep.

'The garage is burning.'

'How bad?'

'The garage is basically gone. Curtis is worried somebody's inside.'

'Shouldn't be anyone. Maddox had some family thing tonight. Cops around?'

'Yeah.'

'Don't say shit. Call me when there's news.'

It's another twenty minutes before the firemen go in to look. They come out empty handed.

'There's nobody in there,' the chief says. 'A couple of cars is all.'

Curtis drops to the curb in front of the garage. Smoke rises up behind him. From where Luke is standing, it looks like it's spuming from him. Like he's burning up inside. Luke figures he probably is.

CHAPTER TWENTY-ONE

Callie opens the Stater Bros. bag, peeks again. The plastic-wrapped pound of crank is yellow-white like an old smoker's hair. They picked it up from Erik an hour ago. The only thing she ever wants to think about Erik again is how they ripped him off. She hopes the debt puts Erik in dutch with the Nazi Dope Boys. She hopes they take one of his clammy, gross fingers as repayment.

She thinks on the garage burning down. No one was inside it. Not this time. She thinks on leaving the Combine behind. She hopes they'll understand.

She looks up at the gunmetal sky. She thinks this time tomorrow they'll be gone – tomorrow night they sleep in Santa Barbara. She wants to put her feet in the ocean. She wants to breathe clean air. She wants to let a little of the money spill through her hands like water.

Pretty Baby hits the indica vape. He messes with his phone, finds the song he wants to hear. A bassline farts from blown speakers. He nods his head to the beat. He smiles – this weird mix of scared and happy. He's been taking more pills these last few weeks. She's been worried they are worming their way into him too deep to root out. But right now, living in hope, a new life and a new world ahead of them, she can imagine him shaking them loose altogether.

They can do it. She knows they can.

They pull into Scubby's apartment complex parking lot. Laundry lines strung up between buildings hang overhead. Dogs barking everywhere – a basso profundo pit bull backed by a chihuahua chorus. Pretty Baby backs into the parking space.

'Ain't nothing to it but to do it,' Pretty Baby says. 'I love you all the way down.'

'All the way down,' she says back.

He kisses her hard. It's what she needs. She breathes deep. Tells herself it's almost done. Their bags are packed. All they need is this one last thing and then they can leave.

All they need is for this to be real.

She gets out of the car. She carries the pound in her backpack.

Just one shot. It's not so much to ask.

It goes bad so fast it's almost funny.

She knocks on the door. The dog chorus reprises. Scubby opens the door. He gives everything away with his face. A trembling lip, a sheen of sweat, this sorry-dog look in his eyes.

Something inside her says *get the fuck out.*

The man standing with Scubby has acne scars like raw hamburger. He has shark eyes. He couldn't look more like a cop if he was holding his badge.

'What's good, Callie?' Scubby says, and she has to hand it to him, his voice almost makes her reconsider what she's seeing with her eyes. 'Come on in. This here is my main man Michael.'

It's a script.

Get the fuck out.

'I left something in the car,' she says.

It's a set-up.

Get the fuck out.

'Come on in,' says Hamburger Face. His voice pure cop.

It's a bust.

Get the fuck out.

'Just a second.' They should have met the man clean first. She shouldn't have been so fucking eager. Greedy stupid sloppy amateur hour bullshit. She steps backwards. Stumbles over her feet. The cop smiles wider. She hates what it does to his face.

'Just remembered, we got someplace to be,' she says, stepping back to the car.

She jumps the car door, thankful he parked backwards, thankful the top is down.

'Drive,' she says. She looks backwards. Scubby hits her with these *I'm-sorry* eyes. The man behind him talks into a cop radio.

'Drive fast,' she says. She reaches under the seat. She pulls out the brick. She tears at the tape with her fingers. 'Baby, go, go, go now.'

He fumbles. He benzo-bumbles.

'He's a cop.'

'Oh shit.'

He puts it in drive. She tears at the bag as they pull out onto the street.

A cop car turns onto the road behind them, maybe a block away.

'I need you to drive faster,' she says.

Pretty Baby pulls a few pills from his pockets, dry-swallows them, lint and all.

She rips at the brick. She fumbles the tape. She breaks a nail. The pain faraway. She bites into the tape, tears it open. Crank spills – toxic waste in her mouth. She spits into the wind.

'Faster,' she says. She turns behind them.

He gets it now. He stomps on the gas. Wind whistles in her ears.

She holds the brick up high. She watches a twenty-grand cloud take flight. It blocks out the cop car. The cop car comes out the other side of the cloud cherries flashing, sirens on. She shakes the bag. She rips it all the way open. It flaps like a plastic flag. This crazy elation fills her. She can't help but war-whoop. She can't help but blast the cops a double-bird.

'Okay baby,' she says, sliding back into her seat. 'You can pull over now.'

CHAPTER TWENTY-TWO

The detective has gray hair and busted blood vessels on his nose. Despite his age, he still has the face of a detestable kid, a hall monitor, a country club brat who'll never know what being trapped is. Her hate for him is pure and clean. It makes what she has to do very easy.

All she has to do is build a wall and sit behind it.

Red lines on her wrists from the plastic ties they'd put on her. Bursts of pain from her broken nail. She funnels her pain into the wall.

Don't say shit.

Silence is the only move.

The interrogation room smells like elementary school – cheap industrial cleaners and piss and dust. Everything murky. Dust is mostly human skin, she thinks, watching motes float in the harsh light. The dust of a thousand hard cases, folks who got pushed too far or came up short, folk with something wrong with them and born too unlucky.

Dumb to think she could ever run. That she could ever get to leave.

'We know what was in the bag,' the detective says.

'We know you deal. We know you're tied in with the Combine up in Devore. We know you've got a juvie record even if it's sealed. We can tag you as gang-affiliated. We can round the whole crew up. We can get really nasty.'

'Cops are demons,' her uncle John had told her once after she waved at a passing cop. 'Open your mouth and they'll reach inside and yank out your soul.'

The hamburger-faced cop from Scubby's place comes in the door. He's breathing hard, this scrim of sweat on his face. Makes him look shiny, even more like meat.

The ground underneath her feet starts shifting.

'Cops don't just lie,' her uncle had told her. 'It's their native tongue.'

'You're going to work for us,' Hamburger Face says. 'That's pretty much your only move.'

She wonders how many times he's given this speech. She wonders if it had been here in this room where Hamburger Face had flipped Scubby.

'A girl like you, you want to do what you can while you look good. And girl, it doesn't last long. You may not know it, but you're at the top of the mountain. What are you, 20? White trash peaks young. You're already on the downward slope. You want to snag a man – I mean a real man, not that piece of shit in the next room – and lock him down with a kid, and you want to do it before you start really rolling down the cliff. Sell high, sweetie. Sell now.'

She squeezes her thumb and forefinger together. She puts all of her rage there and tries to press it into a diamond.

'We know what was in that baggie,' Hamburger Face

says. 'We can hold you twenty-four hours. Your doped-up little friend is talking right now. Maybe you're young enough to think you and him have something real. Something that will last. But it won't. You have to know that. You won't walk out of a real bit to find him waiting for you. You can't believe that, not for a second.'

They'll reach inside and yank out your soul.

'You're young enough to walk from this,' he says. 'You got something in you that isn't dried up. You help me out and I'll help you out.'

He can't know that it's almost word for word what Erik said to her back in his place. She swallows something whole and straightens up in her seat and smiles. The wall is built all the way up. It's safe now for her to open her mouth and say the only thing you ever say in this dusty-ass room.

'Get me a lawyer or let me go.'

CHAPTER TWENTY-THREE

They hold her all night just because they can. The morning air is cold, beautiful. Her phone died in the night – figure cops spent a good chunk of it trying to hack their way in. Maybe Pretty Baby is still in there. Either way the car is impounded.

Eight miles back to the apartment. The walk will do her good.

The streets are already crowded with straight-laced day-job souls on their way to work. She walks north on Sierra, eight lanes of traffic, walking along long grey office complexes – soulless, dead in a way that even graveyards aren't. At the far end of one of the office complexes the side-walk ends and Callie walks in gravel at the road's shoulder, between the road and power lines, the desert on either side of her. No cars pass her. No sounds but the slap of her feet and the rush of her blood. She had been right, the walk is what she needed. Her brain runs on its own while she walks, rebuilding the night.

The cops had nothing on them – the baggie residue was meaningless. And Pretty Baby knew as well as she did never to say a word to the cops. The big problem is Erik, who is expecting ten grand by dinnertime. When he doesn't get it, he'll make noise. He'll come after them. And the Combine can't protect them, not without her telling them they went outside the circle, did business on their own. They'd have to say why. And maybe Del would figure if they stepped outside the Combine, then it wasn't the Combine's problem. And Erik is in with Beast Daniels. Or maybe Del takes their side, and the fight gets worse. Maybe she just made the Combine's problems that much harder.

Erik's debt on one side. Beast Daniels on the other. Hot earth underneath. The million billion particles of sky overhead pressing down on her.

Why's everything got to be so heavy?

By the time she gets back to their apartment building her tongue is swollen from dehydration. She walks up the steps to their place, so tired she has to concentrate on her feet clearing each step so she doesn't trip and fall backwards and die. Even though that would clear up her problems right quick.

She is surprised to find Pretty Baby beat her home. He's sitting on the couch, their suitcases and boxes all around him. He lifts his head slow, like he's floating in syrup. Under the benzo glaze she sees something else. She sees guilt. Face down, eyes up, like Manson after she piddles on the rug.

He scratches at his arm. He wipes snot off his nose. He can't get his eyes past half-mast. He holds up his right hand – the fingers swollen into hot dogs.

'I didn't want to,' he slurs. 'But it . . . it hurt so bad. Even with the bars I popped when they got us, it hurt so bad.'

She remembers Michael, the acne-scarred cop, coming into the interrogation room late, sweat on his face like he'd been putting in work.

She sits on the coffee table, takes his hand in hers. She kisses the fingers gently. She says 'That moon-faced motherfucker.'

He laughs. It trails off into nothing. He slaps himself in the face, slow but hard. Callie winces – maybe she feels it more than he does. He says, 'I'm so fucked up.'

'Baby—'

'I'm gonna get straight. For real I promise.'

She puts a finger on his lips.

'Say it when you're sober,' she says. 'That's the only time it counts.'

He nods like *fair enough*.

'Please don't hate me.'

'Why would I ever hate you?'

'I'm weak.'

'No, baby. No you're not.' She takes him in her arms. 'But you got to tell me what you told them.'

'They wanted a name. Just a name. And I wasn't going to give them anybody in the Combine. I would never. But I gave them Erik. His name and where he lives. I told them he moves weight. I'm a fucking snitch-ass bitch.'

'Look,' she says, 'if I was walking past a house, and the house was on fire, and I saw Erik Montrose inside banging on a window and screaming for help, know what I'd do? I'd pull up a fucking lawn chair.'

He laughs. He sits up a little.

'So I don't really give two fucks if we just made that

scumfuck's life a little harder. But baby, the bad part is – your name, it's on a piece of paper someplace now. Talking even that one little bit, it gets you a snitch jacket. We got to be careful. Nobody can ever hear a word, baby. Del'd take your black heart for this.'

'I'm dragging you down,' Pretty Baby says. 'Even if we get out, I'll just make things worse.'

He wipes his eyes. His eyes are wet above those sharp cheek bones. He rubs his head, the pink hair, the dark circles under his eyes somehow making him even prettier, and she falls on him now, takes his face in her hands.

'I walked home,' she says. 'I thought this through the whole way. We just got to hustle. We got to pay Erik something, get a payment plan going. It means no running, not for a while. Means we're in with the Combine, hook or crook. It means we're not going anywhere. It means we're locked in, we got to lean on each other now.'

And she tells him the plan, how they get out of this alive. And he looks at her with eyes that are soft and it's like she can feel the beams pouring out of them, the love, and she asks him what he's looking at, and he says, *Nothing*. But even if he'd got down on a knee and asked for her hand it wouldn't have meant more to her than those eyes and that *nothing*. That *nothing* was everything, and she knows they are going to be okay.

And they fold themselves up on the couch, limbs entwined, and she feels like they're knotted together even though they aren't. And that's the trick of it, she realizes. Fool yourself into thinking the ties bind, and all of the sudden they do.

CHAPTER TWENTY-FOUR

Luke walks down the gravel towards the gate, looking to see if Callie and Pretty Baby have shown up yet. Callie sounded so weird on the phone this afternoon when he'd called her and asked if they were still down to hang out tonight. Like she'd forgotten all about it. He sees Del on the front porch, leaned back in one of the folding chairs. Del is unshaven, a plastic mug in his crotch. Whatever he's sipping has him relaxed, as mellow as Luke has ever seen him.

'Got a coffin nail?' Del asks. Luke climbs up the steps, hands his uncle a cigarette and then the lighter, shaking out a smoke for himself and taking the lighter back so he can light his own.

'Going out?' Del asks.

'There's a party down in San Berdoo. Callie and PB are picking me up.'

'Get out there and live life while pleasure comes easy,' Del says. 'Enjoy yourself. But watch your six as well.'

'Curtis and them are going to be there too. How's the garage?'

Del shoots twin jets of smoke from his nostrils.

'We'll be all right. The garage can be rebuilt. Insurance is a bitch, though. We're sure to be dry-fucked by the folk in the button-up shirts, seeing as how that's their undying purpose in life.'

'You sure it was Beast Daniels?'

'More likely someone acting as Beast's hand. Peckerwood Nation has a pro firebug down in Victorville, fellow named Half-Hand Randy. Accurate name, by the way. It was probably him or someone like him. But for our purposes, it was Beast Daniels who burnt it down.'

Del studies the contents of his cup, takes a sip. His face gives away how strong the mix is.

'That garage had been part of the Combine from the beginning. Used to belong to this old peckerwood, James Creasy. We used to sell to him. Small-time shit, boosting car stereos mostly – they were worth something back then. Blaupunkt, Kenwoods, Rockford Fosgate. And we were selling nickels of Mexican ditch weed, using cigarette box cellophane as baggies. By the time we graduated to gas station stick-ups we were certain we were the second coming of La Costa Nostra. It was your daddy came up with the Combine name; don't know where he got it from. We built up a nice little operation. Your daddy talked Creasy into selling us that garage for a bargain price, too . . . negotiations took place in the paint bay. So now we were stealing the parts and selling them too. They call it vertical integration these days. And we started to get known. All of us but your daddy most of all. He has that flame, you know? Always did. People want to be close to him. Then he got that first stint inside, it turned out good for us. He went and networked. He made contacts, associates. He came out and we were stronger than ever. It was really something. And then John got killed. Found him there, parked on the side of the road, behind the wheel. Somebody sitting shotgun pulled the trigger.'

Del talks into the night, like he's talking to someone out in the dark instead of Luke.

'Your daddy, he was the one who thought of the black heart, mixing ink in John's ashes. Your daddy wanted to carry him forever. The whole point of the Combine was to keep us all safe. Your daddy wanted to keep everyone safe. And he couldn't stop your momma from herself and those pills, and he couldn't keep John safe. We couldn't even figure out who did it. You ever wonder why your daddy did what he did at Arrowhead?'

Luke tightens his stomach muscles, a reflex now. He still ends every night with blows to the stomach, breaking apart that forever night in his gut until now he can contemplate it without even tasting root beer.

He says, 'I was there.'

'I know you were there. That mean you can make sense of it?'

Even in the dim Luke can feel the lights shifting – a sodium glow coming into the air. Luke worries that despite everything it's happening again. Then he sees it is a car's headlights coming down the road – Callie and Pretty Baby are here. He looks towards his uncle. He thinks their arrival might kill Del's train of thought. He's not sure if he wants it to or not.

Del looks up the road, takes a deep drink. He says, 'Here's what I think. He was so angry about John, and he didn't have nowhere to put the pain. You want to know why he did what he did? You ask me, that's why. He had more pain than he could carry. So he put it in that man. Filled him with it until the man's head came apart.'

CHAPTER TWENTY-FIVE

Callie and Pretty Baby show up stoned and hungry, eyes tired like maybe they've been going hard a few days running. As they pull down the road, he looks back at Uncle Del, sipping his drink, still looking lost to memories. He remembers what Curtis said – that Del only ever does things for a reason.

So what was the reason for that story?

Up front Callie and Pretty Baby are silent. They share drinks from a cup of Sprite stained purple with codeine. Pretty Baby drives like it needs all his concentration.

'How you been?' Luke asks. He doesn't say, *You look half dead*.

'We're just wiped out,' Callie says.

'You sure you want to go to this thing?'

'No, yeah, we had to get out of the house,' Callie said. 'We were going stir crazy.'

The two of them share some look – love and fear all wrapped up together. Something bounces between them – Luke gets this feeling like they're about to tell him something big. And part of him wants to know what it is they're hiding, but the other part is suddenly terrified to know. And so it's a relief when Callie takes a long sip and breaks the moment with a burp.

'You two keep an eye on me tonight,' she says. 'I feel like getting erased.'

Hip-hop rattles the windows in their frames. Voices all mixed together into static underneath it. They cruise past slow, looking for parking. They park two blocks away at the first empty spot. They walk back towards the house. The six packs in Luke's hands swing as he walks, patting his thigh in time with his steps. They move through succulents in the yard. Halfway through the yard Luke stops.

Something's wrong. At first Luke thinks it's something inside him. But that's not it. There's something hanging in the air, some tone to the party babble.

'Bad vibes,' Pretty Baby says.

'Thought it was just me.'

'Nu-uh,' Callie says. 'Something's up.'

'We can just kick it at our place,' Pretty Baby says.

'We ought to go check it out,' Luke tells them. 'Curtis and them might be there. If something's wrong, they may need us.'

Callie agrees. Pretty Baby doesn't look sure, but he follows them into the house. The air inside is thick with vape mist and blunt smoke and used air. It is jammed with people, mostly around their age, mostly already soaked with their chemicals of choice. He scans the room – he thinks about Aryan Steel, the garage burning down – tags most folk as civilians. He laughs at himself – he's been running with the Combine less than a month.

'I got to take a squirt,' Pretty Baby says, folding into the crowd.

Callie and Luke squeeze through towards the kitchen. Luke follows. He sees Apes in the corner, leaning with one hand against the wall behind another girl, leaning so far if she moved her hand she would headbutt her. Luke moves to say *hi*, but Callie stops him with a hand on his shoulder.

'Let her work,' Callie says, pushing through the crowd. 'I want a drink.'

They find the kitchen – the tight nucleus of the party. A plastic trash can full of pale blue jungle juice sits in the center. The floor is sticky with it. People drinking too fast, making faces, gulping, dipping their cups into the punch to ladle up another drink. Laughs like screams, screams like laughs.

One of the Chuck Brothers – Luke thinks he knows them well enough now to say it is Tyson – stands in the corner, talking to a guy with loose corn-rows. Tyson is wide-eyed with drink. He sees the two of them, raises his cup in a *cheers*, too fast so his drink slops down his arm. His smile and his eyes say two different things. His eyes are a warning.

'What the hell is going on?' Callie asks Luke. The bad energy is crackling through him. The crowd pressing against him like a vise. He doesn't know how much longer he can last.

Someone tugs at his arm. He turns. Pretty Baby stands

there. The drug-glaze has burned away from his eyes. He mouths the words *come with me*.

The bathroom is cramped – barely room for the sink and toilet and shower. Sam sits bare-chested on the ratty bathmat, his T-shirt sitting in a soaked wad next to him. The puke stench stings Luke's nose. Sam's eyes are wet and red. Bubbles of tear-snot bursting and rolling down his lips. He gropes for Luke's leg. He presses his cheek into it.

'Aw fuck. Aw shit. Aw shit, brother. She was a good girl.'

He turns his head to the john. He pukes violently. Luke turns away. He studies the sink. Hardened globs of toothpaste speckle it.

Sam stops. He gasps for air. He tells the air *I'm sorry I'm sorry I'm sorry.*

'Jesus, Sam.' Luke reaches over Sam's head and flushes the toilet. The swirling water kicks up even more puke smell.

'Oh god. Oh Jesus. She was a good girl, man.'

Luke takes him by the shoulder. Sam's eyes roll independent of each other. He's past drunk heading towards poisoned.

'Hey man, it's me. Tell me what's going on.'

Sam tells the story through slurred words and sobs.

Luke comes out of the bathroom. The crowd parts easy for him. People glance up, step aside in a way they've never done for him before.

She was a sick thing and they just threw her away.

'What's going on?' Callie asks, trailing him. Luke goes

to the kitchen. Tyson is still there, still telling some story. Luke steps between him and the guy he's talking to.

'Where's Curtis?'

'He just did what he had to do,' Tyson says. 'You better chill out.'

'Shut up.'

Tyson blinks twice. He uses his thumb to crack his index finger. He nods like *all right then*.

'He's out back. But hey, new fish? You better think on the tone of your fucking mouth.'

Luke answers him with his back. For once Luke is sure of the thing he is feeling. For once he has the name for what's erupting inside him.

Its name is *rage*.

The back yard is quiet. It lets Luke hear the roaring of his head a little better. Folk gather around a fire pit. Curtis stands against it, a black shape, holding court over a group of sitting people. He sees Luke coming, waves him over.

'What's up, little brother? Blood is love. Just telling these folk about those peckerwood fuckers who like to start fires.' His vowels all mushed from drink.

He wraps Luke up in one of his hugs. Luke pushes away from him.

'Why didn't you take her to the vet?'

The fire reflects in Curtis's eyes.

'She was past help, brother.' A warning in his voice. Luke ignores it.

'How would you know?'

'I grew up with dogs. And one thing, they know when it's their time. It's in their eyes. You see it and you know.'

'What happened?' Callie asks. 'Are you talking about Manson?'

She was a sick thing and they just threw her away. A part of the family and they just tossed her aside.

'Didn't need a vet,' Ricky, sitting by the fire, says to Luke. 'She needed to be given peace. She was in a bad way.'

'You should have taken her to a vet,' Luke says. Something inside him hums thermonuclear – but still his voice is calm. 'She was sick. Dogs get sick.'

'Where is she?' Callie asks, louder. 'Where's Manson?'

'They took her out to the desert and they shot her.' He watches it hit Callie the way it hit him. 'They gave Sam a rifle and made him do it.'

'Oh my God. What the hell, Curtis?'

'Sam did what a man does. He handled his shit.'

'No,' Luke says. 'No, you should have taken her to a vet. And maybe Sam to a hospital, he's so fucked up he needs his stomach pumped.'

'You put a dog out of its misery, man. Why don't you know that?'

'Because maybe she just needed some help.' *They threw her away at the first sign of weakness*, the rage whispers to him.

'The bitch in you is coming out,' Curtis tells him. 'Thought you squashed it, but I guess I was wrong. You going to have a fucking fit about it?'

Luke's blood retreats to his core. His dick shrinks up

prepubescent. He knows he can't fight Curtis. He knows he can't win.

'You don't just shoot a sick dog, man,' he says. 'That's fucking stupid.'

The crowd around them has fallen silent. Every eye on them. Scared faces. Eager faces. Curtis with this strange smile.

'Watch yourself little brother.'

'Curtis, come on—' Callie starts.

'Between me and him,' Curtis interrupts. He slaps his chest, the black heart over his real one.

Luke knows he ought to walk away. Something in him won't let him.

'It's fucked up, Curtis,' Luke says. 'She deserved better. Sam too. He loved her. And you made him kill her.'

Curtis's voice gets louder. Spittle mists Luke's face as he talks.

'Her time was up. Think I don't know that? This is what it is, man. You got to be strong enough to do what needs to be done.'

He knows he ought to agree. He ought to make nice and beat feet. But this swelling thing inside him won't let him.

Luke says, 'All you had to do was take her to the vet. But you had to be a tough guy about it, huh? You fucked up, Curtis.'

There's no sound but the crackle of the fire. Each flicker of the fire painting their faces a different shape. Callie looks like she's watching someone hanging from a ledge.

'Luke,' she says.

Curtis reaches out for Luke. Luke doesn't flinch.

Curtis's hand is rough against Luke's jaw. Luke waits for the memories to come, to crash in on him. But they don't. The past is just the past. He is living in this razor-thin moment.

'Take it back,' Curtis says. His voice flat.

'No,' Luke says. He is afraid, but he is something else too. 'I can't fight you, Curtis. But I'm not taking it back. You fucked up.'

Curtis's fist lands rocklike in the pit of Luke's eye. Something in his skull pops like some great seal breaking. Luke takes two stumbling steps back. Red pain radiates from his eye. Curtis steps in, his feet never crossing, and he slings a fist into Luke's gut. Luke sees it coming, his stomach tenses in the way he's taught himself, and there's pain but he takes it, and he thinks maybe he can stand it, maybe the nightly punches have toughened him enough, and then the second and third blows come, stuttered so this time they catch him mid-breath, and Luke pukes out all the air in him and bends double like a safety pin. Curtis straightens him up.

'Take it back, brother. Say you're wrong.'

'No.' It comes out a whisper.

He doesn't even see Curtis swing. He hears the celery crunch of his nose snapping. Pain rakes from the tip of his nose to the center of his skull.

His eyes shut and then another blow and he falls hard on his back. He gasps, trying to teach his lungs how to breath, blood draining from his nose into his throat, spit and snot and blood whipped into foam. He spits, feels it run down his chin, into his ears.

The crowd goes *unnnnnngh.*

He opens his eyes, face-up to the night. A ring of black around the world like he's lying in his grave. Curtis steps over him.

'Say it.'

'No.' A word like a cough. All he knows is that someone has to stand up for Manson. The way nobody stood up for him. All he knows is he's found this thing inside him that will not break.

'Fucking say it.'

'*Fuck you.*'

A boot in his rib curls him into a ball. He pukes his air up again. All is blood and crunch.

Somebody says, *Come on, Curtis, that's enough, Curtis.*

A boot to the head fills him with white noise. He comes out the other side like a shipwrecked man washing ashore. He looks up through wet eyes so that Curtis stands over him split into rainbow prisms. Something glitters in his hand.

Somebody says a word that sounds like *knife.*

Somebody says something like *stop, Curtis.* Somebody steps up to Curtis, jumps back the moment Curtis turns to them. Curtis says something. Nobody's words have meaning to Luke anymore, none but his own. He only has one word left but it's the only word that matters.

'No.' The word comes in gasps but he knows Curtis can hear him. 'No.'

The knife traces a sharp line from behind his ear down to the side of his throat.

The tears in his eyes split the world. The fire blurs into

a red sun in the void. Dark shapes cut against the blaze. Inside him little islands of pain grind together.

The rage in him has frozen solid. He knows he will not break. He cannot speak any longer but his lips move anyway.

No.

The knife is small and sharp, made for fitting between ribs or underneath a clavicle. Luke feels the sharpness at his throat, the thin edge that could open up the whole universe. And he wants to beg and plead but the thing in him won't let him. It's stronger than the knife and doesn't care about Luke's life or anything other than refusing to break. And somewhere far away his body thumps with pain but here there is nothing but quiet. And it is beautiful. Curtis and he are the only two things in the universe, connected by this knife. Luke feels foam fill his mouth. This time he swallows it. The way his throat bucks when he swallows sends the knife point sharper against his skin.

Luke, past struggle, waits. This is the moment. The knife makes them both naked. Luke sees Curtis, and Curtis sees Luke. They have their little reckoning. They are both surprised by how it turns out. Curtis stands. He folds up the knife.

'Kid's nuts. Ain't gonna waste a kid for being nuts.'

Hands help Luke sit up. Numbness like storm clouds blots everything. The crowd flickers. Partly because of the bonfire light, partly because he's flickering himself. He sees the Chuck Brothers with their mouths hung open. Like they've seen something they won't forget ever.

'Jesus fuckin' please us,' one of them says.

Luke's mouth has filled with blood again. His stomach tells him not to swallow any more. He spits a red splash into the fire. It hisses thanks.

He is led by hands that are cold in the way that tells him he is hot. Galaxies of pain are birthing all over him. A red sun of pain from his face. A constellation down his ribs.

'Come on, Luke,' someone says.

'Tell him to keep his mouth shut,' Ricky says. At least he thinks it's Ricky.

'He'll keep it shut.' The blood din in his head makes it hard to tell, but he thinks it's Curtis talking. 'Trust and believe.'

He zombie-walks into the night. The hands – Pretty Baby and Callie, he realizes now – get him into the shotgun seat.

'We should go to the clinic,' she says, her voice like she already knows what he's going to say.

'Take me home,' Luke says.

The darkness grabs him with both hands.

CHAPTER TWENTY-SIX

He comes back to the sounds of Callie and Pretty Baby talking.

'Fucking assholes,' Callie says. 'Macho bullshit.'

Luke tries to open his eyes. Only the right one obeys. He looks down, sees himself in the slashes of passing streetlight. Like a body dragged from a car crash.

'I wanted to jump in,' Pretty Baby says. 'Did you see, I tried? I should have stopped him.'

'There wasn't no stopping him. Anyhow, baby, he had a knife. What were you supposed to do?'

The silence is so long Luke starts to drift away again.

'I should have stopped him.'

'Wasn't no stopping him,' she says again. Another long pause. 'That was the most fucked-up thing I've ever seen.'

'I've seen worse,' Luke says. They jump at the sound of his voice. The laugh that comes out of him is too loud, too hard, and when they turn back he sees it on their faces how it scares them, scares them as much as the blood.

*

They roll up to the front gate of the compound. Pretty Baby hops out to get the gate. From his one good eye Luke can see an orange dot from a cigarette flaring up in the dark of the front porch.

'Someone must have called him,' Callie says.

'I'll walk from here,' Luke tells them.

'The hell you will,' Callie says. 'We'll get you to the house.'

They park right in front of the house. Callie helps him up out of the car. Callie and Pretty Baby walk him to the foot of the porch steps. Del stands on the porch looking down. His face more shadow than light.

'Curtis did this,' Callie says. 'Luke didn't throw a single punch.'

'All right then,' Del says, not looking at her.

'He had a knife—'

'He didn't employ it. You let me handle this.'

'Callie,' Luke says mushily. 'I'm okay.'

'No you aren't. I'll call you tomorrow. If something hurts bad go to the clinic, okay?'

He nods like *yeah* even though it's a lie. They let go of him. He sways. He doesn't fall.

Del waits for them to shut the gate and drive away. He comes down the steps. He takes Luke's face in his hand. Studies him. Turns his head to inspect him. Little bombs go off all over Luke.

'Was it one-on-one? Or'd they ratpack you?'

'One on one.'

'Then it was fair and there's nothing to be done. Can you make it up the stairs?'

Luke says *yeah*. He tries. He makes it halfway. At least when he falls, he falls forward.

Luke sprawls on the couch. The pain is coming into focus.

Kathy wipes his face – the washcloth comes back red and black. Her mouth is a tight line. Her eyes are hard. Luke figures it's not her first time wiping up blood. Past her, Luke sees Del in the bedroom, hunched over, his arm deep in a hole in the floor. Luke has a vision of his dad with his arm halfway through the floor in that same spot – some sort of dark magic to a spying five-year-old. Luke remembers waiting until his dad left. He went to the spot, pulled up the carpet. There had been a hole in the floorboard, full of powders and pills, guns and money.

Del gets what he wanted from the stash-hole, moves the carpet back. He comes in holding a baggie of white pills and a glass of water. He hands two of the white pills to Luke. Luke takes them, swallows water – some dribbles out through his split lips. He's way past caring.

'Now let's get you back to your home,' Del says. 'Curtis'll be back soon. You might want to think on how to make amends.'

Luke shakes his head. The little motion carries big pain.

'I was in the right. I got nothing to apologize for.'

Del looks at Luke for a long, long moment. His forehead furrows.

'Ricky said you didn't break. I must admit I didn't believe him when he said it.'

Del tucks the baggie into Luke's hand.

'Watch your dosage. Don't let them get their hooks

into you,' Del tells him. 'Pain's a part of our natural condition. You get where you want no pain, it's the end of everything.'

CHAPTER TWENTY-SEVEN

He wakes up mid-moan. When he keeps still, his whole body is a single sizzling nerve. When he moves, even to roll over, the pain becomes bright flashes, every joint a flashpoint, every muscle sliding rough over his bones.

His guts boil. He tries to bargain with them. They force him up. They march him to the bathroom. The room pans and zooms. He crumples down in front of the toilet. He pukes up whatever is left in his stomach into it. Then he pukes up painful nothing, his body one big spasm.

Please, he begs his body. *Please*.

But he is not in charge.

I'm sorry, he says, not even sure what he's apologizing for.

But he is just a passenger in his body. It shows him that by retching him dry, wracking him, pain and motion he is helpless to stop. If sleep is the cousin of death, then dry heaves are the cousin of dying. When his body is through with him, he drops down to the dirty floor. Bitter dregs drip out of his mouth. His nose starts up bleeding again.

He presses his face against the side of the toilet, blessed cool. He greys out there on the linoleum.

When he comes back to himself the bathroom is hot. The sun fills the room, telling him from the angle of the light that it is mid-afternoon at least. The sunbeams jab into his eyes like thumbs. His head aches like his brain is pressing against his skull. The word *concussion* floats across his consciousness. He pushes it back down. The word is useless.

He wedges himself up. He pushes his face into the sink, sips lukewarm water. He gulps it. He makes himself stop before he is sick again. He takes a few deep breaths to prepare himself for what comes next.

He looks into the mirror at the wreck and ruin of his face. A hematoma like a purple egg of blood swells above his left eye. He touches it. It is hot and tight. It gives a little under his fingers, like if he squeezed it would burst and paint the mirror red. The eye underneath is sealed shut. Gravel scrapes speckle his face. The bridge of his nose is swollen, an arch of a bruise laid across it.

Luke's busted lips creep up into a sickly-sweet smile. He likes how he looks. It feels honest to wear your wounds where the world can see them.

PART FOUR

THE SACRED AND THE PROFANE

CHAPTER TWENTY-EIGHT

The pills wrap him up in invisible blankets. He learns to buffer them with food – granola bars are all he has, and chewing them makes his teeth ache in their loose sockets. But food in the belly staves off the nausea, lets the pills do what they need to.

His phone fills with missed calls and texts. Sam, Apes, Callie. He returns the texts, just enough to let the people know he isn't dead. He remembers his days in the cave apartment, how he had buried himself and let his world fall apart.

He doesn't leave the trailer. It's like his first days here, hearing people come and go, hearing Curtis on the heavy bag. It ought to set something off inside him. It doesn't.

He studies himself in the mirror. How the bruises all over him deepen. How they get yellow at the edges. His nose comes back to normal, a little off-center. He likes how it looks.

He tapers off the pills. They scare him. He remembers what Del said – painlessness is an unnatural condition. He unpacks himself from the cotton. The pain comes back. He lets it.

The knock on the door rattles him – he answers it anyway.

'You look like the walking dead,' Callie says. He steps aside, lets her and Pretty Baby in. He catches her nose-wrinkle at the smell. Whatever it is, he's got used to it.

Pretty Baby holds out a prescription bottle. Luke can smell the reek of weed.

'Mazar I Sharif,' Pretty Baby says. 'Painkiller supreme.'

Luke takes it with a *thanks*. Pretty Baby holds out his other hand – a sandwich bag of chocolate chip cookies.

'Baked them myself. Kind comes out a tube, like Jimmy Dean sausage.'

Luke opens the bag, takes a cookie down in two bites. He's starving.

'They're good,' Luke says. They are still soft, a blessing – his jaw hurts too much to chew. His teeth feel like someone forgot to tie them down.

'The only thing I know how to make is tuna melts and chilaquiles,' Callie says, 'and neither one is sick food.'

'I'm not sick.'

'You're something.'

'How's Sam?' he asks.

'Sam's fucked up. You ought to call him. He feels like shit. Like maybe he's responsible for you getting beat down.'

Pretty Baby shakes his head like *nu-uh*.

'That's not it. He feels like he should have done what you done. He should have stood up for his dog. You made him feel like he was weak.' He's never seen Pretty Baby so sure of something. 'Like maybe not having muscle isn't an excuse. Like maybe he's just weak to the bone.'

Callie takes Pretty Baby's hand. There's that thing again passing between the two. He almost asks them what it is. Instead, he says, 'I just couldn't take it – that she needed help and instead they threw her away. It just got to me is all.'

Callie's eyes light up. She says, 'Oh wow.'

'What?' he asks her. And then he gets it. In his head he sees Callie, nine years old, standing on the porch, standing with Del and Kathy and the others as Luke sits in a stranger's back seat, to be driven away. To be thrown away.

'Oh Luke,' she says. 'Luke, nobody thought they were throwing you away. Is that what you thought?'

'You talked to Curtis?' Pretty Baby asks, like he wants to save Luke from having to answer.

'Haven't seen anyone since that night.' The rising tide inside him ebbs again.

'What are you going to do?' Pretty Baby asks.

'I don't know. I keep waiting for someone to tell me to leave.'

'You're thinking of going?' Callie asks. A look passes again between her and Pretty Baby. But he knows they don't want him to see it, don't want him to ask. 'We like having you here, Luke. It's been good. But if you have to leave, I get it. Believe me.'

'I won't. This is my dad's land,' he says. 'I'm not going anywhere. I'm just waiting for one of them to tell me to go so I can tell them to fuck off.'

CHAPTER TWENTY-NINE

'What the hell is this?'

Erik's eyes are fresh red. His jaw works like a cow chewing hay. His eyes run wild in his skull. He is gakked to the gods. He's at the top of the roller coaster, right before the plunge.

'It's a grand,' Pretty Baby says – his voice down an octave, trying for tough-guy.

Erik's face gets even uglier.

She told Pretty Baby not to talk.

'I don't see a grand. All I see is the nine that isn't there. Now where the fuck is it?'

'We got ripped off,' Callie says.

'You figure that's my problem?'

'I fucked up. We fucked up.' She doesn't touch Pretty Baby. Doesn't give Erik a reason to get more pissed. She shouldn't have brought him. She knows if Erik goes off, Pretty Baby doesn't stand a chance. She just hopes having a man there will reign Erik in. She hopes the calculation is worth it. She hopes they get out of there alive.

'I got to make payments of my own,' Erik says. 'I got to kick up to Stainless and the NDB. I got to fucking worry about Beast fucking Daniels. If I'm getting crucified I'm not going alone. Figure Jesus had a couple of buddies on the cross with him, right? Figure I'll take you down with me. Word is Beast already gunning for the Combine. Hell, I ought to serve you up to him on general principle.'

His glass pipe is stained and old. He drops in a couple chunks of ice, shakes them down into the bowl. He flicks on the butane torch. It hisses. Erik, so big and fumbling, has nimble fingers with the pipe – he plays it, moving the pipe and flame. It crackles. He twists the pipe. He sucks down smoke. He breathes out this noxious cloud, like some smoke-breathing, red-eyed monster.

'Mother's milk.' He holds the pipe up to the air. He squints at the meth as it cools in the pipe, judging the crackback as it forms a pattern like bird feathers against the glass. 'Or maybe I don't give you to Beast. Think I don't know you're running games on the Combine? I did business with Del back in the day. Think he'd like it if I gave him a call? Or maybe I'll just handle this myself. Stomp the both of you and dump you in the Wash. Way I see it, I got a lot of options in fucking you up.'

'Hey man—' Pretty Baby starts. Her hand reaches back, touches him. He's trembling. But he stops talking.

Please baby, be cool, she begs him wordlessly.

'A grand,' she says to Erik. 'Every week for thirteen weeks. That's the nine grand we owe you and four on top. Because we fucked up. But we're here. We're here to make it right.'

'Make it right? You're dry-fucking me and you want me to say thanks?'

He puts the pipe on the coffee table – the tabletop covered with black burn marks. Careful tweakers have a wet rag handy to put the pipe down on. Nothing about Erik is careful.

'It's better than nothing.' She points to the cash. 'You fuck us up and that's all you get. Our way you get paid and make profit on top. That's what we can offer you.'

They'd hustled hard for a week to raise up the grand. They're buying food from the loose-change jar. Any idea of leaving the Empire has blown away on the desert winds.

Please take it.

'Fifteen,' he says.

She looks back to Pretty Baby. He's all the way inside himself now. It's her call.

'Fifteen,' she says. It sounds like a door slamming shut.

Outside the wind is hot. It's drunk the scrub brush on the hills dry.

Pretty Baby sits behind the wheel, hand on the key, not turning it. And it takes Callie a second to see how badly jammed-up he is.

'I'm sorry,' he says. He pulls a white pill from his pocket. Looks like an Atavan. 'I wish I wasn't me. I wish I was Curtis. He would have put his fist all the way through that fat dickbag's head. And it's like I want to be that for you.'

'That's not what I want. I don't need that. I just need you.'

He eyes the pill. He picks off some lint. She wants to

take it from his hand. She knows if she does, it'll just make the shame worse – he'll take more once they get home.

'You've got me,' he says. He's said it lots of times before. But this time there's no sweetness to it. Just weight.

'We'll get out from under this. And we'll get our stash back up. And we'll get out of here.'

He shakes the open soda can from the cupholder. No noise. He dry-swallows the pill. She wants to hold him close. She needs him so badly. She knows if she holds him now it will just confirm his fears.

'It's me and you baby,' she says. 'All the way down.'

She's said it to him so many times. It's never felt like a curse before.

CHAPTER THIRTY

When they come for Luke, they come at night.

The sound of harsh knocking drags him from sleep. He opens the door still half in a dream world. Curtis stands with one foot on the steps. The Chuck Brothers stand behind him. The good soldiers.

'Get dressed,' Curtis says. Curtis's right fist is red and swollen, the only mark on him.

'I'm sleeping.'

The night makes black pits of Curtis's eyes. 'We're going on a little ride. Right now.'

Luke pulls on jeans. He scans the trailer for a weapon he can hide on himself. Nothing sharper than a plastic take-out knife. Crazy to think he could fight them anyway. On his way out the door Curtis stops him with a hand on his shoulder. He reaches into Luke's pocket. He pulls out his phone. He tosses it back inside the trailer.

They walk to Curtis's SUV, all of them in a ring around Luke like he might make a break for it. They steer him to the back seat. He opens the door, sees Sam sitting there, his finger in his mouth, chewing a nail down to the quick. His eyes scream *holy shit holy shit holy shit.*

The Chuck Brothers sit loose in the cargo area, Trent with his back against the spare tire. Someone cracks their knuckles. Someone snorts their nose clean. Bumps on the road jostle Luke and Sam in the back seat. It kicks up fresh pain from Luke's healing wounds. Sam won't look at Luke. His eyes locked on the back of the driver's seat, somewhere below Curtis's shaved skull.

Curtis drives too fast for the roads. He fiddles with the phone, finds some old metal song about a rainbow in the dark with a cheesy keyboard hook. But here and now the song is terrifying.

They drive north on the 15, the hills black humps on either side of them. The same road Luke took his first night here, the road on the edge of the world. Somewhere before Victorville they turn off the main roads. Soon there is nothing but wasteland around them.

'There's something I want to tell you,' Luke says.

'Now he wants to talk,' Curtis says. 'The other night he was fucking mute, but now he wants to talk.'

The Chuck Brothers laugh.

'I was the one talking shit,' Luke says. 'It wasn't Sam. Sam's got nothing to do with this.'

'Shit man, you got more juice from taking that ass-whipping than most people get from giving one. How the fuck do you think it looks? To have some kid get my knife to his throat and still not crack?'

'I didn't—'

'Nobody really thought you were Big Bobby's son.

We figured your mom had herself someone hiding in the woodpile. But now everybody says you're the son of Big Bobby. And you didn't even throw one fucking punch.'

They turn into a large and empty parking lot, only one small building next to it.

A sign says, 'Mount Baldy Recreational Area'.

They get out of the SUV. Above them the whole goddamn universe is spread across the sky. Curtis and the Chuck Brothers put Luke and Sam at the center of their circle. Luke walks so careful through the night. He thinks on how even just walking you're one false move from falling down. They walk towards the building that sits between the parking lot and the desert. The windows are boarded up.

Sam's eyes scream *oh fuck oh fuck oh fuck*. He's sweating faster than the desert night can drink it.

A slash of light under the door.

Luke pictures plastic on the floor to catch their blood. Cleavers to take them apart at the joints. Bags of quicklime to unknit their bones.

Curtis opens the door. The room is filled with folk. Uncle Del stands next to Teller. There's Apes with this wild grin on her face, standing with Ricky and Kathy and men he doesn't know. A man with slick-back black hair sits at a card table. He is inked all over, with glasses thick as drywall so his eyes swim huge in front of his face.

Del looks to Curtis. 'How'd they comport themselves?'

'Pretty sure I smell piss,' Curtis says with a smile. 'But there weren't no tears.'

The room laughs. Luke gets it all at once. This isn't a trial.

It's an initiation.

'Sam,' Del says, 'you've been aiding and abetting the Combine for a while now. You're young and strong, getting stronger. Luke, well, your time with us has been brief. It hasn't taken you long to impress us. It's no nepotism to bring you into the fold in such a short time. It's not Big Bobby's name that's earned you a black heart. It's his blood in you.'

'Blood is love,' Apes says. And then they all say it as one, Luke and Sam too, and it's dumb but it works, it makes Luke feel like he's wrapped up inside of something.

Del pulls off his shirt. Loosening skin on top of ropey muscle. He touches his black heart.

'Dead man's ink will not wash away,' he says. 'It's a stain that sets deep. You don't want to wear it until you rot, now is the time to leave. Nobody will stop you from walking out that door.'

Luke looks back to the door – he thinks on the life he could lead on the other side of it. How grey and washed out it would be. More a half-life than anything. He thinks on the stranger who drove him here, and how that stranger is him, and although he aches from the beating the pain is better than the nothing he's felt most his life. He knows what's on the other side of that door. Nothing. He turns back to face Del.

'All right then,' Del says. 'Disrobe.'

Luke pulls his T-shirt off. Rocks grind under his skin when he moves. Somebody lets off a low whistle. Luke looks down, sees what they see. His torso a purple and yellow sunset.

'Man, I stomped the shit out of you,' Curtis says.

'Goddamn,' Ricky says. 'I would have said anything to get that to stop.'

'See what I mean? You're a fucking legend for that ass-whipping.' Curtis turns to the others. 'And he fucking should be. This skinny motherfucker is hard as scar tissue. He didn't even know it himself. Ain't that right?'

Luke doesn't know what to say. He doesn't know if he hates this or he loves it. But he knows he wants it.

'The usual way is, before we put the black heart on you we give you a trial by fist. But it looks to me, Luke, that you've more than passed that test already,' Del says. Everyone laughs at that. 'Anybody object to Luke not getting another beat-in?'

'I do,' Sam says. Everyone laughs again. And then the circle forms around Sam. Luke moves to the back, catches glimpses between moving bodies.

'We want you to hit back,' Del tells Sam. 'Don't stop fighting until I say.'

Sam nods. His lip trembles. He raises his fists. They vibrate. Del swings first, closed fist to Sam's chin. Sam stumbles. Apes catches him, sends him forward with a thump. It keeps going like that, they hit him and lift him at the same time. And then Sam swings back like he's supposed to and his fist bounces off Curtis's chest. The next punch drops him for real but he gets back up and that's what they're looking for and then it's over and they cheer. They move aside so Sam can sit. He crashes into the chair next to Luke. He smiles. His teeth are pink. Luke leans into him and gets an arm around him, feels his sweat. Hands clap their backs, hard love. Luke starts laughing, not because it's funny but because of how good the night is.

Curtis steps up to the two of them. He kneels between them. He takes out his knife, the same knife he held to Luke's throat a million years ago. Curtis draws a red line down his own left hand. He reaches out to Luke. Luke puts his hand in Curtis's. His body feels so stuffed with blood he worries that when Curtis draws the knife across his hand the wound will spout. But it's just a thin line of red, a thin line of pain. Curtis takes his hand and talks in a sing-song voice.

Talk is cheap and words can lie
but we are bonded til we die
better in hell than up above
because we know that blood is love.

Again part of Luke wants to laugh at how cheesy it is, but he can't, and anyhow part of him wants to cry too.

'Ernesto here,' Del says, nodding to the man with thick glasses, 'he inked the first black hearts on me and Bobby and Teller, and he's done every black heart given outside a prison wall.'

'And maybe someday on the inside, I keep living my sinner's life,' Ernesto says. More laughs – the vibe is pure love.

Del holds up a plastic container filled with black liquid.

'This here is the dead man's ink,' he says. The room goes silent. Luke knows a sacred thing when he sees it.

'Ink mixed in with the remains of our first fallen brother, John Meadows. When they cremated him, before they sent him back to his momma's people in Oklahoma, Bobby took a double fistful of John and mixed some up in a big bottle of black ink and told Ernesto here to give him a black heart over his real one. And that was the first black heart. Me and Teller followed suit the next night. We kept the little sack of ashes all these years, even sent some inside for Bobby when he decided to ordain Curtis and some of the other boys there.'

'Nobody tell me how it got snuck in,' Curtis says. 'I don't want to know.'

Everyone laughs as one, except Del, pissed, his ritual profaned.

'Understand it's not just ink,' Del says, 'it's blood and body. When we say "blood is love", there's a lot of ways for you to take it, and they're each and every one true. So think on that while Ernesto here gets to work on you. Think on what you're carrying in your veins and what will commingle with it when the ink soaks in.'

Ernesto does Luke first. He spreads this gel on his chest with a wooden stick, spreads it thin and cold against his skin. Then he revs up the gun. It stings Luke's chest so that a sweat rises on his upper lip. The stabbing buzz is weirdly familiar to Luke. Soothing almost. First Ernesto sketches the outline of the heart, freehand. Thin as floss, delicate, perfect. Then he sits back and switches the needles on his pen. He fills in the heart, and the pain is greater now, the tingle of perforated skin drinking ink. Luke's skin weeps blood. Ernesto has to pause the machine and wipe it away.

'You're a bleeder,' he says, holding up the bloody gauze. 'Don't worry, it don't mean nothing. Your blood's a little closer to the surface than for others. Your dad's the same way.'

And then it is done. Luke looks down at the black heart inked over his real one. Ernesto spreads a piece of plastic wrap over it. And then Ernesto does the same for Sam and everyone watches Sam and teases him, and Luke is able to zone out, stare off into space, the ache of his chest anchoring him. The ink and ash soak into him. Healing him or infecting him or both.

'Now we got to get down to the Wash,' Del says when Sam's ink is done. 'There's a welcome party waiting for you both, the rest of the family and a lot more besides. But there's one more thing, first.' He takes out a flip phone and hands it to Luke.

'Wanted to do this live, but couldn't risk it. Had to do it by message,' he says. Luke presses play. He puts the phone to his ear. The reception is bad, tinny. The voice is still strong.

'Luke.' Just the one word sets off tidal waves inside him. 'Heard you were getting the black heart. Man. And I know I ain't always been a father to you, and I know why you've stayed away but now you're a part of the Combine, I feel like I'm your father twice over. Come and see me when the ink dries. I'm proud of you, son.'

Luke shuts off the phone. He hands the phone back to Del. Everyone expects him to say something. He doesn't have anything to say.

CHAPTER THIRTY-ONE

They've filled a ring of rocks with old brush and logs bought off the back of a truck and a busted chair with flaking green paint showing the blond ash underneath. Pretty Baby places tinder strategically. One of the Chuck Brothers had gone down into Berdoo earlier and found one of those boxes stuffed with free newspapers advertising call girls and happy-ending massages. They stole the whole stack. Now they rate hooker pics as they wad up the paper for fire starters.

Del gets the honor. He takes a torch made of a stake wrapped in an old T-shirt, doused from the gas can. It's a smell you can see. He touches the lighter to it. It bursts into flame. Del tosses the torch into the pile and there's a moment of nothing and then a sound like something falling. A fist of flame reaches up towards the night.

The fire draws a circle of light. Outside the circle, nothing exists. The sky above them is so full of stars it feels like a cage. The circle is full of people. Bikers with leather cuts and unwashed bodies. Crust punks, even stinkier, their hair in dreadlocks and liberty spikes. Skater kids with shaggy heavy metal hair and Black Sabbath shirts, Mexi gangbangers in snap-front shirts and cowboy boots and handgun face-tats, shitkicker girls with home-trimmed bangs dressed in tank tops and short shorts huddled together for warmth. Luke sees the Chuck Brothers, already wasted, taking turns trading punches, thuds in rhythm, encouraging each other to take it. Laughing, hitting harder, going too far, the scrap turning real until Curtis pulls them apart.

Luke finds the beer coolers. He fishes out a can and pops it. Foam sputters down his wrist. He gulps deep. Pretty Baby comes out of the shadows. He presses something twisted and dry into Luke's hand.

'Happy Combine birthday, new brother.'

'Thanks, man.' Luke eyes the scraggly mushroom.

'It's not a heroic dose or nothing,' Pretty Baby says. 'Just enough to dig up the riverbed.'

Luke eats the mushroom. It tastes as dry and twisted as it looked. He shudders. Pretty Baby laughs. 'It grows on cow shit. Just think on that when it shows you the face of God.'

The mushroom gilds the world. The rocks, the brush, the air itself glints with gold. It lays a carpet of swirling fractals over the dirt and stone beneath him.

He orbits the party. His chest hurts where his new heart sits. He can feel new wet under his bandage. He is a bleeder. Like his dad.

Come see me when the ink dries.

He wanders through bodies. He feels eyes on him. People nod like *that's him*.

The stars above glitter and pulse, a language he can't quite understand, but he gets the gist of it. It all makes sense.

Aunt Kathy comes from the dark, wraps him up in a hug that hurts his chest. She smells like cinnamon and white wine.

'Now you're family for real,' she says. She tips her cup into his mouth, the wine coppery on his tongue, and he closes his eyes to savor it and when he opens them Kathy has turned into Sam, his eyes wild with glee.

'Come quick,' he says. Luke follows him through the crowd. Every step he makes is sure and true. He has always felt like a thing apart traveling through this world, but now the mushroom and the night have shown him that he is as much a part of the world as every rock and stone and star. They reach the edge of the firelight, where it is colder.

'Check that out,' Sam says. He nods towards the dark. In the dim Luke sees a woman on her knees in front of a bearded man. She is wearing a black leather vest with a 'Property of Gator' rocker on its back. Her head is bobbing bobbing bobbing. The man's head is tilted up to the stars, his mouth hung open.

'Just hope that's Gator,' Sam says. Luke laughs, laughs hard, Sam laughing with him until they plop on their asses, howling up at the stars. Laughing themselves clean.

He sees this girl dancing, her hair bounding everywhere, catching firelight. She has a scar down the side of her face. She sees him watching. She smiles. He sees how the scar runs along her cheek all the way down to her lip so you'd feel the gap of it if you kissed her. It sets off this animal stirring in him. And it's like she knows what he's thinking and her eyes are shining in the firelight as she smiles at him and then she's gone in the dark.

The mushroom connects things inside him. He has never been so aware of himself as an animal, an animal who was born and will die, and for once the thought of death holds no fear, because it is a part of this beautiful life and therefore must be beautiful itself.

He sees Pretty Baby sitting in the firelight. The flickering of the flame changes his face second by second. Pretty Baby leans into Callie, singing some song together, arguing over the words mid-stanza, laughing until Pretty Baby falls backwards onto the dirt. Callie pulls him up, fails, joins him on the ground. She's laughing too but there's fear in her eyes.

Apes pours lighter fluid from a metal can into her mouth. She holds a lighter to her lips and blows. She belches a cloud of flam. The crowd cheers.

Kathy pushes her way through people to get in Apes's face.

'That's the stupidest thing I've ever seen,' Kathy shouts. 'Want to catch yourself on fire?'

Apes wipes lighter fluid from her chin with her sleeve. She smiles this heartthrob smile.

'Maybe.'

A guy in a stinking leather coat lifts Luke in the air with his hug. 'I used to rip shit up with your dad,' he says. 'You have a need, you have a brother.'

Luke sees Callie in the murk at the far edge of the

firelight, making a deal with some dude he doesn't know, a quick hand-to-hand and the man returns to the fire. Luke joins her. She's embarrassed, like he caught her doing something wrong. But she pastes over it with a smile.

'The hustle never ends,' she says. 'There is no cure.'

He sees these different things playing across her face in little twitches. His vision is so clear. He knows more than ever that she's hiding something, her and Pretty Baby both, and whatever it is, it's too heavy for them.

'I'm glad to be back here,' he tells her. 'I'm glad we can be play-cousins again.'

'Me too,' she says, and he can tell she means it, but there's still that worry on her face.

'You're my oldest friend, Callie. You'll always be special to me,' he tells her. She smiles at him – she thinks it's the mushroom talking. 'What I mean is, if you want to tell me what's wrong, you can.'

She looks at him for a while, and he knows before she opens her mouth that she is going to change the subject. That she's not going to let him in.

'So you're in for good,' she says. 'Family for real now, huh?'

He pulls up his T-shirt. Shows the heart. The flesh around it red, blood seeping under the skin from the million stab wounds. There's something in her eyes that makes him ask, 'What's wrong? You don't like it?'

'I do like it. But that doesn't mean it's good. It's not all a party, Luke. There's danger, too.'

'Maybe that's what makes it all so good.'

'Maybe,' she says, and again he thinks for a second that

she's going to spill whatever it is that she's carrying. Then she looks up, and he follows her eyes to another beckoning customer, and she turns back to Luke and says, 'Enjoy the night, primo.'

Luke orbits the party. He takes wider loops. He goes out into the night. He sees the crowd around the fire moving as one big organism. He sees Del and Curtis and Teller standing apart. Luke sees them all clear and plain as if it was daylight. And it almost feels like the dead man's ink has soaked into his system, changing him. Whispering to him. He starts putting puzzle pieces together. He sees how Del and Curtis had to put him on the inside. Some of the Combine were angry at Curtis for what they'd done to Manson and for the beating he'd given Luke. Folk were impressed with Luke and how he took it. And they could either shun Luke or bring him in. Bringing him in was the smart choice. This was the move that healed them all. He sees it like he'd been in the room when they'd hashed it out. He sees the whole picture and his place at the center of it, and standing alone in the dark, outside of the fire, he starts to laugh again, that cleansing laugh.

He is a prince. And that is a good thing to be.

CHAPTER THIRTY-TWO

The wood crackles. Dots of flaming ash float in the night. Callie watches an ember faerie float past her shoulder into the blackness. It leaves behind tracers of purple darklight hanging in her vision. Callie swallows carefully. She had passed on the mushrooms, not wanting a heavy night. She'd stuck with Apes's pot brownies, but she miscalculated and ate too much. Now she is deep in the grips of the Fear. This is not her first time grappling with the Fear. But this time she can't deny the Fear has a point.

The fire carves a circle in the night about thirty feet across. Most stay within it. Those outside are drunk up by the dark, bobbing into the light or floating as shapes. She sees Luke go by, an arm around this girl Ramona, who was a couple years behind Callie at Cajon High. They're talking close, Ramona touching Luke on the forearm.

Pretty Baby comes behind her on the rock, squatting and sliding so his torso presses to her, and she presses back, grateful for the warmth and for more, and she reaches behind her and pulls his cheek to her. Music bounces off the rocks so everything is reverbed and eerie, and in the song someone is saying they aren't here, that this isn't happening.

The fire is close but now Callie is cold, so cold, and she tries to wrap Pretty Baby around her like a blanket but he's a person all his own and it doesn't quite work.

The edibles inside her drag her down deeper. She gets the feeling that something is watching her, some alien or some god looking down at her and out from within at the same time, and she holds Pretty Baby close and he holds her and she thinks to the watching alien god, *This here, this love, this is all I can show you, all I can offer of us that is good and worth saving in people. How he holds me and I hold him, leaning into each other so our weakness is strength.*

'How you doing, baby?' he asks her.

'I ate too much of the brownie.'

'Aw, baby. I'm sorry. Everyone always does. Always never eat weed.'

'Why didn't you say?'

'I did, remember?'

'Yeah, but you could have said it harder. We're going to get out of this, aren't we? We're gonna break free and get out of here, right?'

He looks around to see if anyone heard.

'Not too loud baby. Yeah. We are.'

'Promise?'

'I can't control the future. It would be a lie to promise.'

'Do it anyway.'

'I promise.'

At the edge of the fire a scrap of a sex-worker ad floats

down to Callie's feet. A woman's face, painted and posed. A spark lands on the scrap, in the center of the woman's smile. The fire eats her face from the center out, a mouth with lips of black ash that yawns from her face until it swallows her whole. Callie shuts her eyes to it. When she opens them again the woman has turned to ash. It blows away on the wind.

CHAPTER THIRTY-THREE

They're in the backseat of someone's car. Luke's not even sure who is driving. They're in a caravan back to the compound afterparty, windows open, different kinds of music from every car blending into chaos, and the girl with the scar on her face is on his lap, playing with his hair.

Her name is Ramona. She is weird and funny and dark. He had been right about the scar – he can feel it when they kiss, this gap of hardened flesh on her upper lip. He's not sure why it excites him so much. When they kiss her mouth is cooler than his and her tongue strong and probing, her lips soft and dry and then wettened, and he presses against her, hard friction, and later in his trailer they dry-hump furiously and she slaps his ass like something out of a porno and he gets lost in the pulse of her neck and how the shadows spill across her, and he's pulling off her clothes, watching how her hips raise up to slide off her shorts and he kisses down her breasts and belly and down until he can smell her and he wants to taste her there but she pulls his head back up gentle but insistent and he worries he's done something wrong and gets caught in a maze of worries and worries about worries and although they are kissing again it is without his focus and he has to stop, feeling that other world poking at the seams of this one, and she asks him *What?*, worried too, and he says *Nothing* and looks at her in the moonlight, still traces of mushroom sparkles at the edges of his vision, and he wonders why no one talks about this, the fear and the desire to please more than be pleased and how hard that can be, and she touches his face, braver than him, and she lays beneath him posing, hunching her shoulders until her breasts press together and he forgets for a while the fear, and this is enough and for a while they are lost in the moment and it is quiet except the creak of the mattress and the low hum of those still partying on the main house's front porch, and with the forgetting of the fear and himself there is just a moment of this and it is not peace but it is something and she reaches up and touches his face and her own face contorts and she says his name in hushed thrill and he's there and yet he is gone and yet he is there.

CHAPTER THIRTY-FOUR

The GUNSHOTS rip through his sleep. He flings an arm across the bed, across Ramona's chest as if saving her from a crash.

Yells. An engine roars. Luke rises up. He says, 'Stay down.' He pulls on pants in one motion.

Ramona turtles like they taught her in active shooter drills.

Rocks bite the soles of his feet as he runs towards the noise. The Chuck Brothers stand at the gate, pistols in hand, firing—

BANG

BANG

BANG

—at two red pinpricks of vanishing tail-lights. Curtis has started his truck, yelling for someone to open the gate.

'Is anyone hit?'

No one listens to him. Apes on the porch with some girl who is crying, her arm over the girl's shoulders, being strong for her.

'Somebody open the gate,' Curtis yells. *'Hurry up goddamn it!'*

Trent moves to the latch.

'Nobody's going,' Del says from the porch. Trent freezes, caught between them.

Curtis stomps the gas. Gravel sprays from the front wheels. It spatters the house. Apes's date shrieks. The truck bumper kisses the gate.

'Get it open,' he yells. Everyone's shouting. Luke gets to Curtis's truck. Curtis backs the truck up. Luke moves with it. Luke puts his hand on the driver door.

'Curtis, cut it out,' Luke says. 'Either they're already to the highway, or worse yet they're not, waiting to bushwhack whatever sucker is dumb enough to run after them.'

Curtis screams this berserker war cry, pounds the steering wheel. Kills the engine.

The Chuck Brothers count bullet holes in the front of the house. They count thirteen, all up near the roof line.

'Sounded like an AR,' Trent says.

'Since when are you the fucking gun whisperer?' Tyson says. Trent punches his arm.

'Shut up.'

Curtis sits in the funk of an adrenaline crash. His face is buried in his hands.

Del waves Luke over.

'You ran towards the fight,' Del says. 'Guns went off and you ran to the sound. You didn't run away. You did good. That black heart suits you fine.'

Luke nods. He holds back a grin.

Del looks up the hill. Luke follows him. Ramona stands fully dressed at the top of the steps. Luke can read her expression from here. Del can see it too.

'Looks like your friend there has had her fill of fun for the evening.'

They drive in silence, except the occasional *turn here* or *go right* from Ramona. Luke replays the night in his head as they head towards Redlands. Two phrases keep circling through Luke's head.

You ran towards it.

Come see me when the ink dries.

He sneaks peeks of himself in the mirror. He looks exactly the same. He looks completely different. He feels like he just climbed out of a cocoon, ready to see what these wings do.

He keeps sneaking glimpses of Ramona. She looks out the passenger window. Her face reflects in flashes. It brings him back down.

He pulls up to the curb in front of her apartment complex. He turns to her. He wants to kiss her. He wants to learn about her, unearth those veins of beautiful weirdness he just barely glimpsed in her. He wants to hear the story of her scar, and tell her about his invisible ones. She unbuckles her seat belt. This sad smile on her face.

'I'm sorry,' she says. 'You're nice, and I had a lot of fun. But it's just, that was a lot. Guns and stuff. That was too fucking real for me.'

'I get it.' He can't blame her. She climbs out of the car.

And part of him wants to roll down the window, try one more time, see if she's sure.

He watches her go.

He doesn't say a thing.

He gets it.

On the way back, Luke sits at a long stop light, almost asleep. To stay awake he pulls up his shirt. How wet the black-ink heart shines. He presses down on it. The sting keeps him awake. The good kind of hurt.

The afterparty as a war party:

The crew sits in their usual semi-circle. Everyone bleary, half-hung over, sleepless. Apes has pulled her sweatshirt hood up and yanked on the strings so that the face hole is a tiny black circle. They drink energy drinks. They drink coffee fast as Kathy can brew it.

'That fucker Stainless,' Curtis says. 'Beast's number two? He's got himself a little house in Fontana. Cauldwell at the Creepy Crawl, he's been there. He told me where it's at. We can start with him.'

'Once the killing starts, man, it don't often stop,' Teller says. 'It's all about the lab. We find their lab, they're fucked. If they can't cook, they'll have to get on their knees to La Eme. They'll have to get on the Sinoloa pipeline. They'll look weak as hell.'

'You miss the part where they just took a shot at us?' Apes asks. 'We're just gonna sit there and take it? I say we fuck them up. I say this is war.'

Del leans forward. Everyone gets quiet. Everyone looks to Del. Del looks to Luke. Everyone follows Del's eyes.

'I say we hunt,' Luke says. 'I say we look for the lab.'

'All right then,' Del says. 'Let's take a vote.'

Del asks for those in favor of the hunt to raise their hands. Everybody but Curtis does.

Curtis looks around the room. Sees the way it's going. He raises his hand too.

'There it is,' Del says. This smile on his face. Luke understands the trade they just made. Del's tied them up together into a power bloc. Luke lets this feeling wash over him. Power is a new thing to him.

It's such a fucking rush.

CHAPTER THIRTY-FIVE

Now come the soldier days.

They hunt for Beast's lab. Teller lectures them on all the signs to look for. Homemade venting. Padlocked trash-cans. Garage doors with blacked-out windows. He tells them to roll the windows down, let the desert air in, sniff it for the smell of nail polish or cat piss.

Days pass. The winds turn hot. The world turns yellow and then brown. How quick the rain becomes less than a memory, more like a dinosaur, something that once walked the earth but is now extinct.

Some nights Luke goes into San Berdoo on his own, hunting catalytic converters. He doesn't hit another dealership. He looks for pickup trucks parked on the street in nice neighborhoods. Big trucks, easy to climb under, big converters Del can sell for more money.

The truck beds are always shiny and unused.

Luke is always driving, always hunting. Nights are spent driving driving driving. Sometimes alone, sometimes with Sam, sometimes in a big group. Like teenage years spent aimless and cruising. They drive silent. They don't check their phones. They check their rear-views for tails. They might be hunted too.

One day they drive the flats south of San Berdoo, out where the roads turn to dirt and all the mailboxes cluster at the intersection of the main road. The houses have double-tall garages to hold mobile homes. They have green lawns with outlaw sprinklers, illegal in the drought, green grass in defiance of God and man both. Wireless towers taller than any tree in sight. Bikes left in careless piles by the roadside, no fear of theft.

'Some rich folk don't even bother with fences,' Curtis says, and turns the SUV around. Luke thinks on how their impossible lawns are somehow walls enough.

They hunt. They sleep lightly, quick to wake. They wait for Beast Daniels to strike at them again. They watch the winds suck the world dry.

Fire season is coming.

CHAPTER THIRTY-SIX

It started as a night-hunt. It turned into a party. Nobody says it. It just happens. They've been driving quiet too long. If they don't let out some pressure they're going to explode.

They're crammed into the Chuck Brothers' old Jeep. Trent and Tyson up front. Luke, Apes, Pretty Baby in the back, looking incomplete without Callie next to him. They pass the aux cord. They take turns picking tunes. They play drill music. They play hardcore. They play old-school hip-hop. They tell dirty jokes. They dog each other out. They laugh hard. They talk *hunting*. They talk *war*. They drink canned beer. They pass blunts. They pass a little baggie of yellow-white crank.

Pretty Baby waves off the crank. He drinks orange soda. He talks slow, smiles wide. A plastic pill bottle rattles in his pocket. His eyes are heavy-lidded. It seems like he's swimming in the deep end these days.

Luke hits the blunt, gulps canned beer. Waves off the crank.

They cruise down towards Fontana. Locals call it

Fontucky – the Inland Empire's white-trash epicenter. A good bet for a white-trash lab spot.

'A hunting we will go . . .' sings Tyson in the shotgun seat. His eyes in the rear-view glow electric. He snorts like a stallion. He makes ugly faces as he swallows crank-crumb post-nasal drip.

The blunt smoke smells like roast pork. Apes passes it to Pretty Baby. Pretty Baby holds it. He looks at Luke like he's going to say something. But he doesn't.

'What?' Luke asks.

'You seem better,' Pretty Baby says. 'First time I met you, I thought you weren't really there, you know? Like I could pass my hand through you.'

He taps Luke on the chest like *see?*

'You weren't all wrong,' Luke says.

'Is it better or worse, being solid?'

'Better.'

'If you say so,' Pretty Baby says, his voice constricted, holding the smoke in. 'Me myself, I keep trying to melt.'

He lets out a huge smoke cloud. Luke takes the blunt from him.

'Anyway, I'm glad you're with us.'

'Thanks, man. Me too. I feel like—'

'Lookit,' Trent says. His voice high, excited. 'See that purple truck over there?'

'What about it?' Apes asks.

'The guy driving . . . *lookit.*'

Luke looks – some guy about his age, pale shaved head, a tattoo like a sideways Jesus-fish on the side of his head – it looks about as new as the one on Luke's chest.

'Is he—?' Trent asks.

'Yeah,' Apes says. 'It's him.'

Tyson makes jackpot *ding-ding-dings*.

Trent swerves lanes. He rides the purple truck's ass.

Luke reaches up and grabs the *oh-shit* handle.

'Whoa,' Pretty Baby says, stuck in the middle with nothing to grab. 'How'd I wind up sitting bitch?'

'Cause you are one,' Apes says. She punches the roof *rat-a-tat-tat*.

'Who is he?' Luke asks.

'You weren't there,' Apes tells Luke. 'When Beast Daniels came to the house, he had this little new fish driving him. That's the kid. He's with Beast.'

Trent slows, lets the purple truck get a little ahead of them. Trent stomps the gas – adrenaline blooms on Luke – Trent stomps the break.

'Shouldn't we be cool?' Luke asks. 'We can follow him, see where he goes.'

'Oh, good idea,' Trent says. He stomps on the gas. He rear-ends the truck.

CRUNCH.

Trent laughs like *ain't I a stinker?* He says 'Oopsie doo.'

The truck's parking lights come on. The kid climbs out of the truck. He is volcanically pissed. He looks back. He recognizes them. His eyes go from predator to prey in one blink. He hops back in. The truck peels out. It fishtails. It burns through a fresh red light. Trent fumbles the shifter. He gooses the gas too slowly. Cross traffic blocks their path. The truck rabbits around a curve and out of sight.

'And he's off,' Tyson says. He turns to his brother. He punches his arm. 'Nice driving, fucko.'

'Find him,' Apes says. She's got these hungry eyes. 'I want his scalp on my wall.'

They cruise a loose grid. They ride silent. They hunt for real now.

'Aw hell,' Tyson says. 'Little bitch is halfway to Disneyland by now.'

Pretty Baby jostles Luke, shifting so he can dig into his pocket. He maraca-shakes a pill bottle. He rattles a couple of Xan bars into his palm. He washes them down with orange soda. He gets a face like he just slid into warm water – just the act of swallowing them enough to trigger calm.

'Miracle of modern medicine,' he says, and laughs, but his eyes do something different.

'Benzos are for pussies,' Tyson says. He fishes out the baggie of crank. 'Starting to think another bump would smell good right about now.'

'That's what's up,' Trent says. 'Let's pull over so I can get in on this too.'

'Let's get off the street then,' Apes says.

'When the crank starts cranking is about the time I bail,' Pretty Baby tells Luke. 'Fitting to turn into Wild Kingdom up in here. I'm gonna have Callie come get me. You can come with if you want.'

Luke thinks it over. 'Think I'll stay.'

'Free country,' Pretty Baby says as he texts Callie.

'Turn in there,' Apes says, pointing. 'We can park in back. I used to party back there in high school.'

Luke follows her finger.

'That's a grade school.'

'It was my grade school,' she says. 'So what? They've got a playground. I want to play.'

'Isn't it like way worse to get caught carrying on elementary school property?' Luke asks.

'Oh for sure,' Trent says, pulling into the school. 'Way worse.'

They follow the driveway around a dog-leg to the back of the school. They park in the loading zone behind a dumpster. Swings and jungle gyms and see-saws in the unlit dark behind the school. They pile out, laughing in whispers, laughing at how dumb they are to even be here, how stupid a crime this is.

They head into the dark of the playground. Pretty Baby sits in a swing, his phone lighting his face ghostlike. Apes hangs upside down from some monkey bars. The Chuck Brothers busy themselves with the crank. Luke gets on a swing next to Pretty Baby. His feet drag under him. He looks out – empty soccer field, empty teeter-totters. There's something unholy about a playground at night.

'I'm zonked,' Pretty Baby says. The slur in his voice says it again. The pills have grabbed him fast.

'Then come over here and get right,' Trent says, shaking the crank baggie.

'Naw man,' Pretty Baby says. 'Me myself, I like to sleep. Sleep's the best feeling in the world. Don't know what y'all have against it.'

Tyson offers the baggie to Luke.

'You ever get down with this shit before?'

Luke's mouth goes dry. He swallows beer. It's warm, gross and metallic in his mouth. He thinks about Teller and his dad walking into a bowling alley bathroom, coming out snorting like stallions.

'I'll try anything once,' he says.

Trent dumps some on his phone. Scrapes it into a rough line. Trent snorts it. His face goes screwy. He swallows hard.

He holds it out to Luke.

'This shit'll put hair on your chest.'

He holds out his phone, screen up. Trent dumps a little powder on it. Apes scrapes it into a skinny worm.

'You gave him too much,' Tyson tells her.

'No such thing,' Apes says.

Trent passes him the rolled-up fiver.

'Bon appétit, motherfucker.'

Headlights shine from around the corner of the building. Luke freezes.

'It's just Callie come to rescue me from this outdoor drug den,' Pretty Baby says, holding up his phone like *see*? He stands. He stretches.

Luke puts the bill to the line fast. He doesn't want Callie to see him do it. He snorts the line from bottom to top—

a nose full of knives
a mouth full of fish guts
blood full of snakes

—snorting the line lifts his face right in time to see the truck rounding the corner of the school. It's not Callie's car pulling in. It's a purple truck.

It's *the* purple truck. It's the new fish.

Crank and adrenaline collide inside him. The rush is thermonuclear.

'That's that fucker right there,' Apes says. 'He chose the wrong fucking place to hide. Bad luck.' She's already running, they're all already running and Luke is running with them. He could run to Mars and back. His boots thud heavy on the concrete but he is weightless.

Another car comes into the drive behind the truck, blocking in the truck without meaning to – this time it's Callie for real.

'Stay in your car,' someone yells at her. Pretty Baby runs towards her. Everyone else runs towards the new fish. The kid pulls his truck up to the curb facing the playground before he figures out what's happening.

The Chuck Brothers hit the truck running. Tyson hits it with a flying kick. He dents the driver's side door. Then they're all kicking, Luke too, smashing his foot into the door. This wild energy inside him is too much, he's got to get it out of him before he explodes. He tries the door handle. It's locked. He bangs on the driver's side window with his fist. Behind the glass the new fish looks at him. The new fish has this weak look in his eyes. It just makes Luke madder. He kicks and kicks and kicks.

The kid inside panics. He stomps the gas. The engine SCREAMS. The truck goes nowhere. The geek's got it in park. Apes comes around the truck to the passenger side. She's got a huge rock in her hands. She throws it.

CRACK.

The windshield spiderwebs. The kid remembers how to shift. The kid stomps the gas. He jumps the curb into the playground. The truck drives through the swing set. The swings go flying. He leaves tire tracks through the soccer field. He steers left, bottoms out in a ditch, makes it to the street and is gone.

Luke lifts up his head. He howls at the moon. He'd bite its head off if he could.

Sunrise comes on him like an accusation. Luke showers with his eyes closed. He scrubs himself raw. He can feel himself sweating, the cleanliness already gone before he steps out of the shower. He should be deep in hungover sleep but the crank still boils in his blood. The blinds aren't doing their job. He can feel the daylight even when he shuts his eyes. He knows how vampires must feel. He hangs dirty laundry over the windows. He climbs into bed naked and damp. He pulls the blankets over his head. He gets it as cavelike as he can.

Outside he can hear the thump of Curtis on the heavy bag. Luke moans out loud. He can't handle someone who just started their day. He closes his eyes. His heart thumps like boots on a truck door.

It's noon before Luke finds sleep. He wakes up feeling like pure shit. His head feels parboiled. He's hungry and nauseous all at once. He walks down to the main house. He comes into the kitchen. Beer bottles pregnant with cigarette butts, like the old folks had a party last night themselves.

He grabs a bowl from the shelf. He opens the fridge. He opens the meat drawer and grabs the bacon. He digs past the squeeze bottles and cheese squares to the egg carton. He takes two from their cardboard beds. He closes his eyes and presses the eggs into the sockets, feeling the cold they carry, how it seeps into his eyeflesh and maybe carries some soothing to his poisoned brain.

He takes the first egg, cracks it against the lip of the bowl. He tosses the cracked shell in the sink, picks up the second egg and opens it with a single crack so the egg slips perfect into the bowl.

The raw egg is full of blood.

The white of the egg is blood-red. Luke swirls the bowl like maybe it will dissipate, like maybe it's a mirage, or that other world poking through. But the cloud of red around the sun of the yolk shimmers and stays. It looks like a bloody sun, some sort of sign from an invisible world. Luke looks at the bloody egg, and back to the shell, perfect aside from the crack Luke put in it.

He dumps the eggs down the sink. He runs water to wash them away. Tendrils of blood swirl down the drain last.

Luke has never believed in omens. He has to think that this just happened, that it doesn't mean anything. But it seems to Luke that something so strange happening at random is its own sort of omen, an admission from the universe that everything is chance, that everything is a thin sheet away from terror at all times.

INTERLUDE

THE PEBBLE

ERIK

Erik comes to, out of knockout sleep. The kind of sleep that teaches you that death is nothing to fear because death is nothing at all.

He comes to face-down on hot concrete. He is the stump of a rotted tooth.

'Welcome to the world,' a froggy voice says. Erik cracks an eye. A skinny whiteboy sits on the toilet in the middle of the room, his pants around his ankles, taking a shit. His mouth is sucked in like a sinkhole, his teeth gone from meth rot.

So Erik's in jail. That's one question answered. And he knows it's daytime – the sun sticks its thumb in his eyes every time he opens them. But is it Tuesday or Saturday? A.m. or p.m.?

A scream bounces in from somewhere. Someone's always screaming in lockup. Somebody's detoxing or missing their meds or faking it for a trip to medical. Somebody's screaming a promise of split skulls and gang stomps and demon fire.

Erik presses his face into the concrete floor. He begs the gods to drag him back to the nothingness. The gods don't do shit. They never fucking do.

Erik sits up. His stomach flops and splashes inside him. A moan roils out between his cracked lips. His boots flop loose on his feet. COs take your laces when you go inside – they say it's so you don't hang yourself in your cell. Erik calls horseshit on that notion. Erik clocks in at two seventy-five. Even the waxed laces of his boots wouldn't be enough to hold him if he kicked off the holding cell bench. He figures they really take the laces just to fuck with you.

He takes careful sips of the air, like even a deep breath might make him puke. He doesn't make it all the way back to cured but he shifts a little bit in that direction.

'Sometimes you eat the bear,' his suckmouth cellmate says. 'And sometimes the bear eats you.'

'Shut it,' Erik manages. He puts his face against the concrete. He tries to tell himself the story of how he got here. It comes back in weird flashes.

Half wired/half doped.

His front door split in two.

Black masks and bulletproof vests.

Cuffs on his wrists.

A room with flickering lights.

A cop smile in a napalm face.

He's been living out on the far side of things for too long. His heart pumps dirty blood. Ups and downs, powders and pills. Hours unmarked by day or night, unpunctuated by sleep. Living like one of those birds that flies all the way across the ocean not even coming down to sleep, just resting its brain one hemisphere at a time.

The bust came at 3 a.m.– that fucked-up evil hour. They rammed his door off the hinges. His first thought was of Beast Daniels.

I don't want to die in fire.

They dogpiled him. His head full of bad chemicals, tracers and cosmic flashes in his eyes.

A badge in his face.

Thank Christ they're cops—

A fist coming down—

nothing

—and then he was in a room with morgue lighting, watching bruises spread in real-time. He remembers the cop with his face all scarred by acne. He remembers the cop's questions. Asked about buyers. Asked about sellers. Asked about moving serious weight. Asked about moving ice.

Erik doesn't move a lot of weight. Erik doesn't move a lot of ice. In fact he's done both just once in the last few months.

That fucking cocktease and her fag boyfriend.

It starts to make sense. Erik puts more of it together. He remembers the cop with the napalm face. He remembers the badge that dangled from his belt.

The San Bernardino Sheriff's Department badge.

'Where am I?' he asks his cellie.

'Berdoo Jail.'

San Berdoo deputies busting him in Riverside. Doesn't make sense.

Unless it makes perfect sense. Because who lives in San Berdoo?

That fucking cocktease. Her fag boyfriend.

Figure they've paid him back halfway for the pound – the pound the little cocktease talked him into fronting. Figure maybe they didn't feel like paying back the second half. Now he's the one who is in debt for a brick of consignment dope, money owed to Beast fucking Daniels. Now he's been cleaned out. Now he's got charges hanging on him. It's the sort of thing that makes a man like Beast Daniels nervous.

The sort of thing that makes Erik fucked beyond reckoning.

'Montrose.'

Erik lifts his head from the concrete. He sees a CO – *a San Bernadino CO* – standing at the cell door. The CO laughs at him.

'Any idea how much shit I've mopped off that floor?'

Erik moves sloth-slow onto the bench behind him. Everything sloshes, everything moans.

'Get on up – you made bail. Your lawyer's waiting on you.'

He might as well have said it was an angel. Erik's got no one in his life who'd scrape together a bail fund, much less spring for a lawyer. The CO cuffs him and walks him out of the cell.

'*Vaya con dios*,' the suckmouth says.

The lawyer has dark hair, the sort of bad dye job you

barely see anymore. Like shoe polish. His suit pillows around him. Fat purple sacks of blood hang pendulous under his eyes. A smile like he just huffed a fart. He offers his hand for a shake, calls Erik *mister*. Offers him a ride back to his place so he can talk details.

They process him out. An envelope with crumpled papers, a lighter, his wallet, his phone and his shoelaces all coiled up. He bends over to lace them.

Everything sloshes, everything moans. He unbends. He pockets the laces – he'll fix his boots later. He shuffle-steps into the night. He tastes free air. The lawyer offers Erik the front seat, but he climbs into the back so he can stretch out. The cold air snaps life back into him, makes him even half believe there's a time coming where he won't feel poisoned.

'Where are we going?'

'Let's get you home – I thought you might be more disposed to talk legal intricacies tomorrow.'

'Figure I might.'

Erik studies the back of the lawyer's head.

'Who summoned you, man?'

'I'm on retainer from one of your partners.'

Beast had said he had a lawyer on call. Rumor had it the lawyer did all sorts of dirt for the Steel. Rumor had it the lawyer passed messages back and forth between Beast and the Aryan Steel council inside. Rumor had it Beast's lawyer was dirty as hell.

The lawyer passes the exit to Riverside.

'That's my exit there.'

'Oh darn, yeah it was. Hey look, if it's okay, I need to make a stop right off the freeway, won't take ten seconds.'

Like Erik is stupid. Like he believes for a second the Steel paid his bail just because he kicks up to them. No way Beast Daniels just bails out a small-timer like Erik.

Figure Beast knows I took a bad bust.

Figure Beast knows my whole stash got cleaned out.

Figure Beast knows when to cut his losses.

Figure this is a last ride.

The lawyer exits the 10, drives into a corporate-park wasteland. Erik touches the laces in his pocket, the ones the guards didn't want him to hang himself with.

Death is nothing to fear because death is nothing at all.

Fronting the cocktease. Taking weight on consignment. Not running for the hills the moment he saw Beast Daniels and those bottomless eyes. He figures he's been hanging himself these last few months. A slow-motion suicide. You add up the evidence, and you got to say you're looking at a man who wants to die.

So why's everything so clear? Why's the poison gone from his blood, replaced not by the false energy of meth, but something else, some fuel that burns cleaner than crank ever could? Why is he taking the laces out? Why is he wrapping the ends around his fist? Why does he check behind him to see they're on an empty stretch of road? Why does he jump forward and get the lace garrote around the lawyer's neck?

He pulls until the waxed laces bite into his hands. They hold. Erik figures it's true – you can hang someone with shoelaces. He pulls until his palms weep blood. The lawyer kicks and flops. The car rolls slow off the road – the lawyer's feet too busy doing the death shuffle to work the pedals. The smell of his shit hitting air tells Erik the job is done. He's never felt so goddamn alive.

He climbs out of the back seat. He opens up the driver's side door. He pats the lawyer down. He takes his wallet. He shoves the body out in a culvert. He heads east. He drives through the sunset and into the night. He stops at Primm Valley at the California–Nevada border. He pulls into Whiskey Pete's. He buys himself a beer and a shot with the lawyer's debit card. He sees this old green car in one corner of the casino. He checks out a sign – it's Bonnie and Clyde's death car on display. It's riddled with bullets. They've got Clyde's bloody shirt framed on the wall.

It reminds Erik to do something. He goes to the parking lot. He takes out his phone. He searches up Del Crosswhite's phone number. He makes the call. He lets him know.

You've got a rat in your house.

CHAPTER THIRTY-SEVEN

It's Callie's turn to run wild. It's been a week since that grade-school playground madness, pulling into the school to see her friends gang-stomping the truck, seeing that kid do his playground escape, seeing Luke try to hide crank jitters. It's been a week since she crab-walked Pretty Baby into bed, waking up every few hours to put a finger under his nose and feel the heat of his breath just to be sure he was still breathing.

It's been a week of hustling. It's been a week of making sales, stashing cash to pay off their debt. It's been a week of texting Erik, a week of getting no responses from him.

So when Mercedes from back in the day at Cajon High – *go Cowboys* – calls her and says, *You're coming out with us tonight bitch*, she goes. She leaves Pretty Baby with a kiss and a *don't wait up*. He's playing his cowboy game. His eyes are glazed but not too bad.

'Have fun, drink water,' he says. 'Love you.'

'All the way down.'

The night is wild but not as wild as some. There are boys with neat haircuts and muscles and smiles who buy them drinks and dance with them. They are handsome and loud and she has no use for them. Her girlfriends drop her off around midnight. They stopped en route to grab burritos. She'd texted Pretty Baby, asked him if he wanted one.

Nothing.

She walks up the steps careful. She walks up them one by one.

She opens the door – but wait, it's locked. She fumbles for the keys. She one-eye aims for the lock. She opens quiet, figures he's asleep.

She walks through the dark apartment – he didn't leave a light on for her. She pokes her head into the bedroom.

She sees the lump of him in the bed. Relief floods her, then fear. She moves to him, to put a finger under his nose to make sure he's still here. She tells herself, she has to tell him in the morning, has to tell him she's worried enough to do this. But—

It's not Pretty Baby in the bed. It's just an unmade bed with comforter and sheets all wadded up.

She texts again.

where r u?

She drops down onto the floor in front of the coffee table. She unwraps the burrito from the foil halfway down. Chicken, beans – she takes one of the grilled jalapenos, takes a bite, balances it with a radish.

Maybe he went to get food on his own.

Maybe he's out with Luke or the Chuck Brothers.

It's quiet in the complex. Most nights someone would be having a party – there'd be music, maybe EMD from the college kids on the end of the building or Tejano music from the family across the hall.

She looks at her phone.

Nothing.

She finishes the burrito, wipes her wrist where salsa has trickled down.

She looks at her phone. She turns on the TV. She watches mindless bullshit. She wishes she were mindless.

where r u?

INTERLUDE

THEY USED MACHETES, I GUESS

HANNAH

The cop who finds his body will never forget it.

Her name is Hannah Carillo. Her eyes are blurry from a double shift. She heads towards Casper's Diner, where the manager gives cops food on the sleeve. All she wants is a free double chili-cheeseburger and sleep.

She cruises through the office parks on Arrowhead, well-lit, empty, safe. Nothing to jam her up, nothing to stop her from ending duty on-time. She comes up to the T-intersection facing the old Arrowhead Lanes, and takes a left on Orange Show. Dispatch burbles on the radio – just white noise this close to shift change.

She's about to hit the bridge over the Wash when this sun-bitten homeless fuck runs into the street.

Keep driving.

The tweaker has dried piss across his crotch visible in the pre-dawn. His feet are black with street grime, thickened until they could walk noontime on Death Valley asphalt.

Thanks no thanks.

Keep driving.

But then something in his eyes makes her pull over. His eyes are crazy, no shocker there. But there's something else. It's like Hannah can see the sane person locked up behind the crazy. And that sane person is fucking terrified.

She rolls down the shotgun window. She asks, 'What's the problem?'

The man leans in. He brings this wave of stink with him. 'This guy's chopped to hamburger.'

His breath is unholy. The words are too.

Goodbye, free chiliburger.

The young man died with the radio on. It takes Hannah a second to place the song playing as they walk into the scrub of the Wash towards the old convertible. The song is old pop shit her mom used to play. Some guy named Moby. 'We Are All Made of Stars'.

She reaches past the body and twists the key. The music shuts off.

The young man in the driver's seat is covered with tattoos, covered with blood. She reads the words around the rose tattooed on his cheek. It's the universe telling another bad joke. Maybe yesterday the boy was pretty. Maybe in a week, wearing a suit, funeral home makeup airbrushed on, he will be again. Today he is ugly with violent death. His head hangs from his body by threads.

'They used machetes I guess,' the homeless dude says. Hannah pulls back from the car, the bright copper smell of blood in her nose. She's seen bad deaths before, plenty, but something about this carved-up death in the predawn orange and that song echoing, saying that we are all made of stars, it's something that will cling to her always. Every time she hears this song from here on out it will grab her. It will loop in her head for days. This corny-ass song made forever horrifying.

The voice in her head sings about people coming together.

The voice in her head sings about people falling apart.

The voice sings about how we are all made of stars.

But we're made of other stuff, too.

CHAPTER THIRTY-EIGHT

Their convertible sitting in the cop shop impound lot still has streaks of dried blood down the side of the door. Callie should have known the cops wouldn't have cleaned it up. Guess she figured it was just a human thing to do – after they took their evidence from the car that was now a murder scene – to wipe up the rest of the blood. That's what she gets for mistaking cops for humans.

A pulse thrums deep in the meat of her neck. A weird reminder that her body is still full of blood. Unlike Pretty Baby.

The largest streak down the side of the car door is shaped just about like his arm. Like maybe it dangled there when they were done with him. She could read the shape of the smears, see how his arm hung motionless against the car door for hours maybe before the tweaker found him down in the Wash.

The cop with the clipboard hands her Pretty Baby's keychain. The cop doesn't smile. She doesn't say anything a human might say.

'You can call it totaled,' she says, 'for insurance. That's what most do.'

'Don't have insurance,' Callie says. 'Just liability.'

'You can still call it totaled,' the cop says, like this was some favor. 'Send it to the crusher.'

'Only car I got.'

And the cop doesn't say anything that a human being would say. Just nods and says, 'Copy that,' and gives her more forms to sign.

The cop makes her sign here and initial there right in front of the car. The insides of the car are covered in drop cloths. Callie knows what's underneath. So much of Pretty Baby left there for her to clean.

As Callie signs in triplicate she thinks about the sheet that hung over him in the refrigerated room, how they pulled it back to show her the awful truth of it and make her say 'It's him,' even though it wasn't anyone at all, just a cold dumb thing with gaping wounds like red yawns hacked all over it.

The cop is done with her now and leaves her with this thing that can't ever be anything ever again but a death car to her. She uses her phone to find the nearest car wash. Her phone has been electric with texts for two days, ever since they found his body. She has answered enough to tell them she is alive. The Combine stopped texting her last night. It's been radio silence since then.

She thinks she knows why.

She thinks they are on the warpath.

She thinks maybe they are fighting the wrong war.

Only when she's sure of where she's going does she get

in, sits down on the drop cloth. She turns the key, thinking that it probably won't start, how could it start, doesn't it know it's a death car now?

The car starts.

She drives now with her hands at ten and two. She drives safe and slow. She cannot talk to a cop while driving a car full of dried blood. She drives with her jaw locked shut. Her grief is a solid thing battering against the back of her teeth. She cannot let it out. It fills her so fully she's not sure there will be anything left in her if it escapes.

There's speckles of him everywhere. She thinks on how life started in the ocean, and then we learned to carry the ocean inside us, in our veins. That blood is an ocean. And sometimes our oceans spill out. The floorboard is papery with dried blood that once pooled and now flakes.

She parks in the back of the car wash, by the vacuums and trash cans. When she takes her hands off the steering wheel she can see red dust on her palms. Her eyes go blurry, everything turns to prisms and rainbows as her tears split the light. And she cries, cries for him and for the two of them, and she wipes tears from her eyes. She looks down and sees her hands are now bloody – her tears on her fingers have rehydrated his dried blood, brought it back to life.

The floormats she just tosses in the garbage can. She puts a ten-dollar bill into the quarter machine and picks up the quarters in double fistfuls. She buys sponges and wipes. She starts with the vacuum, sucking up what she can. She jams the sucking mouth of the tube into the dried blood, knocking it apart in flakes that the plastic worm gobbles. She takes a towel from the a bag of dirty laundry that she had meant to take to the laundromat and goes into one of the car wash stalls and soaks the towel from the dribbling hose. She goes back to the car. She runs the towel over the dried blood, rehydrating it and sucking it up at the same time.

A pickup truck pulls into the slot to the right. A raised chassis so the driver looks down from on high. He opens his door, stops halfway out with his foot on the runner, gaping down at her.

'Gawd, who died?'

She learns for sure she doesn't have psychic powers – his skull doesn't crunch like an old soda can.

'My man,' she says.

The only man she ever loved all the way down.

She holds his eyes for the moment he can hold hers. He mutters something, turns away.

'That's right,' she says. 'Sin aloud, repent with a mumble, motherfucker.'

She opens the glove box. It is stuffed with old papers, insurance cards, street-cleaning tickets. A deck of cards. A purple metal one-hitter pipe, the insides thick with resin. She fishes out a lighter and hits the one-hitter, the resin softly crackling as it vaporizes, the smoke hollow-tasting and gross. She rotates the one hitter as the flame sucks up into the hole. She's not sure it's working until she exhales a dragon cloud. She coughs, her lungs working against her will like bellows, cleaning her out so her head rings. Right away she knows she's too high and the Fear is coming. Of course it is. She's sitting in the dried muck of the only man she ever loved all the way down. Her too-stoned brain conjures every time she ever grew short with him, every time she turned him down or made him feel small.

She does the only thing she can think to do. She cleans. She cleans the blood up best she can with the sponges and paper towels, scrubbing at the pleather seats until the white paper towels quit coming up pink. She gets more quarters and buys more cleaners, plastic sponges that turn pink almost instantly, wiping and wiping, bringing the blood back to life so she can sop it up. She cleans until her arms burn from it and she's dizzy from fumes, and when she is done she takes off her ruined T-shirt so that the air bites at her belly.

She walks to the trunk again, opens up the laundry bag and puts her face in it and smells, a sourness laced in that old smell. She finds a hoodie, the least rank, the most just soaked with that smell of him, and pulls it on. She thinks on how smell works, that it's not just a reflection or memory. When she smells him, he's still there, really there, flakes of skin and sweat in her nose, running through her lungs. She pulls the sweatshirt up over her nose. It's so full of him, so wonderful and beautiful that she breathes into the sweatshirt until it is wet with her breath and she's dizzy from recirculated air. After a while her brain gets used to the smell and it disappears so that she can't even smell it when she puts her nose right up to the cloth. It makes her sick to think how it will go, how he will fade from her same as the smell did, that there's nothing to be done about it, nothing at all.

In the trunk she finds some old graphic novels,

Blacksad and *Usagi Yojimbo* and *The Humans* and *Teenage Mutant Ninja Turtles*. She never noticed before how the comics he liked were all about animals shaped like people. Samurai rabbits and ninja turtles, ape biker gangs and panther private detectives. What did he see in these animals dressed like men? She wished she could ask him, even if he never was good at saying what was inside him, the way someone is when they were teased lots as a child, every conversation like walking on a creaking bridge. Did he dream of some other life, one cased in fur? What else would she never learn about him? What would be lost forever if she didn't find it?

She goes and buys a soda. She sits against the fence of the parking lot, out of sight of this car she hates and must keep, and she opens one of the graphic novels and starts reading.

CHAPTER THIRTY-NINE

They ride with the windows down so the Santa Ana winds roars in. The thing inside Luke roars louder.

Pretty Baby laughing at the edge of the firelight.

Pretty Baby hacked up in the Wash.

You live your life like you couldn't walk up to a stranger's door and kick it in. It's not the door or lock that keeps you out of it. It's the invisible walls inside you.

There's a forcefield around the people that hurt you that keeps them safe.

You put that forcefield there.

Curtis drives. Teller sits shotgun. Luke is in the back seat with the tools. He would have thought the Chuck Brothers would be there. The good soldiers. But Del said it was to be just the three of them.

Pretty Baby laughing, falling over in the dirt.

Pretty Baby on the news. The bearded crazy who found him saying into the camera, 'They used machetes I guess.'

*

There's nothing stopping you from walking up to the next door you see and taking it down. Pick up a brick and smash a car window and take what's inside. The police? They'd fill out some paperwork for the insurance companies and then go back to writing jaywalking tickets for quotas. It's the cop in your soul that has handcuffed you. These things you don't do, don't say. The dreams you don't even know you want to dream. It's all there right inside you. Standing right behind your inner cop.

Right where it can slit his throat.

There is an aluminum mini-bat riding next to Luke. And a boxcutter. And a ski mask. And a pistol.

Pretty Baby handing him cookies.

Pretty Baby in a box somewhere.

Stepping outside those invisible walls, it's like being thrown out of a plane and learning you can fly.

They move through Fontana's streets. Houses on all sides. Pickup trucks with Confederate flag bumper stickers. Pit bulls barking. Kiddie pools in the front yards.

'Turn right,' Teller says. 'And then we're there.'

'Tool up,' Curtis says. He plays drums on the steering wheel.

Luke takes the bat. He takes a pistol. He pulls on the ski mask.

'Everybody stay cool,' Teller says. 'Just another day at the office.'

Are you even here?
Is this really happening?

When you slip on a ski mask, the patch over your mouth gets sodden from the wet of your breath, so your lips get wet and you lick them and your breath feels heavy in your mouth.

Air is invisible so that sometimes you forget it's more than just nothingness, until you step into a night so thick you could take your feet off the ground and swim through it.

Luke sees the lights burning through the window. There's an invisible wall between him and the house.

He walks right through it.

His brain does its numberless math, the steps measured out as if practiced so his boot lands flush with the full weight of his body behind the kick and the door pops its hinges and he all but rides it into the house. He does not look back to see if his brothers are behind him.

Stainless is there in a dirty Michelob wife-beater, doing some weird jerky dance like he doesn't know if he should run or fight. The butt of Luke's gun passes through the *what the fuck* as it comes from Stainless's mouth. The butt of the gun meets Stainless's closing teeth. The teeth pack in around the butt of the gun like fresh snow around a boot.

Are you really here?
Is this really happening?

The force of the blow doesn't floor Stainless. He drops

anyway, chasing his enamel to the carpet. Somebody cheers. The voice might even have come from outside Luke's head. He switches to the bat. He swings it into Stainless's back. The *thunk* of it goes through his arms. Curtis laughs. Stainless crawls towards his kitchen. Teller stomps on his ass so the man goes flat. Luke steps above him. He sees the blue bolts on Stainless's arm. He swings the bat down into ribs. His hands tingle with tuning-fork vibrations. Something *CRACKS*. Stainless doesn't even scream. He moans. It's funny how he moans, a sad *aww* like the noise you make when a little kid tells you they're sick. Luke shifts his torso so next time the bat will meet skull. He raises the bat over his head. Teller pushes him aside. Luke turns, ready to swing on him. Teller raises his hands like *whoa*.

'Not yet,' Teller says.

Are you even here?

Is this really happening?

Teller kneels down. He takes Stainless's face in his hands. He talks like it's just another day at the office.

'There's two ways this can go, homie. It can go bad, or it can go worse. Your call. You tell us what we want to know, maybe there's a tomorrow, you feel me? Who shot up our compound?'

'Me, man. I did it.'

'Who killed Pretty Baby?'

'He did himself. Such a sad little bitch he cut his head off his own damn neck.'

Teller does something with the boxcutter that makes Stainless scream. The sounds bounce off the walls, ghosts of screams come bouncing back at them.

'Where's Beast gone to ground?' Teller asks. 'He got himself a little featherwood chick or what?'

'Check your mom's house.'

Teller moves his wrist again. A wet noise. Stainless's eyes flutter in his skull.

'Where's the lab, Stainless? Just give us something, huh? Make it easy.'

Stainless spits blood and teeth splinters.

This is the moment.

Luke takes the pistol back out of his pocket.

Are you even here?

Is this really happening?

And there isn't a root beer taste in Luke's mouth and there isn't anything at all except for him and the tiger which is him anyway and somebody says *Luke* and maybe they're saying it like *stop* or maybe they're saying it like *go*. Luke raises the pistol. Stainless raises his hand in front of his face like *stop* like *no* like *don't*.

Luke pulls the trigger.

CHAPTER FORTY

'Give me the gun,' Curtis says. 'I'll wipe it and dump it.'

Luke hands it to him. They ride in silence. They head back to the compound, just the two of them, Teller already dropped home. They'd left Fontana in silence, and it has stayed that way until now.

When Luke closes his eyes he sees a bullet passing through a begging hand.

'First time I killed it was at your dad's say-so,' Curtis says out of nowhere. 'This guy inside, Tommy Caputo. Everybody called him Short Dog, I don't know why. Pretty good guy to party with, he ran with your dad and me but he didn't wear no black heart. This girl who was sweet on your dad was sneaking in dope, riding it in her cooch and slipping it in on visiting hours. And then one day they stop her and take her to a bathroom and some female CO yanks the tampon string out her cooch and out comes a baggie of dope. Somebody had talked. And then it turned out Tommy had a snitch jacket. And seeing as how your dad had done business with him, that he ran with us, it was up to us to put him down. I never had a problem with the dude, not me personally, but him being a snitch, it hurt us in the eyes of the other cons – it's your word that keeps you safe, nothing more than that. You can make phonebook body armor and tape it to your body, but it's your word that really keeps you safe.'

'Like invisible walls,' Luke says.

When Luke closes his eyes he sees Stainless drop like a cord had been cut in him.

'That's it. That's just exactly it. And Tommy, he put a chink in that. We had to patch that chink with Tommy's life. So your dad gave me the shank. Made out of brass so I could walk through metal detectors without fear. The handle was friction tape and duct tape mixed together, maybe just for style to be honest. It had a real sharp point but that was it, no blade. You want to kill someone stabbing, you got to move fast. You got to puncture their liver, their lungs. Stomach's no good. Used to be you stabbed someone in the stomach and they died from septic shock. But those days are done. If you're gonna do it, you got to do it right. So I waited. Like a dude in a deer-stand, days I waited until the moment was right. And when the moment came and there wasn't no one there who would talk and the cameras couldn't see us, I didn't think a thing. I just stabbed. I got him good, and I got away. And then they took him away, and later they told me he died. The call came down after lockup. Whispers carried the news. Tommy was dead. And it stayed with me. Nights in prison are stupid loud, you know. Crazy don't sleep. And for a while my head was loud as any of them. And then one night I slept straight through. Because I realized I spilled that blood for your daddy. Because I loved him. I did it for the Combine, for the family. It showed me the truth of it. That's why when I say "blood is love", I mean it.'

He looks to Luke, searching for judgment. Luke nods like *I hear you*.

'One thing I know for sure is, people are about the opposites inside them. Pacifists, they've got more in common with straight killers than either have with some grunt who fires when he's told and stops when he's told. And I saw it in you from the very start. That thing you let chew you near to pieces, it was in you. That thing that was a weakness because it ate at you, it turned to strength because you turned it facing the other way.'

Curtis claps Luke on the shoulder, hard so it hurts.

'I'm proud of you, brother.'

When Luke closes his eyes he sees blood, black in dim light, spuming from a head like soda from a shook can.

'Curtis?'

'Yeah brother?'

'I think maybe I'd like to take a trip up north sometime soon.'

Curtis smiles.

'To see your dad?'

'I think I'm ready.'

'Brother, I know you are.'

As Luke walks into his trailer his head starts to ache. He realizes he is very thirsty. He realizes he needs to piss, bad. His body put his needs aside for him for a while, but now they are back.

Luke lays in bed for a long time. Hot wind whistles through the canyon outside. He shuts his eyes. The movie plays for him again. It's not the blood that spooks him. It's the begging hand with the bullet hole in it. He crawls out of bed. He finds the baggie of pills Del gave him after the beat-down. He pops two. He washes them down with backwash from an old water bottle. He sits up in his bed waiting for the numbness to take him. When the nothingness comes it feels so good that he gets up and grabs the rest of the pills and flushes them. He knows he can't have access to that beautiful numbness. He gets under the covers and lets it take him for now.

He wakes up to the smell of a burning world.

PART FIVE

THAT YE MAY EAT THE FLESH OF KINGS

CHAPTER FORTY-ONE

The sky is dark grey. The sun is a pink dot.

It has been dusk all day long.

Luke skates San Berdoo. The parked cars all look abandoned, covered in ash. The smoke coats his throat. When he wipes sweat from his forehead, he can feel the grit of it. The wind gusts are hairdryer-hot. Blown-down palm fronds lay across the road, block the sidewalk.

They call it the Mount Baldy Fire. Hot winds from the desert stoke the flames. At night you can see the glow behind the mountains. Far off. For now.

Luke skates hard, searching for that zone where the thoughts go away. Curtis had been right – three nights of no sleep, three nights of Stainless bouncing around behind his eyes. Three nights of getting used to the word *killer.*

Night four he slept. Mostly.

Luke skates through morning traffic. The roads crammed same as always. Folk drive angry – smoke headaches throb in every skull.

The news says the fire sparked from old power lines brought down by the winds. The news says the fire is three percent contained. The news says six separate wildfires are burning in the state. More than last year, which was more than the year before that. The news says evacuations coming. The news says this is one of four California wildfires. The news says Wine Country is a firestorm. They show resort cottages turned black and hollow. The news says some big park in LA is burning – someone is bombing homeless camps, and the fire spread from tents to dry scrub. The news says the Mount Baldy Fire isn't heading this way. Unless the wind changes.

Four days of texting Callie. Four days of no response.

On day four she picks up. Luke's in his car post-skate. He's sweaty, wrung out. He's glad to hear her voice. She sounds smaller than she used to.

He wants to tell her about Stainless. He wants to tell her someone paid for Pretty Baby.

'Stay close to home,' he tells her. 'Some shit went down.'

He drops hints. She doesn't seem interested in picking them up.

'It just makes sense everything's on fire,' she says. 'Like, the world's been wanting to end for a long time.'

'Del wants to have a thing. For Pretty Baby. Like a wake.'

'I know.' Her voice is flat, a robot recording. 'I'll be there. His funeral is in Ohio.'

'You gonna go?'

'I'm not invited.'

'Why not?'

'His mom is a fucking cunt.'

*

The soldier days continue. Del fears big payback.

'This will be the worst of it,' he says. 'If we can locate the lab before they strike, we can press our advantage.'

That night they hunt again. They spread out. Luke rides with Sam. Sam drives. Luke runs his thumb around the edge of the sawed-off barrel. Curtis had told him to take a file to the barrel and smooth it out, but he likes the way it pokes against his fingers.

Sam doesn't ask him about Stainless. Luke can tell by his sideways eyes that he already knows. Neither of them says *killer*. But the word sits between them like a wall.

Luke talks about his trip up north. About seeing his dad. He tries to picture how it will go.

They roll around the edge of the Empire. They cruise Fontucky – they hunt. They hunt for Aryan Steel. They hunt for the lab. They hunt for Beast Daniels. They cruise and cruise and cruise. They get hungry. They stop at a food truck on Baseline. They buy cheeseburgers. They rub red eyes. The whole world smells like a campfire. They grab a bench. They both sit facing the road. They don't talk about it. They're just in deep enough now, the idea of leaving their backs to the road is out of the question.

They lick grease off their fingers. Food tastes better to Luke these days.

Sam puts a thumb to his nose and shoots a snot rocket.

'Think the fire will make it down here?'

'Fire won't come down to the city,' Luke says. 'Maybe sparks will carry to the Wash, but like, this place won't burn. Devore is a different story. The wind shifts the wrong way and the compound is fucked.'

This big black SUV rolls to the light in front of them. Screeching heavy metal pours from the open windows. The man behind the wheel is huge. He is covered in jailhouse ink. Luke blinks like maybe he's an illusion. But there he is.

Beast Daniels.

'Sam,' Luke says, quiet, like maybe Beast has wolf ears.

'What?'

Luke nods to the SUV.

Sam's face: *Is that?*

Luke nods: *Goddamn right it is.*

'Let's go,' Luke whispers.

'Go where?'

'Let's follow him.'

'We should call Curtis.'

Luke stands up. He says, 'When there's something to tell him.'

They speed walk to Sam's truck parked on the curb. Sam turns the ignition – thrash rock blares. Luke jabs it off. They pull out of their spot too fast – horns honk like *hey asshole*. Sam flips a middle finger without looking back.

'Easy,' Luke tells him. Sam grips the wheel hard – Luke knows it's to hide how his hands shake. Luke looks down at his hands cradling the shotgun. They don't shake. Barely, anyway.

They head east on Baseline. They look for the SUV. They roll down the window to listen for Beast's music – hot campfire air floods in. They drive two blocks fast, weaving, getting lucky with the lights. They spot the SUV.

'Not too close. We just got to see where he's going.'

They hang a left on Sierra.

'We're just following him, right?' Sam asks. Luke nods. He ignores the pleading sound in Sam's voice.

Traffic is thinning out. Sam hangs way back, no cars between them now. They take Lyle Creek Road into the mountains. Luke thinks on telling Sam to kill the headlights, changes his mind. He figures that will make Beast notice them quicker.

The blackbrush and owl's clover that bloomed so green not long ago is now grey bones on the mountainside. Power lines loom on both sides.

Horses stand in a dusty pen.

A hand-painted sign: 'Firewood Sales'.

'Not the best week to be in the firewood business,' Sam says, then does a high-pitched giggle.

Luke laughs. He thinks of something.

'Maybe there's nothing up here,' Luke says. He puts a cigarette in his mouth. He doesn't light it – like somehow the cherry would give them away.

'What do you mean?'

'I mean maybe he's not going anywhere. Maybe he knows we're behind him, he's just leading us to nowhere.'

'Should we turn around?' Sam's voice like *please say yes*.

'Keep going.'

It's full dark now. Bad air hides the stars above. No sounds but the haw of the air conditioner, the hum of the road. This faint glow behind the mountains from the far-away fire. Beast's tail lights shine in the distance. They're closer now – Beast driving slow.

Looking for something.

Or reeling them in.

'How far we gonna play this out?' Sam asks.

Before Luke can answer, the SUV pulls over to the side of the road.

'Pull over,' Luke says. 'Now.'

'I'm just gonna drive past him like nothing,' Sam says.

'Then he'll be behind us.'

'Aw hell.'

Sam pulls to the side of the road, about ten yards behind Beast. Beast's brake lights stare back at them like red glowing eyes. The tail lights change as Beast shifts into park.

'I don't want this. Luke for real, I don't.' Sam says.

Luke waits for Beast's car door to open.

It doesn't open. Luke fingers the shotgun.

This is the moment.

'Let's go,' Sam says. 'I'll bust a U-ie, head back into town.'

'We could end this right here.'

'Please,' Sam says. 'Please let's go get Curtis and them.'

'It's just us. We can do this.'

Beast's SUV just sits there. It's too dark to see inside the SUV.

'Please please please,' Sam says. His voice high and childlike.

'Let him make the move,' Luke says. 'I've got the shotgun—'

'No no no no,' Sam says, yanks the wheel – he fucks it up, can't pull the U-turn. He has to back up, do a three-point turn. Luke studies the rear-view best he can, one last glimpse of the SUV. The unblinking tail lights like glowing eyes.

They drive back home on surface streets. They drive through downtown Rialto, four-lane boulevards, families at the Dairy Queen.

Like there isn't a war on.

Like the world's not on fire.

'You think he knew we were on him from the start?' Luke asks.

Sam looks straight ahead. His lower lip quivers.

'Because maybe he was heading someplace,' Luke says. 'Maybe he got suspicious because he was close to where he was going.'

Sam looks at his chewed-up fingers.

'Would you have done it?' he asks.

'Done what?'

'Got out the car? If it wasn't for me turning bitch, would you have done it?'

'I don't know.'

'You know,' Sam says. 'Don't tell no one, okay? Don't tell no one I went bitch.'

'I won't.'

'Don't.'

'Said I wouldn't.'

They drive in silence for a block.

Sam says, 'I didn't know that's the way it would be.'

'What way?'

'I thought I had a choice, if I'm weak or strong. I didn't

know until we were sitting there that I didn't have a say in it.'

'You have a say.'

'I didn't. For real I didn't.'

Luke lets him sit there with it. He doesn't say anything at all. He knows sometimes comfort is a pain, the way it points to your weakness. And he sees Sam and his weakness, and he hates him for it a little, because of how it reminds him of how he used to be. But he can't ever say that.

Sam drops him off with muttered promises of more hunting tomorrow. Luke nods like *okay*. He doesn't say *I'm going without you*. He thinks Sam knows anyway.

He looks to the main house as Sam drives off – all the lights are out. He could wake Curtis. He could wait until tomorrow. But he knows he's not going to do that. He wants this for himself.

He changes into long pants to protect him from brush – his legs start sweating the moment he steps outside. He goes to the side of the house, next to the hose, the gardening tools. He wants the machete in case he has to cut through brush. He can't find it. He picks up the gardening shears instead.

He retraces their drive. He drives up Lyle Creek Road. This late there's no one there, no one at all.

Fire glows behind the mountain. It's brighter now – the fire is growing fast. Dry scrub all around him. Luke thinks about how the more life builds up, the more it leaves to burn in the end.

He passes the handmade 'Firewood Sale' sign. The hills rise up on either side of the road. Luke pulls over where Beast parked a few hours ago. He sees a gravel road just ahead on the right. He thinks maybe Beast was about to turn down this road, looked in his rear-view, saw him and Sam and pulled over.

He decides to go it on foot. He keeps his ears cocked for the sound of engines. He's got the sawed off stuffed into an unzipped duffle bag, his finger on the trigger. If anything happens he'll just fire in the general direction and crawl up the sides of the short steep hills on either side of the gravel road. He walks into blackness. Somewhere a dog barks. Luke stops, waits. He keeps going. He wishes he had brought water.

When he finds it, it's with his nose. Aryan Steel's labs smell just like Teller said they would – cat piss and hot death. He creeps towards the smell, walking in the ditch alongside the road, hunkered down, almost crab-walking. The hills have grown around him into a valley. The road doglegs left. He follows the bend to where the road ends at a gate much like the one in front of the compound. Instead of climbing it he goes to the ridge to his left, scrambles up the rock, his fingers finding crevasses and gaps. The thick dry brush tarries him, tears at his clothes. He looks down onto a little clearing. Chemicals sting his already sore eyes. Trash is strewn everywhere – a dirt bike with no front wheel, a refrigerator with the door removed. A bail of chain link gone to rust. The plastic shells of printers and fax machines, the insides looted.

A man, naked except for a plastic apron and gas mask

on top of his head, smoking a cigarette, sits on the hood of an ancient Volkswagen. His hair is long and dreaded. The lab behind him is a triple-wide trailer, netted over to hide from helicopters. Bad smoke rises from hacked chimneys in the roofs.

Three more trailers just like it fill the little hollow.

He watches until the man heads back inside the lab. He retraces his steps back towards his car. He drives down the hill fast as a falling rock, visions of total war filling his head.

CHAPTER FORTY-TWO

The sky is yellow. The sun is a white dot. You can stare right at it.

The vibe is *totally fucked*.

Everybody wears black, in their own way. Trent in black cargo shorts and a hoodie, Tyson in black jeans and T-shirt. Both of them doped on something heavy, their eyes pinned, their mouths flat lines. Curtis in his court suit – he bulges out of it, his prison muscle making it two sizes too small. Sam in a Metallica T-shirt, tucked into black pants. Apes in a black Dickies zip-up jacket, her hair slicked back.

Everyone's eyes are red. Everyone's throat stings. Everyone's head throbs.

Two million acres of southern California burns. Two million acres of smoke in the sky.

'It's eating Big Bear whole,' Kathy says. 'All those poor deer.'

They eat little smokies from a crock full of barbecue sauce. They drink heavy. They avoid family business. They talk about the fire. They talk about packing go-bags. They talk about forced evacuations.

Luke sits on the porch with his rifle on his lap. He watches the road.

The vibe is *something's coming.*

He'd told Del about the lab this morning. Del had slapped him on the back and said he was proud of him. Del said to keep quiet about the lab until after the wake. He said, *First you mourn, then you fight.*

Callie shows late. She rolls fast through gravel. Emo rap from her stereo echoes off canyon walls. She's got the top down on her death car.

'She's still driving it,' Trent says, like he doesn't believe it.

'What else can she do?' Apes asks.

'Oh man,' Tyson whispers. 'Man I don't know if I can handle—'

Trent shuts his brother up with a smack on his back. 'Handle your shit.'

The vibe is *something's wrong.*

Callie parks in the space they saved for her. She walks up the steps careful, like they might move on her. She swigs from a gas station soda cup – from the smell it's half vodka.

Luke rises to meet her. She looks at him with these eyes, this smile. She gives him a hug.

It isn't until she is past him and inside the house that he clocks what she's wearing.

All white.

Kathy got a cake – 'RIP PB Our Angel'. This frosting cherub underneath. Bad frosting work – the cherub's eyes too big, too wild. 'Looks spun as hell,' Apes whispers to Luke. 'Like three lines of glass deep.'

They eat gas station fried chicken. They mix drinks. They pour heavy.

Del stays sober. He's trying not to smile at a wake. He's sitting on this big piece of news: we're gonna win.

Callie sits in her usual spot. Without Pretty Baby behind her she looks small and alone.

'Pretty Baby's legacy is that he united us,' Del says. 'In life, and now in death. His death revives us.'

'Blood is love,' somebody says.

'Blood is love,' everybody says.

Everybody but Callie.

They mix more drinks. They eat more food. Callie sits staring, watching some movie only she can see.

After the meal, Del takes the first long silence to say, 'There's family business to discuss.'

Everybody puts down their drinks. Everybody looks to Del.

Everybody but Callie.

'Luke found the lab,' Del tells them. 'Up from Fontana.'

'How the hell you do that?' Teller asks.

Sam studies his chewed-up fingers. Luke follows his lead, keeps him out of it.

'Thought I saw Beast Daniel's SUV in Fontana,' Luke says. 'Followed it up the hill. Got lucky.'

Sam takes a long drink.

'Fucking A,' Curtis says. 'Let's hit it. Let's blow up the Death Star.'

'Before they even get a chance to come back at us for Stainless,' Teller agrees.

'We strike first,' Del says. 'Eliminate their source of

power. Illustrate for the other crews that they *are* touchable. Then the rest will rise up too.'

'Why fucking bother?'

Everybody turns towards Callie.

'You want to go up in the hills and wreck shit? The hills are on fire. You think you can wreck them worse than fire can?' she says. 'Maybe the fire's going to eat us all. Haven't you all noticed? The whole world is burning. What the fuck are we even fighting over? A lump of fucking charcoal?'

Del makes a face like he smells something rotting. It's just there for a second, a flicker. Maybe Luke's the only one who clocked it.

'Are you the one who will stop the fires?' he asks Callie. 'Can you do anything at all about them? Or are you prepared to live in the world as it is? Because burning or not this is our place. We can't extinguish the wildfires. But we can do something about these motherfuckers who killed your man. Them, we can extinguish.'

Callie opens her mouth to talk. She thinks it over. She sucks her lips into her mouth to seal it shut.

'I'm not letting a fire do my job for me,' Curtis says. 'Anyhow, wind's blowing the other way, Callie. It's heading east.'

'I want to bust shit up,' Tyson says – his voice dope-thick. 'I want to fuck up their whole world.'

'We go tomorrow,' Curtis says. 'Let's get up with the sun and let's hit it.'

'What sun?' Callie asks. She gets up off her ass – she wobbles – she stands up and heads out onto the porch.

A beat of silence in her wake. Curtis breaks it, starts planning the raid.

Luke goes to the kitchen counter to pour another drink. He feels trapped in something. Drunkenness feels like the only way out. The cake sits half-eaten, chunks taken out at random.

The cake spells out: 'RI B Our gel'.

Someone took a slice of the figure at the bottom of the cake. Luke stares at the carved-up cherub for a long time.

Luke finds Callie out among the junkers, staring at an old sedan. She's hunkered down. She's staring into a rusted-out quarter panel.

'Is rust alive?' she asks him without turning around.

'No.'

'It eats, though,' she says, her fingers playing around the edge of a big rust hole.

'Yeah, but it doesn't die. Nothing's alive if it can't die.'

Then he realizes who he's talking to.

'Shit,' he says. 'Sorry.'

'Don't be,' she says, her eyes still on the hole. He stands there feeling dumb. He thinks the air feels poisoned in more ways than one.

'You wouldn't ever hurt me, would you, Luke?'

'*What?* No, of course I wouldn't.'

She runs her fingers around the edge of the rust hole – the longer Luke looks at it the more it looks like a bruised mouth.

'Just checking,' she says.

'You all right, prima?'

She talks in that slow, steady way of someone who knows how drunk they are.

'I'm a million miles from all right.'

He thinks about the feeling he had before Pretty Baby died. That the two of them were hiding something.

'Do you know something?' he asks her, not even sure what he means.

'Do I know what?'

'Do you know something?' And he thinks he might be asking himself that same question.

She plops back on her butt. She finally turns around to face him.

'I can't take this air. Can we go up to your place?'

He sniffs the air of his trailer as they go in – that sour smell of unwashed clothes, the trash on the counters. He looks back to apologize – he sees from her face she's not here enough to notice.

'How do you feel?' she asks him. He gets what she's really asking.

'Less than you'd think,' he says. 'Is that bad?'

She shrugs. She opens her mouth, her lips moving with the starts of words, but nothing comes out. Tears swell up in her eyes. And Luke thinks she is about to give up, turn around and leave without getting these words out. And part of him wants her to. Wants to not know whatever it is that is so huge she can't yank it out of herself. But he can see how bad she needs to get it out.

'Hey. Prima. You can talk to me.'

'Luke . . . Luke, maybe it wasn't Beast Daniels. Did anybody think of that?'

'What . . . Of course it was. What do you mean?'

'How'd they get him down in the Wash? It's like he was going to meet someone.'

'Who else would it be?'

'I just wanted to be free and clear is all. I wanted a chance to see the world while there's still a world to see.'

'Callie . . .'

'We did this deal, okay? Outside the family. Me and Pretty Baby. We bought a pound of crank, a whole pound, only the guy we were gonna sell it to turned out to be a cop. And we dodged a big bust, but the cops grabbed us, and Pretty Baby, he gave them the name of the guy we copped the pound from. I drove past Erik's place yesterday. His door had a warrant stapled to it, and it was busted out. They got him. Pretty Baby gave up his name and they got him.'

'You think that's who killed him? This Erik guy?'

Stainless raising his hand.

Luke's bullet passing through it.

She looks at him, and it's like she can see what he's thinking.

'Whatever you did Luke, don't try and put it on me. I'll carry Pretty Baby. But I won't carry your load too. What you did, you did for you.'

Luke nods. It's fair enough.

'It could have been the Steel anyway,' he says.

'Maybe,' she says. 'Erik buys his shit from Beast

Daniels. So maybe it was him either way. Only thing is, what was he doing down in the Wash? How could Beast Daniels get him down there? And the only thing I can figure is he was trying to be brave somehow. Brave for me.'

Now her words are thick with pain.

'He did it all for me. Because it was me, I'm the one who made it happen, I'm the one who wanted to do a big deal, I'm the one who pushed it. Pretty Baby didn't care, he only did it 'cause he was dumb enough to love me . . .'

Whatever she says after this is too mangled by tears for Luke to understand.

After a while she is empty and she lays on his bed, and Luke watches as she falls asleep. And her face looks peaceful, but Luke can hear this grinding sound, her jaw working back and forth.

He puts a hand on her arm. The grinding stops. He watches her sleep. He starts to think about what she said. If it wasn't the Steel that killed Pretty Baby, if it was this Erik guy or someone he knew, then him killing Stainless was for nothing.

He gets up, starts moving, like he can leave the thought behind him if he moves fast enough. He sees the gardening shears on the counter where he left them after finding the lab, decides to put them back where they belong. He steps out into the dim – the wildfires have made it permanent dusk. The wake has moved outside. Folk sit on the porch. The drink is taking hold. The laughs are getting wilder. Kathy claps to some song in her head. Sam double-fists a beer and a plastic cup. Tyson and Trent, sloppy, half-wrestle in the gravel.

Luke hawks a loogie into the dust. He heads towards the house. He moves past the red shed. Past his old bedroom window, Curtis's window now.

The side of the house, the gardening supplies. The rake. The trowel. The hand fork.

But no machete.

Tyson drops into the gravel. He says something Luke can't make out. Trent grabs his brother by the shirt. This image comes out of nowhere, from Luke's first days here, when he'd sit in the trailer and watch them all from afar. Tyson chopping the air with the machete.

The machete that isn't there anymore.

His head throbs. It feels overstuffed. These unspeakable thoughts rise up.

How'd they get him down in the Wash?

What had the man who found his body said on the news?

They used machetes I guess.

Down the driveway the twins whisper furiously at each other. In Luke's head, Tyson swings the machete – he chops dead grass. Down the driveway the twins hug each other in the dirt. In his head, Tyson swings the machete – he slams it into Pretty Baby's neck.

This feeling like wanting to vomit, to purge. This feeling like wanting to run. He knows it's all useless. The knowing is in him now.

Little dust devils kick up all around the house. This slithering sound fills the air. Hot air funneled by the canyon whistles in his ears. It runs ghost fingers through his hair. Its hot breath on his neck. Luke realizes what it means.

The wind has shifted.

The fire is coming.

CHAPTER FORTY-THREE

The next morning the sky is brown. The sun is a white dot. You can look right at it.

Luke wraps a bandana around his face before walking down to the main house. Callie had woken up around midnight. She was hungover rotten and mean. He let her leave without talking much. He didn't tell her what he'd been thinking, not yet. Not until he is sure. His sleep had come in knots spaced through the night. He kept hearing Curtis's story, his first kill:

It turned out Tommy had a snitch jacket. And seeing as how your dad had done business with him, that he ran with us, it was up to us to put him down.

He walks down to the main house. He finds Aunt Kathy loading up her car.

'Luke, honey,' she says. 'I was 'bout to wake you up. Best load up your stuff. Looks like it's heading this way.'

'You leaving?'

'Heading up to Bakersfield, gonna stay with my bitch sister and her kids for a spell. My asthma can't take this air.'

She lights one of her skinny cigarettes. She doesn't catch the irony.

'You think the place will burn?' he asks.

'Even if it doesn't make it here, it's too close for comfort.'

'Del going with you?'

She snorts like *you kidding?*

'Del'd rather burn alive than be locked up with my little nephews. He's staying until the fire's on the ridge. But if the fire gets close, you make him up and run. You hear me Luke? He listens to you.'

We'll see about that, Luke thinks.

'Where is he, anyway?'

'He's at the garage, talking to the contractor for an estimate,' she tells him. 'You'd think smoke'd be too thick to do business. Turns out that's rarely the case. Said to tell you, everyone's meeting at the roller rink in Fontana at noon. He called it the base of operations, swear to God. He said to be there.'

Luke heads back to the trailer. There's not much there worth saving. He throws what is in the back seat. He finds his algebra book – like an artifact from a lost civilization. He throws it out into the scrub, where the fire can take it.

He drives down the gravel road. He looks behind him – his family place. He's not sure if he wants the place to be saved, or if he wants it to burn.

He heads down to San Berdoo. Wind gusts rock his hatchback. Smoke gusts cut visibility to zero. He hits the freeway, slows to a crawl. Evacuees jam the road ahead. They drive cars loaded with kids and valuables. They head west. They head east. They jam on their horns. They swerve in smoke gusts. They roll down the window and scream curses to God.

The garage looks a thousand years old. The burnt-out husk is covered in ash covered in dust covered in ash. Del stands out front, leaning against his truck. He sees Luke coming. He waves. Luke gets out of his car.

'This fucker's late,' Del says. 'Typical contractor. Pisses on a job and then splits. That's their modus operandi every goddamn time.'

'Maybe it's the fire,' Luke says. 'I saw Kathy clearing out.'

Del hears something in Luke's voice that makes his eyebrow cock up.

'World doesn't stop because it's burning,' Del says, his eyes searching Luke. 'Shouldn't you be at the base camp? Curtis is counting on you to guide the war party to the labs.'

'I wanted to ask you something first.'

'Ask. Doesn't mean I'll answer.'

'Pretty Baby.'

'Don't believe that's a question.'

'I sort of think it is.'

'Then maybe you have your answer.'

Bombs go off all over Luke. He drops back – the car catches him.

Stainless lifts his hand.

Luke shoots right through it.

Del gets close. Bitter coffee breath in Luke's nose.

'I loved Pretty Baby. Maybe that's hard to believe, but I

did. But he was a junkie and a weak sister and there's no place for weakness with us, not anymore. At least this way he unified us, inspired us.'

'I . . . Stainless . . . you sent me . . .'

'You really going to put that on me?'

Callie said it first: *What you did, you did for you.*

'Pretty Baby though . . . he didn't deserve *that*.'

'"Deserve", that's a child's word. "Deserve" ought to leave your mouth same time as "Santa Claus". But he did deserve it. He talked to the cops. That cannot be permitted. We couldn't have a snitch ride with us, not when we're trying to rise up the way we are.'

'It was the Chuck Brothers, right? The good soldiers?'

Del doesn't answer. But that's the answer.

'They fucking chopped him up, Uncle Del. They massacred him.'

'It had to be an atrocity. That's Beast's signature, isn't it? No one questioned that he was behind it.'

'You lied. You killed one of us and you lied.'

'There you go with your childish ways again. Thought Curtis stomped those from your skull. Try and play it the other way, then. Where I didn't lie. Where I present my case in the open, tell everyone that Pretty Baby is a snitch. Where him and Callie plead and beg and lie, rally some of the family to their side. What then? I bring it to a vote, watch the whole family fall apart at the exact moment we must be united? Lying's a natural part of being a leader. Don't dream it can be some other way.'

Luke coughs – pain in his lungs. He's hyperventilating smoke.

'You got your own mind, and that's fine,' Del says. 'You will run this crew someday as your birthright. And my task is to make sure you are able to take to the throne proper. To be the king you've got to shed these last childish ways. I thought perhaps you had. Reckon I was wrong on that count. But we'll get you there. We will burn this childish streak right out of you. You'll do it today. While the family deals with Beast Daniel's lab, you will deal with Callie.'

It takes Luke a second to figure out what he means.

'No. No, no, no, no.'

'Either she was in with Pretty Baby, or at the very least she knew. You know the rules. You agreed to them when we put that black heart on you. It's got to be you this time, Luke. You're stronger than the rest. Trent and Tyson, they just about snapped doing what they did. The world needs soldiers like them. It needs true believers like Curtis. And then it needs those who stand above all of it and do what needs to be done.'

There is a stampede inside Luke. Things inside him running away from Del and his words. Other things that run towards them. To be the king. To sit where his father once sat. To wear a black heart forever. To be safe and never scared.

'I won't. I'm going to my dad. I'm going to my dad and I'm telling him what you've done.'

Del barks a mean laugh.

'I suppose I should be impressed how long it took you to drag out your daddy's name to get your way. But you picked the wrong moment. Shit, kid. Who do you reckon gave the greenlight on Pretty Baby and Callie both?'

CHAPTER FORTY-FOUR

The sky is deep orange. The sun is a pale grey dot. You can look right at it.

Luke drives like shit. He halfway runs a light – screaming horns wake him up. Cars swerve around him. His brain says *run*. His brain says *fight*. His brain says *hide*.

He's thumbing through his phone. He's sweating – the air conditioner can't keep up with the heat.

He hits the 210. He merges. Clouds of smoke cover the highway. Folk drive slow – visibility is down to car lengths. The mountains to the north are gone. Everything blurry and smudged. He takes the exit to Citrus. He heads south. He calls Callie. It rings so long he starts composing the voicemail in his head – and then she picks up.

'Luke?'

'It was us.'

'What was us?'

'The Combine killed Pretty Baby.'

Fuzz and pops fill the silence.

'Did you hear me?'

'Luke, what do you mean?'

'That Erik guy must have told Del that Pretty Baby snitched on him. And Del and my dad, they decided Pretty Baby had to die. They told the Chuck Brothers to do it. Callie, they told them to make it brutal so we'd all think it was Beast Daniels.'

Telling someone else makes it feel real – like he's not just in some crazy smoke dream.

After a long time she says, 'Okay.'

She sounds far away from okay.

'I'm heading to the roller rink,' he says. 'I got to tell the family. I've got to tell Curtis.'

He'd tried calling Curtis first. Curtis didn't answer. Luke remembered: No phones on a mission.

'I don't care about any of that,' she says. 'Luke, it's all burning. There's nothing to fight for. I'm going to get out of here for good. Come with me, primo. Who cares what happens to them?'

'I can't,' he says. 'I have to try to fix this. Callie, this is all I have. This is my family.'

He sees the roller rink sign up ahead. He cranes his neck, trying to see if the war party is still there.

'Well,' she says, 'Pretty Baby was mine.'

The roller rink parking lot is empty.

'Shit,' he says. 'I missed them.'

'Luke, it's all on fire. Ride out of here with me. I'll sell my car in LA or some shit, I don't know. But I've got to run.'

A flash in his head: the night Curtis beat him down. Sitting on the couch, the fuzzy shape of Del with his hand elbow-deep in the floor, coming back with the pain pills.

'I can't go, Callie, not now. But listen. Kathy's gone and Del's down in the city. I know where his stash hole is. Same one my dad used. I bet there's enough cash down there to run on.'

Luke tells her where it is and how to get at it as he pulls into the roller rink lot so he can turn around. When he is done, he can hear Callie sigh softly.

'Thanks. I hope I see you again, primo.'

'I hope there's something to see, prima.'

'Stay safe.'

'Not likely.'

He pulls back onto Citrus. He drives north.

Into the smoke.

CHAPTER FORTY-FIVE

The red light of the fire behind the hills makes Callie think of lava. Hot winds throw scrub brush across the road. They glow orange with hidden fires. They leave trails of smoke behind them.

There's no one parked in the lot in front of the family land. She undoes the gate, drives through it, parks. Ash like grey snow flits through the air. Sparks come over the hills in great gusts.

An orange helicopter with a dangling hose crosses above her. It is close but blurry. The sky behind it is an impossible orange-brown.

Somewhere, she tells herself, *the sky is still blue. Somewhere a wind is blowing in from the ocean.*

She walks through the gravel to the back bedroom. She uses the palm of her hand pressed against the glass to slide the window up just the way Luke told her to, so it misses the latch. She thinks for a second about her palm print on the glass.

As if Del would ever call in the cops.

As if this house will survive the coming fire.

She boosts herself through the window. The room rank with Curtis's smell, so sour and yet something animal and appealing. She shuts the window behind her to keep the smoke out, then opens it again in case she needs to make a fast escape.

She comes out into the living room – plates on the coffee table in front of the TV and three brands of stubbed-out cigarettes in the ashtray. There is a vape pen and a glass of something mixed with melted ice, strands of brown liquid where the two haven't properly blended yet.

The bed in Del and Kathy's room is unmade. The clothes lie in drifts on the floor. The room has its own tang, different than Curtis's, saltier. Deeper too, as they have been in this room a full decade.

She walks to the corner of the room, the place Luke told her to go. She yanks on the carpet. It untucks itself from the wall the way Luke said it would. She rolls it back. The floor under the carpet has a hole not much bigger than a mail slot. She looks down into it but there's nothing but blackness inside. She tries to use her phone to shine a light down but the slot's too small to get her eyes in line with the light.

She puts her hand down into the dark. Plastic crinkles under her hands.

A sudden gust of wind creaks the house.

She pulls the plastic bag out. Crank, yellow-white, four or five fistfuls. She drops the bag and puts her hand back in the dark. She has no time and no desire for that type of treasure.

Her fingers touch something cold, oily, and her first

response is to draw her hand back, snake-fear shouting in her head. She reaches back in and grabs the pistol by pinching the barrel between her fingers so that she can draw it out from the slot. Chrome that glitters even in the dim of the firestorm. She unlocks the cylinder and checks it to see the brass butts of five bullets. She clicks the cylinder back into place with a flick of the wrist. The clack of it so loud she freezes. She puts the pistol in the center pocket of her hoodie so the belly of it hangs down.

Another gust of wind hums outside, and this time she looks up, but Del's curtains are drawn so she can't see anything. She worries that the fire is too close. She reaches back down into the hole, deep, her whole arm swallowed by it as she traces concentric circles with her hands. Her fingers brush cotton. She teases it with her fingers, drawing it closer. Heavy. She drags the cloth bag with her fingers at first, until she can gather the nap of it in her hand, and she pulls it forward and up until it reaches the mouth of the hole, too big to clear it. She yanks once or twice, trying to figure out how to draw it out.

She lowers the bag back down to the dirt. Del must have put the bag down there when it was less full and fed it over the years. She reaches inside the bag. Her hand touches paper. She grabs as big a fistful as she can and still draw her hand out. It's paper money, tens and twenties mostly. She reaches in and does it again. More bills. Some fresh, others tattered, suckmouth money you'd almost be ashamed to spend. She thinks back to months ago, Pretty Baby showing her Scubby's ratty cash, telling her the man was full of shit.

I'm sorry I didn't listen.

She draws her hand into the bag a full ten times before it's shrunk enough for her to work the whole sack out of the slot. She sits there dazed by the money. She tries to reckon how much it is – thousands for sure, tens of thousands.

I can't run with you, Luke had said. *But I can help.*

She puts the loose money back into the sack. Another gust of wind—

No.

Car wheels hushing up the gravel road.

She stuffs the last of the loose bills back into the sack. Hands trembling. She drops the plastic bag of crank into the slot. She calms herself with thoughts that whoever it is will have to deal with the gate.

But I never shut the gate.

The car comes to a stop in front of the house. She rises, the pistol heavy in the center pocket. She passes the sack to her left hand. She curses her flip-flops as she moves hunched through the house. She hears the front door open as she slips into Curtis's room. She drops the money out the window and follows head first. She somersaults in the air and smacks the ground with her butt.

'You little bitch.' Del stands there at the corner of the house. Behind him the hills are dark, crowned in cresting flame, so Del is framed half in dark and half in fire. 'You goddamn little slit. Your man was a rat and you're a goddamn thief.'

The air is alive with sparks now. The wind stings her like ants all over.

'Come here to bushwhack me?' he says. 'Come here for revenge on your man?'

'I came here to rob you, Del. I came here to take your money. All we wanted was to leave. That shouldn't be so goddamn hard.'

He walks towards her with his hands already choking the air, like they can't wait for her neck. She raises the pistol. He breaks towards her in a run. She shoots three times—

—misses—

—and he's on her. She hits the ground hard. Del gets his hands on her neck. He squeezes. The edges of the world turn grey. Like the smoke is swallowing her. His eyes are pure hate.

'*Bitch bitch bitch*,' he chants to himself.

She gets the gun up next to his head, and she can't get the barrel pointed at him but she pulls the trigger anyway. The gun goes off next to his head. The *BOOM* shatters everything. Gunpowder burns a mask across Del's face. His eyes roll up in his head like she stuck a knitting needle in his ear. He falls off her and onto the ground. Blood coming from his ear. He screams – she bets he can't even hear it. He can't open his eyes. He's gunpowder-blinded. He throws crazy punches. Like he's getting gang-stomped by ghosts. Behind him, the junkers sit in pools of smoke. The brush all around them is starting to catch.

She leaves him there, blind and deaf. Screaming curses that no one can hear, not even himself.

She drives down to Berdoo. She parks on 3rd Street outside the train station. She leaves the keys in the car. She finds a plastic bag in the backseat, puts the bag of cash inside it. She buys a ticket for Los Angeles. As she waits, she looks back at the convertible.

Pretty Baby with his foot up on the dash as he drives.

Top down under a dead sky.

She hopes whoever takes it, it brings them joy. She knows the car won't be haunted for them.

She knows that things don't carry ghosts in them. People do.

CHAPTER FORTY-SIX

The sky is raw meat. There is no sun.

The hills on Luke's right burn. He shuts his vents against the air. He drives fast. He thinks he must only be minutes behind them.

Horses run nervous in the pen by the road. A man in a cowboy hat loads them onto a truck. He turns to the road as Luke approaches. He takes off his hat and waves the other way like *turn back*. Luke nods at the man like *I see you*. He keeps driving.

The 'Firewood Sale' sign is on fire. Luke laughs. A crazy sound. He turns into the gravel road that leads to the lab. Fire on both sides of him now. No sign of the family. He figures he would have seen them coming.

A gust of smoke swallows the car.

BANG BANG BANG.

Spiderwebs crack to life on his windshield.

BANG BANG BANG.

Pebbles of safety glass rain down. Luke crouches down behind the wheel. A bullet passes under the hood. The engine dies coughing. The car rolls a few drunken feet.

The shooter comes out of the smoke.

'Luke?' This froggy voice. Sam's face is pale under grime and soot. His old hunting rifle dangles from his hand. His shoulder is soaked black with blood.

'Luke, Jesus, I didn't know it was you.' He throws his old rifle into the ditch. 'Wasted my last on your car. Shit.'

'Where's everyone?'

Sam looks towards the dog-leg, the road to the lab.

'Aryan Steel was there when we got there. They were loading shit out to save it from the fire. Beast fucking smiled when he saw us. There was a fight like you never saw.'

'We've got to go help them.'

Sam shakes his head like *hell no*.

'It's too late,' Sam says. 'We got to run. The fire's there.'

'It's everywhere,' Luke says. He takes Sam by the sleeve. He leads him towards the lab. Sam follows – he's too broken to fight back.

Fire crackles all around them. The air is greasy. Fat embers float like lightning bugs in the smoke-dimmed air. A scream bounces down the path. A man begging for God and his mother. They turn the dogleg and move to the mouth of the open gate. On the other side of it is hell.

The fighters continue even as everything around them burns. Fire eats the hillside circling the battle. Rolling walls of smoke reveal the scene part by part. A line of three corpses, strangers to Luke, inked up with white power numerology. Jagged lines of divots stitch their chests, as if surprised by some initial barrage of gunfire. Embers rain down on them, and the dead don't swat them out, so little rivulets of smoke rise up off them where already their clothes are burning. Past those dead, Aryan Steel's new fish swings a fireman's axe, red-bladed even before it bites into Ricky's face. The fish releases the axe, which stays buried in Ricky. The new fish looks in awe at his own work. The laugh that comes out of him is high pitched and insane. Ricky stumbles, paws at the blade, puts his hands on the haft to yank it free but it's a part of him now. It muffles his scream.

A lump of a man, fully ablaze, emerges from a cloud of smoke. The flames make him faceless. He falls at their feet. He makes a noise that might be a moan or the creaking of cooked muscle trying to move. The sizzle of cooking fat underneath. The kind thing would be to stove his head in. There's no time to be kind now.

One of Beast's men comes from a smoke cloud on the other side of the gate from Luke and Sam. A bullet has passed through his face, piercing both cheeks. He opens his mouth and blood waterfalls down his chest. His warrior cry is marred by gurgles. He pants wetly. He folds to his knees. Tyson comes behind him with a .22 pistol, battered as if Tyson has been using it as a club. He puts it to the man's head. He pulls the trigger. The pistol explodes. Tyson holds up a mangled hand. The bones of his hand are shocking white in the murk. The man scrambles away, leaving Tyson to scream. Trent, painted black by soot, hauls after the man, tackles him to the earth. Trent raises a stone and cleaves the man's head. Brain matter leaks onto the ground. Trent raises the rock to the sky and screams at the gods. The lab behind him explodes.

Fire like a wave splashes down on him. Too busy killing to stop from being killed.

A huge gust of wind whips the fire to a frenzy. A *CRUNCH* behind Luke and Sam as a tree falls across the road at the dogleg, blocking escape. A cloud of sparks rains down on them as they turn to look. All these pinpricks of fire. Something in Sam breaks. Luke grabs him before he can bolt. Sam turns and slugs him, wild. Luke gets him in a bear hug. He holds him, riding out Sam's struggles.

'Stop it,' he says.

'We gotta go we gotta go.'

The wind pushes smoke around, revealing Beast and Curtis wrestling. Each man dabbed with cuts and scrapes, slick with mingled blood. Exhausted. Fighting over a knife.

'We got to help Curtis,' Luke says. But he sees from Sam's eyes that he will run if Luke releases him, and in his wild state he will not last long. He makes the choice he knows Curtis would tell him to make.

'I'll get you out,' Luke says. Sam stops fighting. Luke lets him go.

He leads him up to the ridge, the way he first used to approach the labs. The one way not blocked by fire or fighters. He boosts Sam into the dry scrub. It smokes but is not yet in flames.

A scream makes him look back.

Beast and Curtis on the ground now. Beast is on top. He has the knife. Curtis on bottom, a cut from his forehead spuming. He has one hand on Beast's knife-wrist.

He gets the knife straight. With his free hand Curtis paws at Beast's face, feeling for his eye sockets. Both men roll again. Curtis on top. 'BLOOD IS LOVE' across his bare back, covered in scratches and dirt.

And then the smoke swallows them.

CHAPTER FORTY-SEVEN

There is no sky.

Luke herds Sam through the brush. Smoke like breathing glass. Eyes wet and blind. The pain of being cooked. A whirling cone of flame dances aside them, and that can't be a face Luke sees in it, and the gobbling noise can't be laughter. An ember the size of a quarter lands on Sam's back. His shirt smokes instantly. Luke slaps at it. Sam turns back at him and his eyes are of another species. He falls. He crouches into a ball.

'Stay with me,' Luke says. 'Sam, you've got to stay with me.'

Sam answers in something that isn't language. Luke holds his hand out. Sam takes it. Luke heaves him up from the earth. Above them embers float above them, flowing faster than they can run.

'I think maybe the fire's leapfrogged us,' Luke says.

Everything lit by flickers. Even standing still everything moves. Luke can't catch his breath. Luke falls face first. The stones somehow still cool. Sam yanks on his shirt. He gets back up.

Luke walks careful now. He sees each rock and each scrub that would snag them. He steers Sam down the mountain. The fire on three sides of them now. The heat unbearable. The lump at the center of his brain screaming *run run run*.

Luke does not let himself run. They walk down the path.

A helicopter roars overhead, close enough for them to feel its wash in the air. A night sun on its belly. It passes over them without stopping.

Snakes slither at their feet. Desert rats and coyotes run with them. All of them prey now with the fire at their backs.

The greedy flames gobble the air. They have to pant like dogs. Every step a thud. Every breath a throatful of nails. But still they move. Luke holds Sam's hand, leads him. A piece of scrub bounces on the wind – it catches Luke flush. Sparks leap up in millions. They pepper Luke's face. He catches a full breath of pure smoke. He goes down. And the things he sees then in the smoke, maybe they are there or maybe he has entered a different world, a place filled with creatures not made of meat who don't live or die or know pain or joy and maybe to them he is nothing, a piece of dust floating past their dull dead eyes.

A stinging pain brings him back. Sam stands over him with his hand raised for another slap. Sam's face is smudged with ash, streaks furrowed by tears from his watering eyes, the rims red as raw flesh, bleeding tears that canal down the black on his face.

'We're going to die,' Sam says as he pulls Luke up.

'Yeah, probably.'

They keep going anyway. They go the only way the fire lets them, knowing it is trapping them, drawing around them, tightening. He lets the thing inside him lead him – he does not let it run.

They come to the edge of a cliff. Below them, a subdivision full of houses. Green lawns and street lights.

How ridiculous. How insane.

The night below them is alive with swirling sparks, embers sent from the mountainside and down onto dried grass and roofs, igniting them so the fire rises from the houses like thatches of hair. Flames reflect in all the windows, give the houses these fearful eyes. Palm trees sway and burn like the torches of an angry mob.

Just below them sits a house in full conflagration. A family stands in the center of a lit swimming pool in the back yard. They see Luke and Sam at the top of the cliff. They beckon like *come on*.

His back is screaming hot. The flames pressing. The thing in his brain screaming *jump jump jump*. He knows if they do not move soon, this dumb animal inside him will take control and he will die.

He breathes in as much as he can. He squints with painful eyes, tries to see a path down.

'Sam, listen. We've got to climb down.'

'It's too steep.'

Luke looks over the side. He fights back against the thing in him that wants to fall. He lowers himself down the lip of the cliff. His feet find holds. His fingers dig into crumbling dirt. He talks Sam through repeating his steps. Sam kicks dirt down onto him. It gets in his eyes. He climbs down blind.

They come down the last fifteen feet fast, tumbling and skidding, sharp pain from his elbows and knees as rocks eat the skin from them. Sam coughs wetly. Pain screams all over Luke. The air here is cleaner. Somehow the pureness of it is a poison to him now. It makes Luke cough, cough until the edges of his sight go white. He spits something thick and black. He stands back upright.

They make it to the burning house's fence. They climb – they fall on the other side. The family eyes them, scared now. The dad puts his skinny arms around his family. His eyes say, *If you make me, I will fight and I will kill.* Luke believes him. Luke falls into the water. So cool on his cooked skin it nearly knocks him out. Luke sinks to the bottom. He opens his eyes. A cloud of black follows him down from the surface. He watches as it washes away into nothing.

PART SIX

APRÈS NOUS, LE DÈLUGE

CHAPTER FORTY-EIGHT

The bus to Sacramento moves through black-stained hills. The fires have been dead for weeks now. Most of the world has forgotten they even happened. Most of the world will be surprised when they come again next year.

Aunt Kathy texted him once before he threw the phone away. He knows Del sits in some hospital bed, smoke-poisoned but alive. The big house burned flat. The news says twelve folk died in the lab fire. It was barely a blip to most people. Trent, Ricky, Teller and Curtis all dead. Apes got out, and so did Tyson, one-handed now, twinless. It took them an extra week to announce Beast Daniels as one of the dead, burned as badly as he was, his body in the heart of the fire. Luke chooses to believe that means Curtis won that final fight.

Luke rides in the back of the bus, families all around him. They chatter. They bicker. They watch blaring videos on their phones.

The bus leaves the scorched lands behind. They ride through green farmlands. Soybeans, orange groves. Long lines of wheeled sprinklers spray water, summon rainbows in the air. It takes a while for Luke not to see it as a lie – for him to accept that there can be green left in the world after the fires.

Luke spat black for three weeks.

Around him families talk and laugh. His seatmate is an old man stinking of whiskey. He sleeps with both his eyes and his mouth half-open.

Luke sits and tells himself a story. It's a story he came up with himself. But he's sure it is true. He fit it together from what he knows, what he was told, and what he read in silences and Del's face.

His dad sitting in prison with a smuggled cell phone in his hands. His dad hearing Del talk about Pretty Baby and Callie. His dad saying something, something like 'It breaks my heart but you're right.' His dad saying, 'Both of them, Pretty Baby and Callie too.'

The bus rolls into Sacramento. While he's at the station he finds the train line that will take him to Folsom in the morning.

He finds a cheap hotel. His money won't last long. After this, he thinks, he'll head north. He's come to miss winter.

He finds a drug store. He buys shampoo and soap. He buys a new toothbrush. He buys gauze. He buys bandages. He buys tape. He buys alcohol. He buys a pack of razor blades.

He sits in his hotel room. He eats take-out garbage.

He takes off his shirt. He turns to the mirror. He touches the black ink heart over his real one. He looks at the muscle that has grown there in the last six months. He looks at the change in his face, the change in his eyes. It is quiet in his head most of the time these days. He does not think of himself as healed. But he is alive in a way he never was before. In a way that maybe he never could have been if he hadn't come home.

He does push-ups. He does sit ups. He rises and lifts his hand over his head and brings it down into his stomach. And again.

When he is done he is sweaty, so he takes a shower. He scrubs his chest. He scrubs his black ink heart.

He tells himself a story. He goes back farther now.

They found Callie's uncle John in his truck with a bullet in his head. Nobody knew who did it. Nobody looked too hard. Big Bobby Crosswhite carried all this rage about it. Burning John up, taking his ashes. Making him a martyr. Making him a sacrifice. Using his death to make the Combine stronger.

Luke sits down at the hotel room's coffee table. He opens up the gauze. He opens up the bandages. He opens up the alcohol. He opens up the razor blades.

Luke tells himself a story.

Maybe John got busted. Maybe he talked. Maybe he snitched big. Maybe he snitched small. Either way he had to go. Whoever killed him had to have known him. Sat there in the shotgun seat and put a gun to his head and pulled the trigger. Maybe it was Del in that shotgun seat. But it was probably Dad. He was the strong one.

They'd thought they could build the family on a crime and a lie and that it wouldn't matter in the end. But the lie grew tumorous in his father.

He had more pain than he could carry, Del had told Luke.

Del lied a lot. But Luke thought that part of the story was true. His dad had all this pain from John's death.

He had to put it somewhere.

So he put it in that man. Filled him with it until the man's head came apart.

Luke looks at the black heart inked over his real one. John's ashes in the ink. All Luke had wanted once was to wear this heart. He had waited to see his father until he felt worthy of it. Until he wore the family's black heart on his chest and proved himself strong. Now all he can see is the lie mixed in with the ashes and ink. Now all he can see is his family's weakness.

He thinks on Ramona, who wears her scars where the world can see them.

He thinks on his dad saying, *Come see me when the ink dries.*

Luke pours alcohol onto his chest.

He takes the wax-paper envelope off a razor blade.

He pours alcohol onto the blade.

He starts to cut.

The pain is tremendous.

Luke tells himself a story.

Tomorrow I will sit in front of my dad in Folsom's visiting room.

He cuts as careful as he can.

Tomorrow I will open my shirt.

He blinks back sweat. He puts the razor in the sink. He pours alcohol down his chest. The pain comes out of his mouth, somewhere between screaming and laughing.

Tomorrow I will show him my wet red heart where a black one used to be.

CHAPTER FORTY-NINE

The day Callie hits LA some Hollywood bigshot gets killed in a carjacking outside a Beverly Hills hotel. It knocks the Mount Baldy fires right out of the news. Callie watches TV reports – chopper shots of a black teardrop of a car, blood and broken glass on a wide pretty boulevard. She eats street tacos and delivery food. She drinks herself senseless. For a little while mere blankness is enough.

LA is a fine place to be erased. Everyone lives in these invisible bubbles that keeps them all apart.

She gets a text from Luke. She texts back that she is okay.

She gets a text from Apes. She looks at it a long time.

Are you my sister, Apes? Would you hug me if I saw you? Or would you strangle me? Or both?

She takes her phone out to the parking lot and she stomps on it.

She starts to understand that the blankness she lives in is not a true numbness. There is a pain at the center of it, the numbness of a hand in ice water. It is the feeling of slow death. She pulls herself out of it.

When she is ready she counts cash by hand until her fingers are black with ink. Forty-three thousand dollars on a cheapo duvet. She sits there among the stacked cash for a long while. She opens her mind to new possibilities. Three days later she buys a one-way ticket to a place where the sky isn't dead. She packs a bag. She hides cash in little lumps she hopes won't get seen by X-rays.

She flies gripping the armrest, scared they'll find the money, more scared they'll drop out of the sky. Halfway through the flight the plane hits a pocket of air, drops like a roller coaster and she grabs Pretty Baby's arm in panic. But of course it isn't him. It's just some stranger sitting next to her and she says *sorry* and looks away before he gets any ideas.

She walks out to Maui at sunset.

Maui. Even the sound is beautiful. The sunset is a radioactive miracle. The colors soak into everything, so every tree and face glows as if the source of light itself.

She finds an apartment far from the beach, among the locals. She knows this place is not a dream to them. It is their home. She knows how white people's dreams have pushed these people to the corners of their own world.

She gets a job at a resort, serving drinks poolside. So many of the women are pregnant – huge bellies absorbing sunlight. The women order mocktails and virgin daiquiris. She learns the word *babymoon.* She thinks on how there are so many words in this world, and how few of them she's even guessed at.

The resort is built on a slope down to a private beach. There are paddleboards and outrigger canoes and boat tours. The boys who work on the beach as lifeguards and surf teachers and tour guides wear red swimsuits and never shirts. They are mostly in their twenties, mostly brown and fatless with smiles made gorgeous by freedom.

The rains come so often she can't believe it, warm and sudden storms that wash everything and then are gone.

Here you'd hardly know the world is on fire.

For now, anyway.

She makes a friend, a hostess at the resort named Judy, a wild-child who spends money like spilling water from a cup. A girl from Minnesota whose past is not a debt. Callie lets herself be seduced by it, not looking at prices on the menu before ordering, paying with cash. She knows the money will go fast if she lives like it won't. That it's only powerful if she uses it right. She knows this life is a lie, but she could use a lie right now. She's had enough of pure truth for a while.

Of all the horrors she lived through, somehow it's Erik's eyes that come to her most often. Maybe because she sees those eyes riding in so many other men's skulls. Sometimes the vacationing men pinch her ass or whisper room numbers to her, and things seize up in her throat and she is flooded with it all again. She goes to the resort kitchen and grasps a butter knife by the blade until the little teeth bite furrows in her palms. This little pain is enough and she puts the knives in the sink and goes to fetch the men their beers or mahi-mahi sliders.

Sometimes she thinks about Pretty Baby. Sometimes he is next to her, tingling like a phantom limb.

She watches television at night, rich women screaming at each other and throwing drinks. She thinks on how strange and soft our blood sport has become.

She thinks on how when she was a kid she lived with the world rubbing right up against her skin, but now there's something between her and the world. Something like a pane of glass. And she worries it will always be there, that she'll never laugh as hard or cry as hard or love as hard again.

One December day Judy texts, says: *Come down to the beach. The whales have come, let's say hey.*

Judy has already bought the tickets with no mention of the price. They climb aboard an outrigger canoe with a honeymooning couple and one of the red swimsuit boys, his hair bleached by sun and curled by salt water.

They row out onto the bay, so Callie can turn around and see how the resort fits itself just so into the rolling green hills. A dolphin crests through the water near them. Callie plugs her ears against the *oohs* and *ahhs* of Judy and the honeymoon couple. She'd push them all overboard if she could. She has some sudden need rising in her.

The boy in the red swimsuit tells them to look at the mountaintop. He says some god with a name she'll never hold onto put the mountain there, and the boy has timed it just right because just as he's talking the sun cracks over the top of it, light spilling out sudden and too bright so when she looks away the purple memory of it still hangs in front of her face.

They paddle deeper into the ocean, chasing splashes and glimpses of tails. *Paddle left side*, the boy says. *Paddle right side*. He talks about whales, how they swim across the sea in great circuits. How they are vast but live on tiny little krill. How they come to these islands every winter to give birth so their babies will be safe. That there are no predators for them here. He talks about how whales are mammals like us who once walked on land. How they turned back to the sea. How they still carry hipbones inside them, the unseen ghosts of long-forgotten legs.

He is about to say more when a whale vast and grey rises from the water to their left. Bigger than you'd ever know. Its face masked in barnacles. White scars on its back from some ancient battle. It breaches close enough that Callie thinks she could reach out and touch it. Its fluke spumes a white jet and it slips back under. The mist of it kisses her face, leaves it cool.

Something unlocks in her. Tears come out in jagged chunks. When she is done, she feels a good sort of empty, like after puking up something rotten.

'You all right?' Judy doesn't know much of the story, but she knows that Callie had loved a man who died bad.

Callie doesn't know how to explain it. Something in the way this giant came from the deep, something huge and hidden right there under the surface. What else is swimming unseen underneath it all? How many things are hidden?

The guide tells them to paddle. She paddles hard. This joy and this grief all mixed up inside her. The guide tells them to look down and there it is right under them in the depths. How easy it could breach right now and spill them into the water. And her tears blur everything as she cries again, smiling, laughing and snorting back tear-snot. And the guide hands her a water bottle with a smile, and she knows all at once that she will love again, maybe not this boy but one like him. Maybe not now, but soon enough.

They paddle. They chase the whale for an hour, guessing where it will breach next, sometimes close, sometimes far. They paddle until the whale surpasses them and their arms burn useless, and the guide steers them back towards the shore.

Callie paddles and watches the beach grow bigger. She wonders if we will really strangle the sea the way they say we will, strangle it until it lies fishless and dead. Or will the sea rise up first and wash us away?

And she thinks that it is too bad that we have bet the one way and whales the other. She wonders what whales saw on land that made them turn back. What told them the sea was a better home after all? She thinks on what the boy said, that whales carry the ghosts of legs in their bodies. Those forgotten bones wrapped in the meat of them. She thinks that sometimes quitting a thing is best. She thinks maybe we too could fold our ghosts up inside us, let them grow vestigial. That maybe we too could learn a new way.

Discover more from Jordan Harper . . .

A Lesson in Violence

WINNER OF THE BEST FIRST NOVEL
AWARD AT THE EDGARS 2018

'Striking . . . visceral, violent and utterly compelling, it nevertheless shines with humanity' *Daily Mail*

A GRITTY, PROPULSIVE DEBUT ABOUT A FATHER, A DAUGHTER, AND THE HARDEST LESSONS IN LIFE . . .

'If nowhere was safe for her, then the only place he could let her be was with him'

Meet Polly: eleven years old and smart beyond her years. But she's a loner, always on the outside, until she is unexpectedly reunited with her father.

Meet Nate: fresh out of jail and driving a stolen car, Nate takes Polly from the safety of her quiet existence into a world of robbery, violence and the constant threat of death.

And he does it to save her life.

SIMON &
SCHUSTER

Love and Other Wounds

A BLISTERING COLLECTION THAT UNSPARINGLY CONFRONTS THE EXTREME, BRUTAL PARTS OF THE HUMAN HEART.

A man runs away from his grave and into a maelstrom of bullets and fire. A Hollywood fixer finds love over the corpse of a dead celebrity. A morbidly obese woman imagines a new life with the jewel thief who is scheming to rob the store where she works. A man earns the name 'Mad Dog' and lives to regret it.

All are thirsting for something seemingly just beyond their reach. Some are on the run, pursued by the law or propelled relentlessly forward by a dangerous past. Others are searching for a semblance of peace and stability, and even love, in a fractured world defined by seething violence and ruthless desperation. All are bruised, pushed to their breaking point and beyond, driven to extremes they never imagined.

SIMON &
SCHUSTER